OUR LOVE IS THE REALEST III

SHVONNE LATRICE

FIRST CLASS

PUBLISHING GROUP

ABOUT THE AUTHOR

<u>Other Works by Me:</u>

Good Girls Love Thugs 1-5
Falling for a Hood King 1-4
Married to a Distinguished Thug 1-3
She's Gotta Have It 1-2
Me & My Dope Boy 1-3
Yazir & Nina 1-3
Forbidden Love with a Thug 1-3
You Needed Me 1-3
Shorty is in Love with a Real One 1-4
I Got Your Back 1-2
My Baby Is a West Coast King 1-4
Our Love Is the Realest 1-3
She Got It Bad for a Heartless Gangsta 1-4
She Got It Bad for a Heartless Gangsta: An AK Christmas
Hood Boyz Fall In Love Too 1-3
Nobody Can Love You Like Them Roughnecks Do 1-4

$19.99

ISBN 978-1-966375-30-2

YIKAYLA GOODE

"I love you, Waayil."

"Come here." He let my legs down and pulled me up closer to him so he could kiss me as his dick still sat inside of me. "I love you more, Kay."

Finally, we snapped out of our Romeo and Juliet shit once we'd kissed for a million years, so I went to clean myself up and re-brush my teeth, before he hopped into the shower. I left out, and on the way to Brynn's, I called Miss Laughton because I already knew she had Lonan instead of Roscoe. When my suspicions were confirmed, I told her I was coming to get him after my lunch, instead of tomorrow. I was missing him too much anyway, and loathed having to split my time.

When I got to Brynn's house, I texted her to let her know I was outside. She told me she'd be a minute since she messed up her makeup putting on mascara, so she offered for me to come inside. Her home was nice, and she told me it was a rental like what Waayil had.

"Almost done!" she shouted from her bathroom as I paced the living room, looking around. I saw her daughter's toys, which made me smile.

"Where is Haven?" I asked about her daughter.

"Oh, she is over her cousin's house. Or my sister's house. They're going somewhere... I forgot the name."

I nodded in response, even though she couldn't see me. I saw a picture of her daughter on the table, and picked it up to look. She was super adorable, but looked like a handful. I placed the picture back, and then picked up another of her daughter but when she was a little baby.

"You ready?" Brynn walked into the living room dressed.

"Yep!" I replied, just as someone started viciously beating on the door. It was almost like they were kicking it.

Suddenly, I realized I didn't know much about Brynn, or what she had going on in her life. This bitch could have been into all kinds of shit, and I was a bit afraid now.

"What the hell!" Brynn's brows dipped as she darted towards her door. I discreetly pulled my iPhone out, ready to dial 911, when she pulled the door open.

"Where is my fucking daughter, Brynn!" Roscoe shouted, just before I caught his eye. His balled-up face immediately returned to its normal position as soon as we made eye contact. "Yikayla." He exhaled lowly and shook his head like he was disappointed in himself.

"How do you know Yikayla?" Brynn pointed behind herself, using her thumb.

I was standing there, still as hell and not knowing what I should or could say. I didn't know if I was angry, sad, shocked, or all of the above. All I knew was that I couldn't move, and I was feeling like I was having an outer body experience. This couldn't have been real, what was going on in front of me. If this was some kind of cruel nightmare that my brain wanted to bring upon me, I needed to wake the hell up now.

No one else said a word as my stomach felt like it was balling up into the smallest tiny knot that it could. I was speechless as I stared at Roscoe, who was glaring at Brynn now for some reason.

"How do I know Yikayla? Really, Brynn?" His brows furrowed as he closed her front door and started towards her a little bit.

For a moment, her confused expression stayed put on her face, before finally she rolled her eyes and glanced my way. At that moment, when she looked at me, I saw a different person than I'd been seeing all of this time. I almost didn't recognize her because she didn't bear a single resemblance to the sad, low self-esteem having co-worker of mine. Right now, I saw a conniving, mischievous ass slut.

"What umm... what is going on?" I inquired so lowly that I barely heard it myself.

"That's what the fuck I wanna know!" Roscoe hollered down at Brynn who was now frowning as she looked up at him.

"This is all of your fault! You cheated on me with her and you made me do this! You made me act crazy!" Brynn barked.

My head began to pound because I still couldn't wrap my mind around the fact that not only did Brynn know Roscoe, but she had a child by him as well.

"How many times do I have to tell you I was with her first, Brynn! How many?"

"Then why is you guys' baby only one year old, huh? Our baby is older, so that's how I know you're lying! We've been together for years, Roscoe!"

"Oh my gosh," I said to myself, leaning on the table to hold myself up so I wouldn't collapse to the floor. Right about now, someone could knock me over with a feather.

Yet again, I'd met another woman who Roscoe had cheated on me with. Yes, I was in a new relationship, and happy as hell to be in it, but this hurt and a lot. I may have hated Roscoe's guts, but there was a time when I *did* love him. And just thinking back to the days where I was so deeply in love with this man, having no idea that he was making babies all over Tennessee, made my heart physically ache. I couldn't imagine how I would feel right now if he was still my man.

And then Brynn making friends with me for malicious reasoning? I wanted to whoop her ass, but then I wondered for what? Did I really want to fight over Roscoe? Had this been prior to me resuming my relationship with Waayil, then yes, I would have dragged that stupid scheming bitch out of her house by her dry ass ponytail.

"I'm gonna go." I started across the living room, bumping the shit out of Brynn and then Roscoe too. Okay, I know I said I wouldn't touch her, but I swear that shoulder bump was a reflex I couldn't control.

As I walked to my car, I heard Brynn calling after Roscoe and then I felt him grab my arm. I snatched that shit back so damn quickly that he stumbled a little. He threw his hands up in mock surrender, and momentarily closed his eyes as he exhaled.

"Yikayla, I just wanna talk to you. I just want to explain everything to you, ma. Please."

Shaking my head at him, I folded my arms and took a couple deep breaths. I didn't want to cry, especially in front of him, but unfortunately, I did. The tears just flowed freely from my eyes, and when he stepped towards me, I put my hand out to let him know I didn't need anything from him, especially not to be consoled.

"This shit with Brynn is the same type of situation as RJ's mama."

"Oh, Christelle?" I laughed through tears as his lips parted in astonishment. "Yes, I met her. She came up to my job to let me know I needed to leave you alone," I spoke calmly. Feeling enraged, I began to yell. "She came to my fucking job and told *me* to leave *you* alone! I have been with you for five years, and you have all of these newbie ass, rookie bitches coming up to me like I'm some side chick! You disgust me, Roscoe! Really! And Shamaria, her sister, are you fucking her too?"

"Yikayla, baby, relax," he replied as I began to hyperventilate. He ignored my question, which gave me my answer. I hoped Christelle wasn't still messing with him or she'd be in for another rude awakening like myself.

"No! Get back!"

I looked behind him to see Brynn in her doorway wearing a

smirk. To think I actually saw this bitch as a friend. This was why I stuck with my sisters and my sisters only. Bitches were way too shady for my liking. Thankfully, God brought me a man now that would never have me out here looking like Roscoe had.

As Roscoe called after me, I ignored him and got into my car. I drove straight back home, and once I parked in front of the house Waayil and I shared, I paused. I needed to get myself together before going inside. I needed to clean up so that I could tell Waayil what happened and then go get my baby from Miss Laughton.

"Okay, you're okay," I told myself as I looked into my rearview mirror, after putting in some eye drops to cure the redness. No way I could go in there this broken up over another man.

Entering the house, I heard Waayil singing in the kitchen, which made me smile, even though I didn't want to. I loved his voice so much, and how soothing it was. Lonan did too, and now it was the surefire way to get my baby to sleep.

"Hey." I stood in the archway of the kitchen as Waayil made himself a sandwich while shirtless. The upgrade I'd done was crazy. Roscoe didn't hold a candle to Waayil in looks or personality, and I'm sure he couldn't fight like Waayil either. I'd never actually seen Roscoe get down, but he talked a lot of shit, so I hoped he could do a little something.

"Hey." Waayil turned to me, showing his beautiful perfect smile that only enhanced his sexy chocolate face. Those dimples dug deeply into his smooth cocoa cheeks just before his brows dipped, and he placed the knife he was using for the spread down. "What's wrong?"

"Huh? Nothing." I shook my head repeatedly. I caught a glimpse of myself in the microwave, and I looked pretty normal, so I had no idea what he was talking about.

Nearing me, his cologne hit me first, sending a tingle down to my womanhood. Towering over me, Waayil placed his big hands on the sides of my face as he stared down into my eyes with his hazel ones.

"Your body language, Kay. What's wrong with you? And why are you back so damn early?" The sexy scowl on his face was full of confusion.

"Umm." My eyes darted off.

Don't cry, Yikayla.

"Aye, come here." Waayil pulled me into his chest as I started to cry. I really tried to hold it in, but I couldn't. My chest began to heave up and down, so I had to let it out. "Baby, what happened? Do I need to have the homegirls stomp that bitch out?" he inquired, making me chuckle for a quick millisecond.

"My *friend* is a—no—nother one!" I stammered.

"Another what?"

"Of Rosc—Roscoe's baby mamas. He came over to find his daughter while I was there." I broke down.

"What the fuck is wrong with this nigga?" Waayil asked lowly to himself.

"I'm sorry, Waayil. I shouldn't be crying about this in front of you."

Waayil leaned my head back some and just looked down at me. He was so handsome, and believe it or not, one of a kind. Yes, he had a twin, but he was the one and only to me. Even if he didn't have dimples, I could tell the two apart just from the way Waayil walked, and his demeanor. He was like the cool kid in school that didn't try to be, and who everyone wanted to be like.

"What were we before anything, Kay?" he questioned.

"Best friends."

"Exactly, and that shit hasn't changed just 'cause you're my girl now. I told you don't ever fake shit for a nigga. I love you, and if any muthafucka in the world should have to comfort you, as ya man, it should be me."

Sniffling, I poked my lips out, up at him, making him smile and snicker lowly in his sexy deep voice. He kissed me a couple times, and then I laid my head back onto his hard chest that smelled like pure, sexy, clean man. Like always, he'd made me feel one hundred times better. For a while, we just stood there in the archway of the kitchen and hugged, while I thanked God for sending me someone like Waayil Christian.

2

WAAYIL CHRISTIAN

Late That Night...

That conversation with that muthafucka, Gavin, replayed in my mind constantly since the shit happened. I hadn't said anything to Alba or anyone else about it. I was angry that the bitch lied to me, but I can't say I wasn't a bit relieved.

I never allowed myself to get used to the idea of having a kid of my own that wasn't gon' be birthed by Yikayla, so there was no attachment there. However, even though I was relieved as hell, at the end of the day, Alba Micel tried to play a nigga, and that didn't sit well with me at all.

I looked down at Yikayla lying on her stomach next to me, facing the other way. The covers were down by her legs, letting her nice round ass show. I started to think nasty shit, even though it was covered by a gown, making me completely forget about the bullshit Alba had done for a moment. Licking my lips, I reached over to touch her and she quickly turned to look me dead in my eyes, scaring the shit out of me.

"I thought you were sleep," I frowned.

"I was, you pervert!" She slapped my arm. "But I felt someone trying to touch on me!"

"Well, now you don' fucked up because you could have gotten yo' ass ate if you hadn't have woken up," I grinned, as she burst into laughter.

"Okay, I'm sleep now."

"Aye, ma, I was joking, but now I know yo' nasty ass likes getting yo' ass ate. Who the fuck been eating yo' ass?"

"You've done it before though, Waayil."

"You're lying like fuck. I ain't never ate no ass in my life. I just got the muthafuckin' idea a minute ago to try something new, but like I said, you fucked that up."

"Nope, nope." She shook her head. "The other night I felt your tongue slip." She laughed loudly when I glared at her.

"That's not the same as me deliberately eating yo' ass, ma. Learn the fucking difference before you go around spreading rumors and shit."

"Your tongue touched my ass, which means you ate my ass." She said that shit with a straight ass face so she probably believed it.

"Fuck did I just say, huh?" I clawed at her side, making her squeal because her fine ass was ticklish.

"Okay! Okay!" she hollered. I kissed her lips as she panted heavily, and she pushed me away. "Don't kiss me when you know you be eating ass. I'm kidding!" she shouted the last part while cheesing, when I touched her ribcage again. "Why are you up, baby? It's 1 a.m."

Glancing down at her again, since my back was against the headboard, I sighed. "Remember how I said we're best friends and shit?"

"Always."

"So when I tell you this, I don't want you to get mad at me, aight? I've known something for a minute, and now I kind of don't know anymore."

"Waayil."

"So, awhile back, Alba got a DNA test done, but I didn't go with her. She used my hairbrush or toothbrush. I don't quite remember which one."

"Oh." Yikayla propped her head up using her forearms.

"So anyway, uh... she showed me the test results and they pretty much said that I was the father but—"

"Waayil! You told me—"

"Listen, Yikayla— Aye, listen! Lay yo' ass back down until I'm done with my muthafuckin' story, ma," I hissed when her little ass tried to hop out the bed. She rolled her eyes and laid back down. "I didn't believe the test so I didn't say shit, and also, I was afraid of yo' reaction. But the other day when I was at the shop, I got a call from an inmate and he told me he was the father."

"What? So, Alba lied?"

"I mean, I think so. I don't wanna just believe some random ass nigga, but I can't help but to. How did he know to call me and say that shit, unless he was fucking with her some kind of way? I mean, he knew to call Monarch and everything with his bitch ass." I looked to Yikayla before turning my attention back to the turned off television.

"Well, what did she say?"

"I haven't talked to her. The day I found out I wanted to kill her, so I decided to stay away until I could get my shit together. Not to mention, I didn't wanna roll up in there and do something to her ass if that nigga was lying."

"I can beat her up," Yikayla offered sweetly, which made the shit funny as hell.

"I know, my lil' ridah, but I got it." I pinched her chin. "You mad?"

"A little. You have to stop keeping secrets, Waayil, or this will never work. I have enough to deal with, with Roscoe and all his skeletons jumping out of the closet. I can't have you keeping shit away. You never kept stuff from me when we were just friends."

Sliding down under the covers and turning to face her, I replied, "I know. A nigga loves yo' ass a lot, probably more than you know, and I guess I be paranoid as fuck that you gon' *try* to leave me."

"Why did you say try like that?"

"Because you'll try, but you won't be successful."

"Get that ass beat by my new man then, Waayil." She rolled her eyes playfully and pursed her sexy lips. "It's Eric Bellinger, by the way."

"Aight, I'm really gon' have to stomp that nigga out. Then again, his wife is fine as hell, so I guess he and I can switch." I then looked off like I was in deep thought and added, "I'll fuck the shit outta her sexy ass," before turning back to face Yikayla. I laughed when her mouth fell open. "Yeah, shut yo' ass up 'cause you know you can't take it."

"Goodnight, asshole." She roughly fluffed her pillow and slammed her head down onto it. "I can't sleep now." Her eyes flew back open.

Without another word, I sat up and turned her onto her back. Standing on my knees, I got between her legs and moved my hands up her thighs to grab her panties. Moving them down her sexy cognac colored legs, I tossed them to the floor.

"What are you doing?" she asked, smiling.

Again, I said nothing, as I lowered down and spread her legs. Palming the backs of her thighs, I pressed them lightly into her stomach before starting to place sloppy pecks on her pussy. In no time, she was wet as hell, so I flicked my tongue over her clit for a few, before sucking it softly.

"Mmm," she whined, as I licked and sucked her pussy passionately as hell.

I pressed her thighs into her body harder, making it so she couldn't move and so that I had unlimited access to my pussy. I dipped my tongue into her opening, making her shriek lowly, and then dragged it back up until my lips collapsed around her button. I moaned against it, loving how wet her pussy was and how good her juices tasted, as she released twice damn near back to back. I felt her body tense up, so I went harder, making my mouth become one with the pussy as I ate like a muthafuckin' show dog.

"Oh my gosh, baby," Yikayla sniveled as I yanked a third orgasm from her. I took pride in making her cum with just my mouth, no fingers or anything.

Finally seeing that she was spent, I let her legs down and licked her one more time before climbing out of the bed. I left to brush my teeth, and by the time I came back, Yikayla was knocked out like someone had hit her over the head with a Billy club.

Smirking 'cause a nigga was feeling himself a little bit, I got in the bed next to her and hugged her body into mine.

The Next Morning...

Alba had gotten off work about fifteen minutes ago, so I was here in the parking lot waiting on her ass. My initial plan was to wait at her crib until she got there, but I was too on one to do that shit. I needed to talk to her ass now, and shit, she was lucky I didn't bust up in her job trying to talk.

As I sat there waiting, I saw Nusef was calling me and decided to answer. I'd been dodging his calls for a minute, and scheduling myself at the times and on the days I knew he wasn't gon' be at the shop. I didn't feel like hearing his ass plead for Wednesday, and in a minute, he and I were gon' be at odds over that shit.

"What's good?" I answered.

"When you gon' check on Wednesday, man? You shot her in the fucking foot, Waayil."

"She's lucky I didn't put that muthafuckin' bullet elsewhere. And I'll see her when I feel like it. I don't need you on my head about checking on her ass. Why don't you get on her head about lying, my nigga?"

"Calm yo' ass down, Waayil. She knows what she did was wrong so I don't need to go there with her." He sighed and then said, "She's sorry and she just wants to talk, bruh."

"And I don' already said I'll get at her ass when I feel like it, Sef. Stop calling me about this bullshit before I shoot yo' ass in the foot too," I spat as I watched Alba leave the bank and start towards her car.

"Nigga, you shoot me in the foot, I'll—"

"What? Get yo' ass beat afterwards too? If you want a hole in yo' foot and a cracked face to go with it, be my guest."

"Waayil—"

"I gotta go, muthafucka. Go do a tattoo or get bossed around by Rebecca to keep yaself busy."

I hung up and shook my head at my iPhone as if it were him. He was getting on my fucking nerves with that shit. He was my brother, my fucking twin, and he should understand how I felt. He was letting lying ass Wednesday come between us, and I ain't like that shit at all. No fucking way I'd ever take a muthafucka's side over Nusef's, and he needed to learn that part of the game.

I hopped out my whip after pocketing my iPhone, and as soon as I closed my door, Alba and I made eye contact. She was afraid at first, but then she smiled softly. I admit the pregnancy had her looking pretty as hell, and before that, she was already fine as fuck. I just didn't understand why such a pretty ass girl had to scheme and lie; that's if what that Gavin nigga said had any truth to it.

"Hey, Waayil, what are you doing here?" She walked up to me and tried to hug me, but I was still as hell, staring down at her. "You okay?"

"Who is Gavin, ma?" I squinted my eyes as I glared down at her, pushing my hood off of my head.

The way her mouth opened and closed let me know she knew exactly who that nigga was.

"He's nobody to me, so I don't know why you're asking about him." She cleared her throat. "Why?"

"Because I got a nice courtesy call from him. Wanted to thank me for helping you and *his baby* out."

Shaking her head 'no,' she responded, "Absolutely not, Waayil! I don't even know who this guy is!"

"Then how in the entire fuck does he know to call me, huh? How he know my muthafuckin' shop, my name, and the fact that we got this baby situation poppin' off, Alba!" I roared.

"Alba, you okay?" some Oreo ass nigga walked up.

"Man, if you don't mind yo' own damn business, I'll bust yo' shit open," I gritted to him. He stood there, contemplating, before finally walking his ass off in them high-water pants.

"Waayil—"

"I'm getting a DNA test just to be sure, and like I told you before, Alba, if that baby ain't mine, you better have ya running shoes on, ma."

I yanked my car door open and got inside before she could say anything. I started backing up before she moved, so she darted out of the way, tripping a little.

All I knew was that bitch had better bribe the whole medical staff if she wanted to live.

3

ALBA MICEL

I watched Waayil speed out of the parking lot, while trying to hold back the tears. This shit was becoming way too much, and it seemed like the more that I did to try and convince him, the deeper hole I dug myself into. I didn't even recognize myself when I looked in the mirror because I wasn't this type of girl. All my life men have basically bowed down in my presence, yet, here I was lying and manipulating people to get a man to believe I was pregnant by him.

At this point, I knew full well that Waayil would never be with me, regardless of whether this baby was truly his or not. For years he'd been in love with Yikayla, and I knew it. I knew it before he went to jail, and it was even more obvious now because he was blatantly telling me. But I loved that man, even if he didn't believe that I did, and I just couldn't fathom a life without him. I couldn't imagine waking up knowing that he and I had nothing to discuss or talk about. I couldn't live with the fact that we'd have no reason to see one another, so this baby was the only chance I had at having anything with Waayil.

At this stage, I just wanted him around. I didn't care if he was married with kids to another bitch; I wanted whatever I could get from him. Shit, I'd even take up a few hours on the weekends at Monarch Tattoo if that would keep him near. I just had to look at him, hear his voice, smell his cologne, and watch him in deep thought with his lips tucked in and his dimples making an appearance.

I realized I was standing in the parking lot of my job at Regions Bank, watching what used to be the direction of where Waayil's car was going. I got in my car and drove to get myself something to eat.

I texted Ashley to come over, so once I got home, I saw her new, used car parked in my driveway. When she saw me, we got out at the same time, and once inside my house, I damn near ripped my food bag open to start eating.

"So what was so important, Alba?" Ashley inquired, sipping on her water bottle.

"Can I get something in my system first? I am pregnant!"

"I know, but you made it sound urgent, so I've been anxious to know what's going on with you." I didn't say anything as I kept tearing this fried chicken apart like a lion to its prey. "Alba, you stress too much. Didn't your doctor say you need to relax? It's not good for the baby, all this—"

"All this what?"

"All these games and plans you keep coming up with. And aren't you seeing that none of them are working?"

"Ashley, when I want your advice, I will ask for it." I dusted the chicken crumbs off of my hands and then balled up my trash. "Now, I need you to do something for me. I told you Waayil *did* believe the paternity test I showed him, but I learned today that Gavin fucked that up."

"So what do you want me to do?"

"I need you to tell Waayil that Gavin is an ex of yours who had a thing for me, and when I turned him down, he must have felt the need to try and sabotage me."

"No, Alba. I am not getting in the middle of this shit with Waayil. That boy ain't wrapped too tightly at all, and if I help you, he may come for me."

"So what, you're just gonna let me go down for this alone?" When she opened her mouth, I cut her off. "Well, you can't! You're the one who convinced me to fake a DNA test so what do you think he'll do once I tell him that?"

"I did not tell you to do that!"

"Oh yes you did... in a way. You said that it was too bad I didn't know anyone who could falsify some medical documents for me. Do you not remember that?"

Now I wasn't a terrible person, and I don't care what you think, but Ashley had me fucked up. In a way, I felt like she and I were in this together. And she was my close friend, so she should be willing to do anything I asked her to in order for me to stay alive. I understood she was scared, but if Waayil was gonna kill anyone, he'd be killing us both... or just her if I could somehow swing that.

"I just said it was too bad, Alba. I didn't say to go hire someone to do it! I can't do this for you. And doesn't Waayil know Gavin? You said Gavin's girlfriend was Rori Goode, Yikayla Goode's little sister."

"Yes, he knows him, kind of, but it's obvious that he hasn't put two and two together. And before he has the chance to, I need you to tell him this or I will say it was your idea to get the fake test once all of this unravels."

Ashley thought I was fucking around but I was dead serious. If she didn't do what I was asking, as soon as Waayil got the real DNA results, I was throwing her ass under the bus like a bowling ball.

"Fine. When?"

"Today."

"Alba!"

"You said it yourself that Waayil and Gavin are dangerously close, so we need to act fast before his little girlfriend tells him who Gavin is."

I was actually surprised Yikayla hadn't spilled the beans, but I just assumed Waayil had kept this all a secret. I mean, he didn't even want Yikayla to know the paternity results, so I doubt he was laid up with her, discussing Gavin's phone call.

I texted Waayil and asked him to come over so I could explain who Gavin was. He, of course, told me that he was busy and didn't work on my time, so I needed to come to him. So after changing out of my work clothes, me, and a-nervous-wreck-ass, Ashley, drove over to Monarch Tattoo.

When we walked in, some wannabe Beyoncé looking bitch was sitting behind the honey colored wood front desk, giggling with some guy who I assumed was a customer.

"Have a nice day." She grinned and handed him a receipt. She almost snapped her neck to look at me when I slammed my purse on top of the bar like desk to look down at her. "May I help you?"

"Yes, actually... Chiara." I looked at her name necklace. "I need to speak with Waayil."

"Waayil is booked, babe." She turned her attention towards the computer. "We have some others that could help you if you need it done this evening, but Waayil won't be available until next week."

Damn, this nigga is doing it like that? I thought to myself.

"No, *babe*, I don't want a tattoo. Waayil and I have a much more personal relationship, so please go let him know that I'm here or escort me to the back."

"Personal? Well let me go and see if he's taking any *personal* visits right now." She got up. She's lucky I didn't punch her in her smart-ass mouth.

"Name's Alba."

She nodded before going to the back, just as Nusef came walking into the front. He saw me and shook his head, making me suck my teeth.

"Ashley, this is the other one," I said, purposely taking a shot at him. He flicked me off and I gave him a smile.

"Hi, it's Nusef, right?" Ashley reached her hand out to shake his.

"Yeah. What you doing hanging out with Satan, Ashley?" Nusef quizzed.

"Fuck off, Nusef. I'm sure you have some buzzards to tend to." I rolled my eyes. Nusef seemed to love ugly hoes, then again, there was a time where he was just smashing everything moving. So maybe that was why he was always seen with a bitch that looked like shit on rye bread.

"I'm gon' let that slide." He looked to me and then turned his attention back to Ashley. "Have a nice night, Ashley."

"Yes, same to you." Ashley nodded, still nervous about speaking to Waayil.

"Where is this stupid bitch?" I spat and started towards the back once Nusef left out. Just as I did, I saw Chiara was coming back up the hallway.

"He said you can come in once he's done wrapping up his client's tattoo," she said with too much attitude. Something told me that she had a thing for Waayil because she seemed upset for no reason. I knew that feeling all too well, so it was easy to recognize. Anytime a woman wanted to even ask Waayil a question, she was immediately on my hit list. Chiara was acting the same way I used to.

Smirking at Chiara, I simply said, "Thank you." She scoffed and shook her head before switching to the front. "Does she have on any panties?" I asked Ashley as we both watched Chiara's ass jiggle wildly as she walked.

"If she did, they must have gotten swallowed up by her ass earlier today."

We both roared with laughter as Waayil's tattoo room door came open. His client, some biker looking chick, walked out licking her lips at me, which made me turn my lip up.

Waayil nodded for me and Ashley to come in with his cute ass, and I happily did. His cologne permeated the air of his room, and I just basked in it as I sat down in one chair, and Ashley in the other. I glanced at her, and she was watching the door with her eyes wide as Waayil closed it. She needed to calm the fuck down for this to work.

Without saying a word, Waayil sat down on his chair and stared at me, fingers intertwined. He yanked down his sleeves, but before he could, I saw *Yikayla* tattooed on his inner forearm. For a moment, I lost my train of thought.

"Wh—when did you get that tattoo?"

"None of yo' damn business. Now you got 'bout eight and a half minutes before my last client comes in, so talk."

"Well, when you told me about Gavin earlier, it truly disturbed me, Waayil. I had no idea, at the time, who he was or why he would even try something like that. That was until I told Ashley, and we realized it. Ashley, explain to Waayil, please."

"Hi." She chuckled awkwardly at Waayil. He turned his attention from me to her, with his brows slightly furrowed. He tucked his lips in like always, causing his dimples to show as his eyes beamed on her. "How are you this evening, Waayil?"

Was this hoe serious?

"I'm great, Ashley, but I got about six minutes left, baby, so say what you gotta say to me."

"Right. Of course. Don't want to waste your time. I'm sure you're a very busy ma—ow!" she shouted when I punched her thigh. "So, Gavin and I used to be in a relationship. It wasn't anything too serious, but we did like each other. So, he umm... well, one day I was..." She looked at me, and even though I wanted to snap, I played it cool. The thigh punch was already suspicious enough. "I was umm... we actually were at my house and Gavin came over. When I went to the bathroom, Gavin tried to get with Alba, and when she turned him down, he got angry."

"Ma, you're babbling right now. But I'm guessing what you're trying to say is that old boy is hating, so he lied."

Smiling widely as if she was relieved, Ashley replied, "Yes! That is exactly what I'm saying!" She pointed to Waayil and then looked to me grinning. "He just couldn't take it, so I guess he called you."

"Well, ladies, thank you." Waayil got up and opened the door for us to leave.

"Wait, what does this mean?" I inquired as both Ashley and I stood up.

"Well, this open door means get up outta here so I can get back to work." He licked his lips. Ashley and I walked out of his room, and when I looked back to him, he responded lowly, "I'll be in touch witchu." His pretty eyes scanned me as he held onto the back of the door.

I didn't know if it was the pregnancy hormones or what, but the way he said what he'd said, had me wanting to pull my dress up and let him do some things. Yeah, it had to be the pregnancy because what he said wasn't even sexual. I think it was the low tone and the way he looked me up and down.

I smiled, feeling like I'd finally been victorious, and then I started back down the hallway. I glanced over my shoulder at Chiara before I left, and sure enough, she was watching me. If I couldn't get Waayil, she damn sure couldn't.

Middle Of the Night… A Little After 2 a.m.…

"Fuck," I groaned, throwing the covers off of my body.

Sitting up, I looked at the clock but then turned my attention right back to my bed. The deep maroon colored blood spot between my legs signified my worst nightmare.

"No." I jumped up from my bed, only to double over in extreme pain. "Noooo!" I screamed, staring at the humongous bloodstain in the middle of my bed.

Blood continued to drip down my inner thighs.

"Nooooo! Noooo! Noooo!" I shouted, clearing everything off of my nightstand before falling back down onto my bed to sob, hysterically. "Noooo, God," I whispered through the tears. "Noooo."

4

———————

JONAYA GOODE

I was on the edge of my seat as my professor talked and talked about what was to come next class. He'd said the shit five damn times already, and I didn't need to hear it a sixth. As soon as he said class was dismissed, I hopped my ass up and damn near sprinted to Leighton's class. I wanted to catch her as she walked out because it would be the only way I could see her.

I'd tried calling and texting, even though I knew that wouldn't work, and then I dropped by her house, but her parents blew me off per her request.

I hated this because I felt really bad for what I'd done. I wished I could go back in time and just be honest about my feelings. That night of the double date, I should have told Leighton what Nusef said to me, even if I didn't feel the same at that time; or at least I thought I didn't. All my lying, in order to protect her feelings, only made things worse. The look on her face when she saw us together was still etched in my mind. And I loved Nusef, I did, but honestly, this was making it hard to enjoy my relationship with him. It just didn't feel the same now that Leighton knew and hated me.

"Hey!" I called out, sticking my hand in the air since some tall ass nigga and his friends had walked between Leighton and me.

Leighton glanced my way, and when she saw me, she rolled her eyes and started off with some girl. I speed walked to catch up, and then tapped her shoulder so that I could get her attention.

When they both turned around, I said, "Hey, Leighton, can I talk to you for a minute?"

"Talk, Jonaya, and make it quick."

"This is your break between classes though, so why the rush?" I cocked my head, glancing at the girl who was standing next to her.

"Because I don't want to spend my whole entire break talking to you. If you haven't noticed, me and you aren't friends anymore."

"Okay, I'll catch you later, Leighton," the random said before walking off.

"Leighton, I'm sorry about everything. You have every reason to be mad at me because I should have told you. I wanted to, but by the time all of this happened, you really liked him and had slept with him."

"So during the whole time I expressed wanting to be with Nusef, you didn't have feelings for him at all?"

"I did, but I didn't know, if that makes sense. He'd been my best friend for a long time, so I'd confused my feelings for friendly love. If I had felt this way and knew it from day one, I would have told you."

"I don't believe you. From what I saw at that party, y'all appeared to have been in love or together for a while, Jonaya."

"Well we haven't been. It's new."

Grunting, she said, "You don't even like him as much as I did! You only want him because I had him, Jonaya!"

"What?"

"I saw the way you looked every time I told you something he and I had done. I just thought you were worried about me because he was a hoe and a player, but no, you were upset about it because you wanted him. I never once heard you express feelings for him, but now all of sudden, they were just hidden this whole time and only recently surfaced?"

"You're right, I was upset, but it's because by that time I'd realized I had feelings for him. Leighton, I even tried to suppress them so that this wouldn't happen, but I couldn't help it. And then Nusef was persistent!"

"Of course, blame it on Nusef." She rolled her eyes and shook her head.

"I didn't mean to blame him, I was just saying that his persistence didn't help me any."

"Well, Jonaya, I don't know what to say. If you were really my friend, none of this would have happened. A real friend would have told me that he had feelings for her, and to move on."

"I am your real friend, alright? Stop fucking saying that. I can barely enjoy my relationship because of all of this! If I wasn't your real friend, I wouldn't even give a fuck!"

"Oh, poor Jonaya. She can't enjoy being laid up with a nigga I was falling for because she did me dirty," Leighton mocked me. Everything I was saying was coming out all wrong right now.

"Okay, Leighton, how can we fix this? We can't let a man break us up. We've been friends for a long time and I don't want to lose you, and I know you feel the same."

"No, I don't wanna lose you. I love you, Jo."

Grinning widely, I said, "Okay, good. So maybe later we can go—"

"No, no, no. Before we resume being friends, I need you to do something for me. If you don't, then don't ever talk to me again."

"What?"

"Break up with him."

"No, Leighton, you can't ask me to do some shit like that. I love him, why would I break up with him?"

"Well." She shrugged and threw her arms out before allowing them to lazily fall back at her side. "If you can't break up with him, then we can't be friends. But whatever you do, just know you can't have us both. Either you want your friend, or you want Nusef."

"That's selfish as fuck and you know it!"

"Bye, Jonaya."

I watched her walk off and thought about jumping on her back and punching her in the head. Instead, I took a deep breath and went to get some food. By the time I finished eating, which I barely did because my appetite had somewhat vanished, it was time for my last class of the day. This was the day Rori and I finished classes at the same time, and since she drove, we went home together.

When I got to the house, I saw Yikayla and Dree in the den playing with Lonan. I loved when Yikayla visited because now that she lived with Waayil, I didn't see her or my nephew as much as I liked. I was used to seeing them every day, and I missed that a lot.

"Byyyye!" Lonan sang to me as he walked up to me and handed me a chip. He loved saying 'bye' to people and it was so cute.

"Thank you, cutie." I smiled and took the chip.

"It's 'hi,' Lonan. Can you say 'hi'?" Yikayla said to him as he made his way back over to her.

"Ugh, Lo, why is the chip wet?" I frowned. I looked to see him leaning against his mom's legs, smiling at me smugly as if he understood.

"You are gonna be a little heartbreaker when you grow up," Dree said to Lonan's handsome self before we all chuckled.

Dree got up to leave since she had to go meet with her study group, so she hugged both Yikayla and I before I sat down.

"Leighton hates me," I sighed.

"Of course she does," Yikayla chuckled. "I don't know why you just didn't tell her that Nusef was crushing on you. She's embarrassed, Jonaya."

"Embarrassed about what?"

"This whole time she was bragging to you about him liking her, and expressing her feelings for him, when in actuality, you knew he didn't really want her. Wouldn't you be a little ashamed? If you were bragging on some nigga, yet, the entire time we all knew he didn't really fuck with you like that?"

"Yeah." I exhaled and shook my head. "I didn't try to do this though. I really thought I didn't like him. And then I assumed my feelings would fade, and when it got worse, I just hoped they'd break up and she wouldn't care if I slid in her spot."

"Yeah, *all* bad ideas." Yikayla ws quiet for a moment but then she said, "I would have beat your ass if I was her."

"Yeah me too," I chuckled.

"That's how you know she loves you because she didn't. And Leighton is no punk."

"Well, she wants me to break up with him or we can't be friends."

"In that case, you have to decide which relationship is more important to you or give her some space and hope she comes around."

I nodded in response before Rori came in and changed the subject. I wouldn't dare ask her opinion because she was always about doing the right thing. That's why I was so surprised yet happy as hell that she'd slept with Gavin's right hand. Not only did Gavin not deserve Rori, but also, she seemed so much happier with Eko.

After chilling for a little bit with my sisters, I had something to eat and then decided to go to Nusef's shop since he said he'd be working a little later tonight. I felt like maybe being around him would make me feel better, or at least help me decide. I knew I didn't want to break up with him, but I wondered if that was selfish of me.

I walked into Monarch, and the girl at the front greeted me. I just gave her a faint smile because I knew she didn't like Yikayla. And if you didn't like one of my sisters, I didn't like you.

I walked straight through, and down the hallway until I got to Nusef's tattoo room. The door was closed, so I contemplated if I should wait or knock. He'd let me sit in on his work before when it was something chill, but this could have been an ass tattoo or something, so I didn't wanna barge in.

I heard laughing and low conversation, so instead of waiting, I just knocked and slowly entered the room. I saw he was in there with Rebecca, and it looked like she was helping him clean up.

"What the fuck, Sef?" I frowned, shooting daggers at him.

His smile faded quickly as fuck upon seeing me. "Oh nah, baby, Rebecca was just helping me straighten up is all."

"Why does the door need to be closed for that?"

"I guess I will go. I'm not trying to be in the middle of any mess. See you tomorrow, Nusef." Rebecca walked to the door.

"Oh you're definitely trying to be in the middle of something; this relationship. Don't think you're slick, bitch."

"Jonaya," Nusef called my name.

I waited for Rebecca to reply, but she just left out, shaking her head. I closed the door behind her, and leaned up against the sink with my arms folded.

"Why was the damn door closed, Nusef? You know she wants to be with you, yet, you're closed off in here with her, alone."

"Jonaya, you're acting like you walked in on us fucking or some shit. She was helping me out so I can get home quicker."

"What you're doing is disrespectful and you need to be able to see that. If I was somewhere closed up with Marquise, you would have been trying to fight him."

"Yeah, because you don't know how to tell that nigga no. How many times have you seen me get in her ass about pushing up on me? A lot. So don't act like I just be letting her make moves and don't say shit."

"You know what, fuck you, Nusef. You lock yourself in a room with that hoc all day if you want to."

"Jonaya—" He reached for me.

"No, move." I snatched my arm from his reach, and then yanked the door open. Walking back to the front, I told Rebecca, "Let me catch you sniffing around my man one more time and it's gon' be over for you."

She chuckled but I didn't care. I didn't need her to be intimidated at all. In fact, I was happy she wasn't, because that meant she'd fuck with my nigga again and give me reason to knock her out. But Nusef had better watch that shit before I gnaw off his balls. Yes, I said gnaw!

5

____

RORI GOODE

"Come in here with me, baby, please," I begged Eko as we sat outside in the parking lot of this big business building downtown.

I was in my senior year of college, which meant I had to bag this internship or it wouldn't look good for me. My ultimate dream was to work in politics, and even become mayor or something like that. I don't know, I wasn't sure, but I loved politics and wanted a job within it.

Today, I had an interview for an internship working with the campaigning team of some important man who was gonna be running for mayor later this year. It was the perfect internship for me, which is why I was so damn frightened to even go inside. If I didn't get it, I may be depressed for weeks.

"What the hell am I gon' be able to do, ma?" Eko chuckled as if I wasn't sweating bullets in this ugly ass skirt suit I was wearing. I looked like a complete fool with my hair pushed all the way back into one of those buns with no part, that only old bitches wore.

"I don't know. If they don't give it to me, maybe you can beat them up. Oh! Or while I'm interviewing, just stare at them with that glare you have. It's pretty scary."

"Rori, get yo' ass out my car, mane." He shook his head, laughing at me as I exhaled heavily.

"Fine. Fine. But if I don't get it, I'm blaming you."

"If you get it, we can celebrate over dinner or something. If you don't, I'll just dick you down real good, make you feel better." He nibbled on his lip, giving me that look that always made my panties want to slide down my legs.

"Can I get dinner *and* some dick if I get it?"

"Oh, of course."

"Okay." I giggled before kissing his lips a few times and hopping out of his car.

Once Eko had driven off, I straightened up my clothes and took a few deep breaths. I'd been practicing what I was going to say for over a week now with my sisters' help. They were great, but I wished I hadn't listened to Dree and wore this damn outfit, especially now that I was inside, seeing all the other potential hires dressed a little more casually.

"Fuck," I mumbled as I sat down, feeling like a loser.

I realized I needed to sign in, so I got back up to do so. On my way back to my seat, I scanned the area and saw the posters of the man running for mayor. He looked way younger than he was, which was forty-six. He could pass for early thirties definitely, which I guess wasn't surprising because black didn't crack too often. Nodding my head in approval, I sat back down, next to the girl I originally peeped when I came in.

"Handsome, huh?" She grinned and nudged me. I didn't like the nudge part because she didn't know me, but I needed to be professional.

"Who?"

"Troy Garrick," she replied with a look like she knew that I knew exactly whom she was talking about.

"Uh, yeah, in a fatherly type of way," I lied. Nigga was fine as fuck, but again... I had to remain professional.

"Yeah, he can be my daddy anytime, okay?" She laughed lowly, and I just nodded because this was awkward. I didn't want anything I said or did to make me lose this job. "Scarlett." She put her hand out to the side so I could see it.

"Rori."

"Pretty."

Thankfully, she didn't say anything else, and then got called in before me. I went to the back about five minutes after her, and when I entered the interview room, I was close as hell to shaking. The room was empty, except for a big round wooden table, surrounded by a bunch of people dressed in the finest suits. They told me to stand by the white board and face them, as they shot question after question at me like balls in a batting cage. As I answered with as much poise and intelligence as I could, I tried to read their faces but I got nothing.

"Well, Rori, as you know, we expect you to treat this internship like the job of your dreams if we hire you. No, it's not paid, but we need you to act like it is. That means showing up on time and working, not only efficiently, but also effectively. If we were to hire you, do you think you'd be able to dedicate yourself to this? Regardless of the lack of pay?"

"Absolutely. I love politics, and this is the perfect job for someone like me. I just want the experience, I'm not really worried about the money at all."

And I need the college credit...

The guy who asked me the question stared at me for a minute, along with his colleagues, and then said, "Okay, so go next door and fill out some paperwork for us. We're gonna call your school and verify a few things from your application, and if it all checks out, we'll give you a call."

"Oh my gosh. So that means I got it?" I smiled.

"Yes, but this hire is contingent upon whether or not what you put on your application is valid."

"Right, yes, of course."

I was so damn happy I wanted to hug all of their uptight asses, but I refrained. After going next door to fill out some paperwork, which was just some personal information and emergency contacts, I was free to go. As mean as it may sound, I was praying Scarlett didn't get it because I didn't feel like being bothered with her ass for the next couple months. But of course, with my damn luck, she was hired with contingency as well.

Eko had some work to do this afternoon, so Yikayla agreed to pick me up. When I got outside though, I saw Waayil's car instead. Walking to it, I smiled when Waayil got out to open the back door for me. I hugged him, and then got in to see what my nephew was doing. Of course, Lonan was passed out in his car seat, with his little hands hugging his sippy cup. His soft curly hair was wild as usual, and of course, thanks to Waayil, he was wearing some baby Yeezy 350s.

"How'd it go?" Yikayla looked into the back at me as I placed a kiss on Lonan's plump little cheek.

"Great. I got hired, so all they have to do is verify some details and I'm good. I will start in a week. And remind me to never listen to Dree about what to wear. I was in there looking like a damn 1950's schoolteacher compared to everyone else."

Waayil and Yikayla burst into laughter as I rolled my eyes.

"Congrats though, ma." Waayil glanced in the rearview mirror at me.

"Yes, congratulations, Rori." Yikayla smiled as she looked back at me, still snickering lightly about my outfit.

"Thank you very much."

I let my head fall back against the seat, enjoying the masculine but not overwhelming smell of Waayil's cologne. My mind of course drifted to Eko because, outside of school, he was all I thought about with his fine ass. He was so perfect sometimes, too perfect, and it made me feel like I needed to watch him. But I realized that he was just a gift to me from God. I'd endured enough, too much actually, dealing with Gavin and now I was getting a break.

My phone started ringing, interrupting my thoughts, and I looked down to see it was Gavin's ass calling from prison. I knew it was him because every time my caller ID read *Unknown*, it was his ass.

"Is there a way to block unknown numbers?" I asked, staring down at my phone, waiting for the ringing to cease.

"No," Yikayla replied. "Why?"

"Gavin keeps on calling me from prison and I'm getting annoyed with it. And it doesn't give me the option to ignore the call, only slide to answer. Nor do I get the option to block."

"Gavin?" Waayil repeated but in question form.

"Yeah, you know Gavin, Waayil. That boyfriend I had for years. I'm sure you met him through either me or Eko before."

"No, Waayil was in jail by the time you got with Gavin, Rori," Yikayla corrected me, and after pondering for a moment, I remembered she was right.

"That's where I know that nigga from. Fuck. When Eko and I used to be corner boys, he had a homie named Gavin that used to play tough and wanna get on but couldn't. What a small fucking world," Waayil chuckled, but not like he actually found what he was saying funny. "That's the muthafucka who called me from jail, Kay."

"Gavin?" her eyes bucked. She was turned, facing him, so I could see the side of her face.

"What am I missing right now?" I inquired.

"Gavin called Waayil and told him that Alba's baby is his," Yikayla responded to me with a look of sympathy.

"Wait." I laughed and sat up straight. "Gavin and Alba? How? When? And as obsessed as she is with Waayil, why in the hell would she?"

My mind suddenly drifted to the golden blond curl I'd found on that nigga's shirt that day. It was all making sense now, why Alba was so eager to tell me about Gavin's *other woman* that he loved so much, inside of Victoria's Secret that day. Bitch was talking about herself.

"I don't know how true the shit is, but I'm definitely gon' find out.

That bitch brought her homegirl in with some bullshit ass story about why he hit me up, but we gon' see."

I shook my head, processing Waayil's words. That was one nigga whose bad side I didn't want to get on. Nusef was crazy too, but a lot of people didn't fuck with him because he talked more. People saw Waayil as quiet and assumed he was soft. It was funny because he was definitely crazier than Nusef. And in my opinion, Waayil *looked* crazier too. Maybe it was because I knew the twins, but Waayil just looked like he didn't take any shit, and Nusef looked like the nice one.

I used to live for seeing niggas press Waayil, only to get the ass whooping of their life and be confused as hell. Then Nusef, who they thought was the more psycho one, would just be looking at them shrugging. As we got older though, word spread around and niggas would show Waayil respect in order to keep from getting knocked out. I chuckled at my memories.

"I'm sorry, Rori." Yikayla broke me from my trip down memory lane.

"Oh, I don't even care anymore, Kay. I'm surprised because of who it is that he'd possibly gotten pregnant, but I really don't care."

Yikayla smiled and nodded before turning around in her seat.

A year ago, I would have been crying; shit, maybe even a few months ago. But after coming to terms with my true feelings for Eko, and expressing them to Gavin, I didn't give a fuck who Gavin stuck his dick in. I just wanted him to forget about me and never talk to me again. Maybe this baby with Alba would help him focus on something other than me. So not only did I *not* care, I was hoping and wishing that the baby *was* his.

Waayil stopped and got me something to eat before dropping me off at home. As I got out the car, I got a text from Eko asking about the interview, and telling me that he'd be to get me in half an hour.

Me: *I got it. I want a steak from Mesquite's and some head.*
Eko: *I got you. In that order.*

I bit down on my lip, just thinking about what was to come as I ascended the stairs. Eko would eat my pussy until I told him to stop, and I loved that.

"Hey, Mama." I walked into the house and saw a big ass bouquet of flowers. "Whose are these?" I touched them.

"Hi, sweetheart, and they're for you," she responded, wearing a look like she'd just sipped some piping hot tea that was none of her business.

"Me?" I pointed into my chest and she nodded with her brows raised. "Eko," I smiled to myself as I pulled the card that had obviously already been read, thanks to my mom. Nosey ass.

Congrats on the job. Enjoy Eko while it lasts bitch. —Jenni

6

YIKAYLA

I'd just come back from my break and as soon as I got into my workroom, my cell phone started ringing. I saw it was Waayil, so I closed the door behind me and sat down in the far corner so my voice couldn't be heard. I knew if Jerica found out I was talking on the phone during work hours, she would have a fit.

"Hello?" I smiled like a little child as I sunk down in the seat.

"What you doing?"

"Waayil, you know what I'm doing. I'm at work, and I'm supposed to be working, nigga."

"Then why you ain't working?"

"Because you called me!" I shrieked as we chuckled in unison.

"Nah, I'm fucking with you. I wasn't gon' call you, but I got like forty-five minutes before my next session and I started thinking about last night."

"Oh yeah?" I licked my lips.

"Yeah. I want you on my face again tonight. I swear that was the best fucking view I've ever had while eatin' pussy."

"Waayil, stop," I whispered, feeling my clit start to throb. I didn't have time to be getting horny as hell.

"You were riding my face, and I was just watching you, sweat dripping down the front of ya body and shit."

"Waayil," I whined, crossing my legs tightly to stop the feeling emerging.

"You remember how hard you came?"

"Yes."

"Shit, me too. Pussy was so wet and tight when I first slid in it. You gon' cum like that again for me tonight, right?" he asked, voice sexy, low, and raspy. The same tone he used when he would whisper in my ear before sucking on it, while stroking me deeply as hell.

"Mm hmm." I nodded as if he could see me, with my eyes closed and my teeth sunken into my bottom lip. I was already feeling the pain mixed with pleasure I got whenever Waayil beat it up. The way everything appeared to be effortless on his part, as he stared down into my eyes while making me cum.

"Shit, I gotta go. I need to eat before later."

"Are you serious!"

"Yo' panties wet than a muthafucka, huh?" He burst into laughter but I was too horny to find anything funny. "It's okay, you ain't gotta answer, Kay. I know my pussy," he said more so to himself as he moved around.

"Bye, asshole."

"Bye. I love you." He waited and when I didn't respond, he said, "Say it back."

"I love you, Waayil."

"Nah, say that shit the way you say it when I'm digging you out, ma. When I'm killing yo' shit from the back. That little cry shit with a slight stutter you do," he replied, just before mocking my voice and moans.

"Boy, get off my phone!" I quickly hung up and then went into the bathroom to use one of my wipes. He was right; I was very ready to go down below.

I washed my hands, and as I came out, I saw Brynn was in my workroom, leaning up against the door. Me and this bitch hadn't said a thing to one another since I found out she too had a child by Roscoe. I didn't know what kind of sick fucking game she was playing, but in a minute, it was gonna get her ass whooped.

"You need to go. I'm sure Jerica has plenty of things for a bottom feeder like yourself to do," I said.

Laughing, Brynn shook her head. "Look, I was just doing, or trying to do what you did to me in a way."

"I don't know what you're talking about." I plugged up the steamer. "And did you get this job because you knew I'd be here? No, I was here second... fuck. Just get out."

"Yeah, don't flatter yourself, Yikayla. It just so happens that Roscoe likes girls who aspire to be in the field of fashion. It was just my luck when I saw your name added to the schedule. Your name isn't too common, so I knew it had to be you."

"Brynn, what the fuck do you want? Because I'm very close to causing harm to you."

"Well, ever since Roscoe met you, he doesn't want to be with me."

"If I'm not mistaken, he told you he and I were together *before* you two, dummy. Roscoe had been my man for five years up until recently."

Ugh, I was so damn sick and tired of saying this shit. I mean, how many hoes did this nigga have? And how did he pull it off? All of us couldn't have been that oblivious, but then again, he had a lot of free time doing 'music.'

"Yeah, that's what y'all say, but I don't believe it. Plus, my child is older than yours so that makes what Roscoe and I have stronger."

"Keep telling yourself that."

"Anyway, just like you stole my man, I'm gonna steal yours. I know everything I need to know to get Waayil, and that's all thanks to you."

I didn't say anything for a few moments, and then I started to roar with laughter. Not only because I would never let her steal anyone from me, but Waayil wouldn't let this bitch see the waistband of his boxers, let alone smash or even date her. If she wanted to get her feelings hurt from trying to push up on my man, then she could be my guest. I wasn't insecure at all, and Waayil made sure of it. I was extremely confident that once she tried to make any kind of moves, Waayil would hurt her feelings, embarrass her, or worst-case scenario, shoot her ass.

"Girl, you couldn't even keep Roscoe, and he's at the bottom of the nigga food chain. But good luck with trying to steal Waayil."

She started moving towards me. "Don't you tell me— ah!" she screamed and jumped back when I pressed the button on the steamer and let it shoot out into her face.

"Make that the last damn time you try to walk up on me, bitch. Next time, I'm clocking your stupid ass over the head."

Before I could even finish, she was scurrying out like a roach when you hit the lights. I laughed thinking about how she was covering her big ass eyes up on the way out.

I cut the steamer off, went to lock the door, and then got back to work.

A couple hours later, I was finally off and ready to go get my baby from my mama. But before I left, I wanted to check something, so I slipped back into the bathroom after letting Jerica know I was gonna head out, and retrieved the pregnancy test from my purse.

I'd been really tired lately, more than usual, which was exactly what happened when I got pregnant with Lonan. I didn't really want to be pregnant because Lonan was so small still, but when I thought about whom the baby came from, it made me smile. Plus, I just couldn't ever see myself getting an abortion.

I did my business and then washed my hands before hitting my iPhone to start the timer. The five minutes seemed to fly by, and I guess that was because I wanted it to go slower, giving me a minute to think. I slowly looked down at the test, and sure enough, it read that I was pregnant. Now that I was facing fact and no longer guessing and wondering, I felt weird as hell. I was happy, but also afraid too.

"Oh, sorry," Jerica said when she accidentally walked into the bathroom. "I thought you'd gone home, Yikayla."

"Yeah, I just had to use the bathroom. But go ahead. See you next week, Jerica."

"Same to you, darling. Oh, do you know what happened to Brynn? Her face was really red and she asked to go home early."

Shaking my head, I replied, "I haven't the slightest idea."

"K. Have a good one."

I left work and went straight to my mom's place so I could get Lonan. I noticed Buddy wasn't there, and he'd been coming over less and less. Like usual, my mother was gradually cutting him off since my stepdad was gonna be back soon.

I got my baby and strapped him into his car seat. When I closed the back door, I almost jumped out of my skin seeing Roscoe standing all close to me.

"What the fuck, Roscoe! What are you stalking me?"

"No, I dropped by and ya moms told me you'd be home soon to get Lonan, so I waited outside."

"You waited outside instead of chilling with your baby? Of course."

"Damn, you're always complaining! A nigga can't do shit right! I came here to talk to you, not to intrude on yo' time with our son."

Excuses.

"Talk to me about what, Roscoe? I honestly don't have the time to talk right now. I have things to do."

"About the shit that happened while we were over at Brynn's crib. Shit wasn't supposed to be like this. I—"

"You what, Roscoe? I'm sure the story is the same as the one you had for RJ's mother, Christelle. You slept with Brynn and made a baby by accident, only this time we'd been together for a year, and you'd already impregnated Christelle."

"But I don't love either of them. I mean, I love my kids, but I ain't trying to be with either one of them like that, ma. I was stupid when I made them mistakes, and young. I didn't wanna be tied down, but now I do."

I stood there, leaning up against my car with the most unenthusiastic expression ever. I didn't care about none of the shit he was saying right now, and it was just going in one ear and out the other. I was actually a bit baffled that he thought there was something he could say to me to make me even contemplate being with him again. Plus, I was in love with Waayil, so even if Brynn and Christelle didn't exist, I still wouldn't want to be with him.

"Roscoe, I am done with you, sweetheart. I need you to really understand that. The only thing I want from you is to be a father to Lonan. I have no interest in being in any type of relationship with you, ever again. We were barely hanging on before I found out that you had not one but two babies on me. If you loved me, that would have never happened."

"We were new, Yikayla! Damn!" He stomped his foot like a bratty child. I could tell he was very upset and frustrated, but I didn't know what to tell him. "I would never do no shit like that now."

"Move so I can open my door. I have to go."

"Yikayla."

"Move!"

"I ain't done talking to you yet!" He gripped my arm.

"Roscoe, stop! I'm not fucking around with you!" I tried to push him off. We were moving a lot, but both stopped when we heard something light hit the cement of the driveway.

Roscoe immediately snatched up my positive pregnancy test, that I'd hurriedly shoved into my back pocket earlier when Jerica burst in on me.

"Yikayla, no." His voice trembled.

Is this nigga about to cry?

"Roscoe—"

"Baby, please don't do this shit to me." He dropped down to his knees like he was Sisqo from Dru Hill, and hugged my waist.

"Yikayla, please don't have this nigga's baby. I swear to God I'll do anything," he cried.

For a moment, I was frozen, but then I tilted his head back to see this nigga had real life tears flowing down his caramel cheeks. He looked just like a grownup Lonan, minus the adorable part.

"Roscoe, stand up, you look a mess," I replied lowly.

He sniffled and paused for a moment like he was pondering on whether or not he should stand up. I guess he chose not to, because he slammed his head back against my stomach and hugged my lower half tighter as he sobbed.

"Please, baby. I'll pay for the abortion, ma. Whatever you need. I'll cut Brynn, Christelle, Shamaria, and all them other hoes off."

There were more outside of Brynn, Shamaria, and Christelle? Damn! He was so hysterical he didn't realize that he'd finally admitted to dating Christelle's sister, Shamaria.

"Roscoe, get up!" I began smacking his head with my purse until he finally let go of my body to block the blows.

I continued hitting him until he was back far enough for me to quickly get into my car. I hit the lock button just in time, because he'd hopped to his feet and tried to yank it open.

"Lonan! Tell yo' mama to forgive me!" Roscoe banged on the backseat window, wailing as I sped off. I glanced at Lonan in my rearview, and he was looking at his father like he was the biggest fool in the world.

"Promise Mommy that you won't be anything like that, okay?" I said to my baby before exhaling heavily and continuing home.

Roscoe honestly, truly, wholeheartedly... never ceased to amaze me.

7

NUSEF CHRISTIAN

I was on a break, basically because my next tattoo wasn't for a couple hours, so I wanted to check on Wednesday and see how she was doing. Her foot had been slowly healing, so she was using crutches and shit to get around at the moment.

I still couldn't wrap my damn mind around the fact that Waayil had actually shot her ass in the foot. I mean I didn't put shit past my brother, but I never thought he'd go there with Wednesday. I understood he was angry, but the least he could do was see how the fuck she was doing.

"How is everything?" I entered Wednesday's room. She was lying on the bed with her foot propped up, watching some bullshit on TV.

"My foot feels okay, I guess, but I'm just wondering when Waayil is gonna come around," she sighed.

Sitting on the edge of the bed, I said, "Yeah, me too. I'm gon' holla at his ass though and see what's up."

"I don't think it will work. He hates me now."

"Aye, aye, don't say that, ma. He doesn't hate you, he's disappointed, which is a big difference. And, baby, I think everyone is disappointed because of what you did. It's just that your actions affected Waayil the most, so it's taking him longer. Harry too, but he can't quite complain."

"I just wish I could go back in time or something. I hate being at odds with Waayil like this."

"Look, don't worry, Wednesday. I'm gon' see him today when I head back to the shop, and I'm gon' get his hard-headed ass together, aight?"

"Okay." She smiled, just before I kissed her face.

I chilled with Wednesday for a little longer until she started watching one of them VH1 reality shows that I couldn't stand. That shit made me think about Jonaya and how she'd force me to watch that shit.

Speaking of my baby, I hadn't talked to her really since we'd gotten into that stupid ass argument over Rebecca. I understood where she was coming from, but she needed to realize that I could control myself. Not only that, but I had no interest in being with anybody else but her. And yeah, I loved Jonaya, but I wasn't about to let her control who the fuck I hung around, especially since she knew I wasn't gon' do shit.

Before leaving the house, I decided to say what's up to Emil since I rarely saw him. Nigga acted like he was too good for the rest of the family and shit. I saw his door was cracked, so I just walked in but immediately regretted that shit. He was right in there, kissing the fuck out of some nigga that looked like one of the little homies named Mooney.

"Get the fuck back!" Mooney barked once he saw me, shoving Emil off the bed and onto the floor.

"Nigga, what the fuck is wrong with you pushing my broth—"

"Sef! Stop, man." Emil cut me off and jumped in front of me, in order to stop me from charging Mooney's bitch ass.

"Fuck you let him push you like that for, huh?" I hissed. I was hot as fuck right now.

"It's fine! I'm grown! I can handle my fucking self! Damn! You and Waayil just need to back the fuck off!" Emil roared.

I stared hard into Emil's eyes, trying to calm myself down. I wanted so badly to Allen Iverson his ass so I could get around him and to Mooney. Instead, I gave Mooney eye contact to let him know I'd be seeing his ass around, and then I made an about face before leaving the room.

I drove like a bat out of hell back to the shop because I was so damn pissed. I knew Emil wanted to handle himself, but it was hard for me to just step back. He was way too damn soft, and I wasn't used to being related to anybody like that. Shit, even Midori would get down if she needed to.

I spoke to the few patrons waiting in the lobby as I walked to the back where my office was. I still had another hour before my next person, so I decided to check some emails and handle some other computer work while I waited. About twenty minutes into me handling correspondences, I heard a knock on my door.

"Come in!" I shouted, keeping my eyes on the screen.

"Hey, Nusef." Rebecca came in and closed the door behind herself. "I'm off now, and I've clocked out already."

"Oh, okay. You need something?" I turned from my computer and leaned back in my chair some.

"Can I sit down?" she inquired and I nodded. "I wanted to talk to you, and yes, this is about something personal. But before you even say anything, I'm not here to argue or accuse you of anything, Sef. The way things ended with us was so abrupt, and I think that was why I had such a hard time just letting it go. Yes, I love you, a lot, but as a friend now. I've realized that the relationship we *did* have was not what I thought it was, and now that I see that, I'm okay with you moving on with Jonaya. Like you said, I need to be with someone who loves me and only me, and I will be. I'm actually excited to meet that person, wherever they are.

I umm... I also wanted to say that when I see Jonaya, I'm gonna apologize to her because I was wrong and she was right to be angry. I was acting out because I felt like she was taking something away from me, but in reality, I never had you. I mean, I did, but not in the way that I thought. So yeah, I just wanted to tell you that, and let you know that from here on out, I hope we can be cool and continue to work together. I won't be causing any more problems with you or your relationship."

I took a moment to process what Rebecca was saying, and even though I was happy to hear she wouldn't be on her *woe is me* tip, I would be lying if I said I didn't feel some type of way. Don't get shit twisted, I didn't want to be with her like that at all because I loved Jonaya more than anything, but hearing that Rebecca was pretty much washing her hands completely, fucked with me and I didn't understand why. Maybe it was because a nigga had become a bit attached to her over the years we'd spent together, but I'd rather be cool with her than be at odds.

"Well good, ma, I'm glad to hear all that. But I thought you were fucking with Sax."

Tittering, she replied, "Yeah, I only started dating him because I thought you'd be jealous and want me back. But no, he and I aren't anything special."

"You fucked him?" I had to know.

"No, Nusef, I didn't sleep with him. We shared a kiss or two, and we cuddled some nights but that's it."

Nodding, I said, "Oh, aight."

"Alright. Well, you have a good rest of the day, Sef. And remember your first client is at 9 a.m. tomorrow so don't be late." She rose to her feet and went to open my door.

"Yeah, yeah, yeah. Get outta here."

She chuckled before leaving and after thinking about what had happened for a moment, I got back to work. Just thirty minutes later, I heard thirst bucket ass Chiara saying 'hi' to Waayil, so I knew he was here. Getting up, I came out of my office and met him in the hall-way. We dapped one another up, and then I followed him into his office where he placed some of his shit down.

"Before you go out there, let me get at you, Yil." I stopped him. Not saying a word per usual, he folded his arms and looked at me. "You need to go see Wednesday. Aye wait, listen." I palmed his chest when he tried to walk past me and leave. "Man, you know she didn't mean what the fuck she did, so how long you gon' be mad?"

"As long as I want to, my nigga." He started off but then stopped. "And how the fuck you know what she meant and meant not to do? Oh 'cause she told yo' ass that?"

"Yeah, and because that's my sister too, muthafucka. I know her personality and she ain't do that shit because she hated you!"

"Oh my fucking gosh, bruh." He laughed, clapping his hands together. "Nigga, you need to learn what the fuck loyalty means. You my muthafuckin' blood at the end of the day and whoever I ain't rocking with, you don't need to either. In this case, I understand because she's our sister, but how dare you bring yo' dumb ass up in here and try to convince me that I should forgive her? I don't work on nobody's muthafuckin' time but Waayil Christian's!"

"You being mad at first, aight... I understand. But now the shit has gone on too long!" I barked at him, getting just as angry as he was.

"Gone on too long?" He bucked his eyes and chuckled. "Did you spend six fucking years of yo' life in prison? Did you fight for six months straight and get thrown in the hole because niggas wanted to test you? Did you miss out on six years of being with the woman you loved, only to come home and find out she had a whole fucking life without you? Nah, you didn't, nigga, I did!" He hit his chest.

"And that's yo' fault! Didn't nobody tell you to kill that nigga!"

"Nah, they didn't. I chose to murk his ass because I thought he'd done something foul as fuck to a person I loved more than anything. See, Nusef, I protect the people I love and I hold them down regardless. That's some shit yo' bitch ass needs to learn, bruh. Straddling the fence ass nigga."

"Fuck you, bruh. That's yo' damn sister, and you over here acting like you hate her ass!"

"Because I do! Right now, I hate her muthafuckin' guts! Every time I hear her name, I wanna wring her neck. But because I *do* love her, I'm trying to keep my distance until I can control myself. And because I *do* love her, when I found out what she did, I didn't take my ass down to the police station and let them know she put the battery in my back by lying. But nah, you muthafuckas don't see it that way, huh?" he grinned. "Nah, y'all are too busy worried about poor ass Wednesday and how she's feeling."

"Waayil—"

"Sef, don't come at me about this shit no more. Because you're letting this shit come between what you and me got going on, and that ain't ever supposed to happen."

Before I could respond, he shoulder checked me and left his office. Feeling defeated and like there was nothing I could say to convince him, I just went back to my office until it was time for my next tattoo.

When I was done with my last client, I texted Jonaya to see if she could come over, and once that was squared away, I went home without saying shit to my brother.

Jonaya got dropped off about ten minutes after I got home, so by that time, I had just gotten out of the shower.

"How you doing?" I asked her as I pulled her down into my lap. We were in my bedroom, with only the TV on.

"I'm fine, Sef."

"I'm sorry about the shit I said about me and Rebecca. You were right about us being in the room with the door closed."

"What made you come to that conclusion?" She turned to look at me.

"Believe it or not... Rebecca made me see it."

"What?"

"Yeah, she came in and gave me this whole damn speech and basically said you were right and all this shit."

"So you believe it when that bitch says it, but not me?"

"Nah, I think I was just upset when I was talking to you, so I wasn't really hearing what you were saying. But from now on, I'm gonna make sure I respect what we got at all times."

"Thank you."

I kissed her lips, her cheek, and then her neck.

"I love you." I placed her on her back.

"I love you too."

8

DREE GOODE

"Ahhh," I whimpered as Canyon hammered into me.

He had my legs over his forearms as he dug deeply as hell inside of me. I felt like I'd cum one thousand times by now, and was on the verge of letting go of another as he slammed into me with force. We were both sweating profusely, moaning together in perfect harmony, just before he delivered a few more quick pumps and exploded.

"Shit." He grumbled against my lips as he sucked on them one by one. "I don't think I'll ever get tired of this pussy, Dree."

"You better not." I panted as he slowly pulled out and rolled off of me. My body was still reacting to his sex game, causing my legs to tremble a little.

I watched him remove the condom, and then we both went to the bathroom so he could flush it and then we could brush our teeth. We were literally in the bathroom brushing while butt ass naked.

"Ugh, Canyon, stop!" I jumped when he pressed his dick and balls up against my ass.

"Wait a minute now. Yo' ass was just hollering and crying in pleasure when I had this shit bumping ya cervix, but now it's 'ugh?'"

Spitting out my mouthwash, I replied, "Yes, because now I'm out of the sex zone. I'm back in my right mind and recognizing that our fornication was a sin."

He looked at me like I was crazy for a few moments before speaking.

"If you don't get the fuck outta here."

We laughed in unison as he turned the shower on.

We cleaned up together, and then returned to the bedroom so that I could get dressed for class, and he for work. It was funny how I tried to tell myself that he was beneath me, when clearly Canyon was ahead. He was the one with two degrees and working a career already, and here I was only with an undergrad degree and in law school. I was really tripping out before.

His phone beeped on the nightstand, and since I was closer, I picked it up. I saw it was a message from Jodi on what looked like Twitter.

"Damn, nosey." Canyon snatched his phone from me to check the notification on the screen.

"I thought you said you blocked her, Canyon."

"I did on everything else, but I ain't used this Twitter shit in a minute, so I couldn't figure out how to do it. But fuck that shit, I'm just gon' roll up on her and see what the problem is."

"What? No! That's what the hell she wants you to do! She's doing all of this in order to get your attention."

"Dree, I'm not about to keep blocking this bitch on every damn social media page. And shit, I can't even figure this one out and she's been blowing me the fuck up. Nah, I'm stepping to shorty and letting her know the deal."

"No, baby, I can do it," I smiled. "Yeah... she works at my mom's waffle house as you know, so I can drop by there after class and let that bi— young woman know that she needs to leave you alone."

"Baby, that ain't gon' be enough."

"And all this time, I thought you knew me. Clearly you don't realize who you're talking to, because once I let her know to step off, she's going to."

"No—"

"You got in Sean's face, so let me do this." I raised a brow as he placed the tip of his tongue against his molars. "Yeah, you didn't think I knew that you talked to him, did you?"

"Nah, I didn't, but I'm not surprised he ran and told." After snapping his watch on, he asked, "Have you seen him recently?"

"Now that you mention it, no. He hasn't been to class and the teacher asked a classmate to get him his assignments. I would have inquired about him, but I remembered I didn't care."

Canyon chuckled and nodded.

"Aight. And yeah, you better not care." He draped his arm around my shoulders and kissed me gently. I inhaled deeply, loving the scent of his body wash mixed with his cologne.

"You're so clean, baby."

"Well, you know." He winked, making me roll my eyes.

After kissing and feeling one another up a little bit more, we got in separate cars to head to the same place basically. When I got to class, I spotted Monroe so I went and sat next to her.

"Guess who's back?" she whispered.

"Wh—" I scanned the room so before I could even fully ask, I already knew who she was referring to. There Sean was, sitting across the room, watching me like a hawk. "Damn, he must have not been getting any sleep with all those days off. Do you see the dark circle around his left eye?" I frowned.

"Girl, someone whooped his ass." Monroe looked over her shoulder and then leaned in more. "Supposedly, he was hit across the face with a bat."

"Damn!" I clenched my teeth, not even wanting to know what that pain felt like. "Did your source say why?"

"Sean told Cary that some guy was manhandling some woman in front of a liquor store, and when he stepped in, the guy pulled his bat out and started swinging. I guess it was a brave thing to do."

"Monroe, come on. This is Sean we're talking about. That boy probably couldn't tell you where a liquor store was if you pulled a bat out right now and threatened to give him a part two."

We both fell out in laughter, just as the professor came in and told everyone to quiet down.

"True. Well then I wonder what happened."

I shrugged before getting one more look at Sean. I tried to think about what the real story could have been, when suddenly it hit me. If Canyon didn't do this, it'd be one hell of a coincidence. I just thought he told him off, I didn't know he went back and fucked him up too. I was hoping he hadn't, but I admit it was kind of sexy knowing that he might have reverted to his old ways to protect me. Not to mention, there was some deep rooted hated for what Sean had done to me.

About forty-five minutes into class, the professor made us get into groups of threes to work on some section questions and choose a case to argue as a group for next class. Once situated, he stepped outside to take a phone call.

"Hey, Dree." My classmate, Cary, came to where Monroe, this girl named Andrea, and I were grouped up.

"Hey, what's up?" I glanced up at him in confusion. I'd never talked to him before and vice versa, so I didn't know why he was getting up to come greet me.

"I was wondering if maybe we could go out sometime."

"Uh, no, I—"

"And yes, I'll have a nice steak dinner and plenty of *champagne,* which is your favorite, right? That's all it takes to smash, right? I mean according to my man, Sean, over there." He grinned, just as Sean and his other friend, Derek, started to roar with laughter from across the room. "I have one condition though; if I get you pregnant, you *cannot* kill my child. I don't believe in that." He palmed his chest. Cary, Sean, and Derek started to crack up again.

Every student in the class's eyes were on me as my heart beat quickly and seemingly out of my chest.

"I don't know who the fuck—"

"Okay, sorry about that, class. Cary, I hope you guys have all your ducks in a row since you feel the need to get up." The professor walked in, cutting me off, and prompting Cary to rush back to his seat by Sean and Derek.

I was angry as hell, but also, I was embarrassed. I looked to Andrea and Monroe who were obviously surprised by what Cary had told the whole damn class. Monroe knew about the possible rape, but not the abortion.

The professor gave directions for the last ten minutes of class, but I could barely pay attention.

"Dree, don't—"

I left as soon as the professor said we could, not giving Monroe a chance to finish her sentence. I wanted to pull a paper bag over my head at this moment, but I also wanted to fight.

Rushing to my car, I hopped in and took my cellphone out. I tapped Canyon's name because I needed someone to talk to, but I quickly hung up. He was the wrong person to tell, especially right now, while he was working. I wouldn't be surprised if he marched over to this side of the campus and whooped Sean's ass on the clock. I loved Canyon way too much to have him jeopardize all that he'd worked for in order to protect me. And from the looks of Sean's poor face, Canyon had stood on the line for me enough.

"Hello?" Yikayla answered after a couple rings. I despised talking to my little sisters about things that bothered me because I felt like as a big sister, I was supposed to be the smart one, the one they came to for advice and help. However, right now I was panicking, and if I had to choose out of my sisters, I was gonna go for the oldest one after me.

"Hey, are you really busy?"

"I actually am just leaving the doctor and about to head to work, but I have some time to talk."

"The doctor, for what?"

"Just an umm, regular gynecologist appointment."

"Oh yeah, I forgot you were getting banged by Waayil every day now. Gotta get that vagina looked at and make sure it's still intact," I half joked, causing her to suck her teeth.

"Bitch, what do you want?"

I couldn't do it. I couldn't tell her what had happened to me and how weak I felt. I'd taken too long to express my feelings, and now I'd snapped out of my temporary vulnerable state. I just couldn't allow anyone outside of Canyon to see how broken I was within right now. I knew Yikayla, nor Rori, or Jonaya would see me differently, but I saw myself differently. There was no way I could let them in on that.

"You know what, it was nothing. I just wanted to see what you were doing. But I have my next class, so I will see you later for dinner... at the house?"

"Yes, and please be on time."

"Always."

I hung up the phone and just stared out the window for a moment, before getting out of the car and going to my next class like everything was okay.

A Few Hours Later...

I entered my mother's waffle house and spotted Jodi cashing out a check by the bar area. Making my way over, I sat on the barstool that was directly in front of her and stared. She pretended not to see me, or at least, I believe she was pretending, so I dropped my purse roughly on top of the bar.

"Oh, hi, Dree," Jodi smiled.

"Hi, Jodi. Can I talk to you for a little bit?"

"Sure, just let me take my customers their change." She pranced off before I could respond, and went to handle her business.

When she came back, I led her to my mom's office since I knew it was empty. My mother was never here, and if it weren't for the new manager she'd hired, this place would have probably gone down in flames.

Closing the door behind me after letting Jodi walk in, I lied and said, "Jodi, I like you. You're a sweet girl and you're one of my mother's top employees."

"Yes." Jodi nodded, folding her arms.

She was a pretty girl, with a vanilla complexion, and the light brown hair that she sported didn't come out of a box. Her frame was slim, and overall, she was pretty basic.

"Another thing, there are a lot of guys that would love to date you. I could even recommend a few if you'd like," I cheesed. "We just have to dust you off a little bit, but that's nothing."

"Dree, what is this about?"

"This is about my man, Jodi. This is about you constantly messaging Canyon and stalking his social profiles. I don't appreciate it, and frankly, you should be ashamed of yourself for even doing what you're doing."

Glaring at me hard, she said, "I don't have the slightest idea of what you're talking about."

Laughing because this bitch must have thought I was a fool, I replied, "Yes you do. You just messaged Canyon this morning! Isn't your twitter name Pretty Jodi?"

Shifting her weight from one leg to the other, with a frown, she just sighed and shook her head.

"Like I said, you must be confused. Tell your mother and sisters I said hello, will you?" She sauntered past me and out of the office, leaving the door open.

For a moment, I stared at the spot that she'd been standing in prior, utterly perplexed. This bitch was really crazy.

9

WAAYIL

This evening was the day of the damn DNA appointment and I was beyond ready to get this shit done and over with. If this was my kid, I wanted to know so that Alba and I could work on being cordial towards one another. I ain't want my kid growing up thinking I hated their mama, even though true enough, I did hold a strong ass dislike for her. However, at one point in my life, I did have love for her, and I knew with work I could at the least get back to that. She and I would never be shit anymore, not just because of Yikayla, so hopefully shit would work out.

Alba and I were just two totally different muthafuckas who saw shit differently. She liked to be the center of attention and all that bullshit, where as I liked to hang back. The only thing we had in common was in the bedroom, and unlike most of these muthafuckas, I needed more. I needed a female to stimulate my mental and *then* give me some of the best head and pussy of my life. That shit right there was wifey, not a female that could suck yo' dick with no questions asked, but then start stuttering like Porky Pig when you try to hold a conversation. Alba wasn't dumb by any means, but we never talked. All we did was argue, fuck, chill in silence, and repeat. She just wasn't Yikayla Goode.

"I wish you could snap your dick off so I could take it with me today." Yikayla stood in the doorway holding Lonan.

"Ma!" I laughed loudly because her face showed that she was dead ass serious. "You know it ain't no need for that. I do not wanna smash that bitch."

"I know. But see, Waayil, she's the type to slip something in your drink and then when you wake up, your dick is in her mouth and you're tied up."

"That doesn't sound half bad. I'm kidding, Kay, damn!" I shouted with a chuckle when she punched my chest with her free hand. "You gotta admit that was some freaky ass shit you just said."

"Whatever, Waayil."

"See you, little man. Can I get a hi-five?" I put my hand up and Lonan hit it before smiling widely as hell with his seven teeth in his mouth. Yeah, I knew how many teeth the little nigga had. He loved brushing them muthafuckas.

"So she finally answered your call?" Yikayla asked as I slipped my Jordans onto my feet.

"Nah, she actually hasn't, but she's coming to this damn appointment. I had to do the most to get it since this place was booked weeks out. Who knew all these muthafuckas needed DNA tests?" I frowned thinking about it as I pulled my hat down onto my head. I had to settle for a late ass 6 p.m. appointment, which I really didn't want, but I was desperate. I didn't even know appointments ran that late.

I kissed Yikayla's lips and then pecked Lonan's cheek before ruffling his soft ass hair up. After that, I was out the door and on my way to Alba's spot.

When I got there, I saw her car in the driveway and just shook my fucking head. She played too many damn games for me, which was another reason I didn't fuck with her like that. She knew damn well she'd seen my fucking call, yet, she didn't answer not a one, nor a text.

I banged on the door hard, and once people started to come out of their houses to see what the fuck was up, I picked her flowerpot up and used the spare key to get in.

Closing the front door behind me, I called out, "Alba!"

I got no response, so I patted my waist to make sure I still had my gun on me before calling her name again. I heard light sniffles as I neared her bedroom door, which was cracked, so I just touched it lightly to open it.

"Alba?" I said in a lower tone. She had the covers pulled up over her head, and her body shook lightly as she cried softly. "Alba, shorty get up we gotta... go."

I wanted to be demanding as fuck and snatch them covers off of her, but I was baffled as hell right now. Alba only cried if some deep shit happened. She cried when she found out her dad died, and then when I got a life sentence, but outside of that she remained stoic.

I peeled the covers back and saw her hair was down and her face was drenched. She still hadn't acknowledged me, not even when I turned her onto her back so I could look down into her eyes.

"Baby, what happened to you?" I questioned, worried as hell by this time. For the first time in a long time, I felt something for this woman. Not love or anything, hell nah, but I cared, which I hadn't in a minute.

"It's gone, Waayil so there is no point," she sobbed.

"It's gone? What's gone—" I stopped myself when it clicked for me. "Aye, come here." I sat her up and hugged her body before kissing her forehead. "Can I ask what happened?"

"I don't know." She sobbed into my chest. "I went to sleep and when I woke up, I'd bled everywhere. I called the ambulance and when I got to the hospital, they told me what I already knew."

"Damn, baby." I exhaled heavily as I rubbed her back gently. "How you feeling physically?"

"I don't want to talk right now, Waayil, I just want to lie down. I don't even wanna be here anymore," she sniveled.

"Aight, look." I pulled back some and looked down into her face.

"Stop talking like that. I know I don't get it because I didn't carry the baby, but taking yo' own life ain't the way to go, ma. You just need to chill out and relax. It's aight to grieve and shit, but don't get depressed."

She pushed her hair behind her ears as she nodded.

"I know I'm not gonna hurt myself, but sometimes I just want to disappear."

I honestly didn't know what the fuck to say, and honestly, I was feeling a little bad about this shit.

I stayed there with Alba for about an hour and a half longer, just because I didn't know if she'd try to make good on her death threat. I didn't wanna be with the bitch, but that didn't mean I wanted to walk in on her swinging from the plant holder on the ceiling.

After leaving her spot, I decided to stop by Monarch to see what was going on. I scheduled today off for myself for obvious reasons, but I wanted to make sure no shit had popped off and that the place wasn't running like an old beat up ass car since Nusef and I weren't in the building.

As soon as I pulled up, parked, and got out, a big black Yukon Denali rolled into the parking lot. The rims were shinier than a muthafucka and the windows were tinted darkly as fuck. I stared for a minute since they'd swooped into the park right next to my shit and damn hear hit me.

"Fuck wrong with you!" I hollered, not giving a fuck who was behind the wheel.

"I missed you, baby." The back window rolled down and there Zia was in the back seat, smiling hard at me. She reminded me of a younger, prettier, and thicker version of Zoe Saldana.

Fuck.

"Look, Zia, now ain't a good time for me. I'll hit you up at a later date or some shit, aight?"

She climbed out of the car and switched over to me wearing a dress that clung to her body like a latex glove. I wasn't turned on like I used to be in my prison days, so she looked dumb as fuck to me, trying to switch all hard and shit.

"I just want to get some things straight, Waayil. My daddy offered to do it for me, but I love you so I told him no in order to protect you."

"Protect me? I don't need no muthafuckin' protection from nobody, ma. Especially not yo' old decrepit ass pops."

"See, that's what I love about you, Waayil. That's exactly why Daddy wanted me with you because he knew that you wouldn't let anyone scare you; not even someone as vicious and powerful as my father."

"Zia, look, man, this right here ain't gon' work no more. I don' told ya pops that already. When I was in jail, thinking I would never get out, I agreed to fuck with you heavily, but now that shit has changed..." I shrugged trying to find the right words. "I don't want you. I got a girl now, and I'm not leaving that."

Chuckling, she asked, "So you used me?"

"Yeah, pretty much."

Fuck was I supposed to do, lie? That's exactly what the fuck I did, and if she or Neo couldn't see that, then they were dumb as fuck. I was a nigga locked up in jail for a life sentence and agreed to some long-term shit with a bitch I'd never met. It should have been beyond obvious as to why it was so easy to convince me. Muthafuckas can't be that damn blind and stupid.

"Wow." She shook her head as tears welled up in her eyes. "Can I meet her then?"

"Meet who?" I was frowning so hard that I felt that shit. "My girl? You better get yo' ass up outta here with that, Zia. Fuck I look like letting the bitch I was smashing while in jail meet my girl? I thought yo' ass was smarter than that, but I'm realizing otherwise."

"Waayil—"

"Nah, check this out. What we had was a convenient ass situation for me, ma. I fucked you because I needed some pussy and you were the only female I could get to. That's fucked up, but let's be honest, you knew what the deal was deep down. You knew I was busting you down because I didn't have anything else to do. You knew deep down, that I had no muthafuckin' feelings for you once I nutted."

"Yeah, but I thought that after a while that I'd grown on you. I didn't even know you when my father made me get with you, but over time, I started to fall for you, and I thought that was mutual."

"It wasn't." I shook my head. "I was in love with the same girl I'm in love with now, ma, and as you can see, that shit ain't gon' ever change. I didn't see or talk to her for years, and when I touched down from the pen, I was *still* in love." I wanted her to understand just how deeply my feelings for Yikayla ran.

Zia looked off and exhaled heavily while scratching her forehead.

"I—" she stopped talking and just hopped into the back seat of the truck before it pulled out.

"Waayil! You be having all the fine ass hoes!" some nigga leaning on the wall of the shop yelled to me.

"Man, get yo' ignorant ass off the wall of my shit and mind ya damn business."

"My bad, Waayil. Aye, you got like five dollars? A nigga is hungry as fuck." He rubbed his gut.

"Nah, I got some trash to be taken out and some floors to be swept. I'll give you twenty dollars for that."

"Aww, man, nah, come on!"

"If you want a little pocket money to help you take care of them triplets you 'bout ready to birth, you can sweep these fucking floors and take out the trash."

Sucking his teeth and looking off for a moment, he replied, "Aight, aight. Yeah, I can do that."

"What's ya name, man?"

"Dawson." He grinned widely as hell and stuck his hand out for me to shake. I just looked at it as if it were smothered in shit.

"Wash yo' damn hands first, my nigga. Come on." I opened the door for him. "And how the fuck you know my name?"

"Everybody knows the twins that own Monarch tattoo," he replied as I led him to the bathroom to clean his hands.

We walked back to the front once he dried them, and I handed him the broom.

"Aye, everybody, this is Dawson. He's gon' sweep the shop and take out all the trash around here. Once he's done, give him this twenty dollars." I pulled a twenty-dollar bill from my pocket and handed it to Rebecca who nodded.

"Nice to meet you, Dawson." Rebecca half smiled, and he licked his lips at her making her frown subtly.

"Get to work, bruh. If I come back tomorrow and shit is looking dusty, and that trash ain't out, it's yo' ass, mane."

"No worries. And you shady as hell for talking about my stomach earlier, Waayil!" he hollered after me, but I just kept it going out the door.

When I got home, I heard Lonan talking in his baby language, as the smell of seasoned meat hit my nose. I entered the kitchen to see Lonan in his high chair, and Yikayla making tacos.

"You remembered." I came behind her, pressing my dick against that plump ass. I sucked on the side of her neck as she smiled softly.

"You're home early. Ow, Waayil, I told you, you grab them too hard," she whined when I gripped her breasts.

"You just started complaining about that shit. You aight?"

"Yes, I'm fine, just be more gentle."

"I'm sorry, ma. Gentle like this?" I reached my hand down into the front of her tights and began to strum her clit.

"Baby," she moaned lowly. "I don't wanna burn the food."

After playing with her bud a little longer, I took my hand from her tights and washed them in the sink before scooping Lonan up.

"Say 'hiiii,' Lonan." Yikayla grinned over her shoulder. "He said it earlier but now he's acting shy."

He looked to me with his cute ass, placing one of his small fingers in his mouth.

"Say it, man. Say 'hiiii,'" I repeated after Yikayla.

"Hiiii," he replied before shoving his small face into my shoulder bashfully, which caused me and Yikayla to laugh.

"Baby, Jonaya said Wednesday got robbed and shot in front of your parents' house recently. Did you know that?"

"Shot?" I furrowed my brows.

"Yeah, and in the damn foot! Can you believe that? I swear Memphis ain't safe nowhere, even in the good parts of Midtown."

"Ohhh." I nodded. I'd wrongly assumed Wednesday's scheming ass had gotten shot again, which had me hot. Placing Lonan back into his high chair, I replied, "That was me, ma, but I ain't rob her."

Yikayla turned to look at me with her eyes wide and her sexy ass lips parted. My mind immediately drifted to her sucking my dick.

The silence lingered for a few seconds longer, before the both of us guffawed loudly.

"Oh my gosh, I shouldn't be laughing!" She covered her face as she continued to chuckle. "We ain't shit for laughing, Waayil."

"I know." I pulled her into me and kissed her lips.

10

———————

JONAYA

I was in the library typing the last paragraph of this paper that I'd been working on for the longest. I couldn't do it at home because there were way too many damn distractions, and then, Nusef would pop up and try to feel all on me even though he clearly saw I was working. This shit was worth 30% of my grade so I couldn't even let Nusef's good ass sex game get in the way of it.

Just as I hit save three times in a row to make sure that it went through, Leighton came and sat down next to me smiling. Wednesday came on the other side of me. Wednesday didn't have her crutches anymore, just this big ass black thing on her foot so she could walk. What happened to her made me feel not as safe as I used to on my quiet upscale street. All of my neighbors were well to do like my stepfather, but then again, I guess that's why some knucklehead was over there trying to rob folks.

"Hey." I smiled, turning my head to each side so they could see me. I saved my paper to my flash drive, and then safely removed it before shoving it into my purse.

"So did you do it?" Leighton quizzed.

Fuck. I thought she'd changed her mind or had at least forgotten about what she'd asked me to do because the three of us had been hanging out at Wednesday's just like the old days with no problems. She hadn't mentioned Nusef or wanting me to break up with him since she'd asked me to do it.

"Do what?" I inquired, hoping she was maybe talking about something she'd asked for that I'd forgotten about.

"Break up with Nusef, Jonaya. You know what I'm talking about."

"Wait, why would she do that?" Wednesday frowned and then turned her eyes onto me, waiting for an explanation.

"Ask her!" I said.

"Ladies, I need you to quiet down or leave the lab, please." Some lady with big fish tank glasses scolded us before walking off.

The three of us gathered our things back up, and I shut the computer down that I was on so that we could leave. When we got out of the computer lab, we sat down at one of the vacant tables outside.

"I told Jonaya if she wanted us to be friends again, then she needed to break up with Nusef, Wednesday."

"That's stupid though. They want to be together and have always wanted to." Wednesday shrugged as Leighton shook her head.

"Look, Leighton, there has to be a way that we can be friends without me dumping Sef. I love him a lot, and he loves me too. If we break up, I'm gonna be miserable. You want to hang out with me when I'm miserable?"

"So it's settled then. You've made a decision." Leighton stood up.

"Wait, what? What are you talking about?" My brows dipped.

"I told you to make a choice. And since you claim you'll be miserable if Nusef isn't your man anymore, then it's obvious you're choosing him over me."

"Leighton, that's stupid! You're acting like you were deep in love with Nusef or something and we all know you weren't!" Wednesday spat.

"So what! I liked him, and a lot. I made a fucking fool of myself pursuing him when the whole time he didn't even like me! And you..." She pointed to me. "...the person who has been my best friend for almost a decade, knew that shit and didn't even tell me. And now you want me to come be around you and your new man? Then be happy for you? Well, I can't. If you wanted the best of both worlds, you should have done your job as my friend and let me know what was going on."

"Leighton—"

She walked off before I could even say anything, so I grunted while running my fingers back through my hair.

"She's dumb, Jonaya. Hopefully she will get over it, and if not, oh well." Wednesday shrugged.

"Wednesday, you cannot tell me that everything she just said was wrong. She's right, I should have told her. If the tables were turned, I would have expected her, as my best friend, to pull me to the side and let me know this nigga was just using me to get back at her."

"Yeah, I guess that's true. Give it time. When she starts to miss you, she will get over it."

"I hope so. I really do." I nodded, staring off.

Wednesday and I went to get food from the student union food court, and then Rori gave us a ride home in my mom's car. Once home, Wednesday went across the street to her house and I got the keys from Rori.

"Where are you going? To see Nusef?" Rori smirked.

"Yes, I am. You didn't have plans, did you?"

"With Eko, but he's coming to get me." She was talking while backing up towards the porch steps. "I have to go take a shower though." She turned around and rushed up the steps.

"Freaky ass," I mumbled.

I was going to see Nusef, but first I wanted to go see Marquise. No one was giving up any information on who had possibly shot

Nusef, and we both felt like we knew exactly who it was. Nusef didn't have any enemies, but the one minor beef he had was with Marquise. It was pretty obvious if you asked me.

I parked in front of where Marquise stayed once I saw his car sitting in the driveway. I went up to ring the doorbell, bobbing my head to the loud ass music he was playing in his living room. When I realized he couldn't hear me, I knocked on the window a little. He peered through the blinds with his cute ass, and sucked his teeth before getting up to come open the door. The music cut off just before he did.

"Fuck you want?" He hissed down at me, staying behind the screen door.

"Can you open this so I can come in?"

"For what, Jo? We ain't no longer, so we don't have shit to talk about. Go take ya shady ass on somewhere."

"Please, it's important." I pouted playfully. He smirked a little and then unlocked the screen door to allow me inside.

"You look good." He smiled as he closed and locked the door.

I sat down on the couch before saying, "Thank you. Marquise, I came here to let you know that you can tell me what you did. You can be honest."

"The fuck are you talking about, Jonaya? I ain't ever did shit to you. If I remember correctly, you did me dirty, ma."

"Okay, I see you want to play dumb. You shot Nusef!" I rose to my feet abruptly.

"I ain't shoot no fucking Nusef. You out yo' damn mind. And don't be coming up in here accusing me of shit, Jo."

"Who else would have done it, huh? Nusef doesn't have any enemies! You're the only one he has, basically. If that even counts."

"If that even counts? What does that mean?"

"It means that he whooped your ass so you're not really a threat. Now it makes even more sense! You couldn't fight him like a man, so you shot him!"

"Jonaya, yo' crazy ass has got to go. I don't know if you've been watching too many damn detective shows or what, but you're way off ya mark."

"And all this time I thought you cared about me. The shooter was trying to kill me, but thankfully, Nusef hopped in front of me. And then the shooter just riddled him with bullets anyway! Not even caring!"

"Do you hear yaself? If I was gon' shoot somebody, I'd be targeting that nigga specifically. I did care about yo' ass before you fucked me over, and right now, I'm off you, but I would never kill you or try to. I can't stand yo' ass, but I still got love for you! Plus, before I met you, Nusef was the homie. I don't like the nigga, and I may have wanted to shoot him in the leg or something, but kill him? You fine, but it ain't that deep."

The look in his eyes appeared to be very sincere, but this couldn't be right. He had to be lying to me. I mean, who else could have done this?

"You promise you didn't—"

"No, ma, I didn't. And you're looking stressed as fuck right now. That nigga already got yo' ass on one. That's why you should have never stopped fucking with me."

"Marquise, stop." I moved past him and he grabbed my arm. "Stop." I yanked from him.

"You for real don't love me at all?" he questioned somberly.

"No, Marquise. I liked you when we were dating, but things just moved way too fast for me. You were ready for something that I wasn't."

"Yet, now you're his bitch. So it looks like you *were* ready."

"Because I've known him longer, and I... I love him, Marquise."

"Yeah, aight." He pulled the door open wider, so I continued out and to my mom's car.

I stopped to get some food for Nusef and myself since I didn't feel like making him anything tonight. I knew my mother had probably cooked, but I didn't feel like going back home to pick it up.

"You were supposed to be here like twenty minutes ago, Jonaya," Nusef said to me as I set the food on the coffee table.

"I went to see Marquise. Not for what you're thinking, Sef, so you can calm down." I put my hand out as I sat on the couch next to him. "I went to approach him about what he did to you. Or at least what—"

"Why the fuck would you go by yourself and do some shit like that? Nobody asked you to do that shit. I told you to stay away from that nigga multiple fucking times. What if he had have shot your ass when you got there, huh?"

"Calm down, Sef! He didn't even shoot you! And I went because I wanted to find that out! I'm not gonna sit and wait for you to tell me what to do about it!"

"I don't want you to do shit about it! I want you to move on with yo' damn life while I handle the shit!"

"The shooter was coming for me, so no! I'm not gonna just sit back!"

Nusef looked away from me and inhaled before exhaling sharply like he always did when I upset him.

"How you know it wasn't him?" he inquired after a while, tone and demeanor much calmer than before.

"Because think about it, Sef. Why would he want to shoot me? I know you don't want to hear it, but he cares about me."

Nusef shook his head.

"Well, that's yo' opinion. If I hear he did do it, or get a feeling about the shit, I'm coming for that nigga, and it won't be shit you can say to stop me."

"I know."

"Jonaya, I wanna eat." He sighed when I straddled his lap.

"Kiss me first. I don't like when you're all mad. You start being quiet like Waayil." I chuckled and so did he, even though he tried to suppress it.

"That nigga got the right idea, I'm starting to see." His big hands moved up and down my back before he kissed me gently.

"One more."

"Get yo' thirsty ass of me, bruh."

"Nusef!" I laughed before crushing my lips against his.

For now, I would leave this whole shooting thing alone, but that wouldn't last forever.

11

EKO BENNET

I was able to get into the prison to see Gavin today, even though I knew his bitch ass didn't wanna see me. He was still feeding them same muthafuckin' lies to Neo about how I set him up and shit. I didn't want Rori in the middle of it, but Gavin was a weak ass nigga, so of course he threw her name around like a hoe to support his case.

He made it sound like I chased Rori purposely and only because I was a shady ass nigga. Hell yeah, my efforts were on purpose, but I did the shit because for one, Gavin tried to play me himself, and secondly, I'd always had a thing for shorty. Wasn't no point in me fucking Gavin over and leaving her to starve with him. So in the process of taking his shit, I got Rori too.

Anyway, Neo hit me up to confirm, and when I told him I, in fact, was fucking with Rori, I could tell that he was kind of looking at me sideways. Nigga even tried to lecture me about loyalty, but I nipped that shit in the bud.

It was finally my time to speak with Gavin, so I sat in front of the glass where the phones were. When he came to sit on the other side, his face immediately twisted up as he shook his head. I'm sure he was wondering how I got on his visitor's list; he could thank Neo for that.

I knew Gavin hated me, and shit... I would hate me too. I wasn't in jail, nor on trial for a lengthy sentence, and I had his prized possession, Rori Goode.

"What's good, bruh?" I grinned, knowing I was getting under his skin.

"Fuck you doing here, mane? I don't fuck with you. You set me up so you could swoop in on my bitch and my work. You wanted to be me all this time."

I chortled heavily because I couldn't help it. The only thing Gavin ever had that I wanted was Rori, and I been knew she felt the same. Rori was just the ride or die type of female, so she would never just jump ship over a few feelings.

"Negro, please. I don't want shit you got, especially now. But I came to talk to you about—"

"You don't need to talk to me about shit unless you gon' stop smashing my bitch. If you gon' keep that shit up, then we ain't got nothing to discuss, patna."

"Aight, fuck it." I stood up and he looked surprised.

"Wait." He looked around and then back towards me as I sat down. "Eko, as my nigga, my brother, I'm begging you to please back up off her. You're breaking the fucking code, man!" he shouted in a whisper.

"I don't live by no damn code with you no more! Once I found out you were trying to cut me out of some shit we were doing together, it was a wrap for any loyalty I had to you!"

"I don't know what you're talking about."

"You think I ain't know you were trying to get Neo to work with you exclusively? Telling all the trap workers how they needed to pick a side because you were about to be running shit? Yeah, some of them weren't so loyal to you either, *patna*, because they told me that shit as soon as it left ya lips, damn near."

For a moment, he was silent, confirming everything that I'd just said to him.

"And you gon' believe them niggas over me? We're like brothers, Eko. You should have confirmed that shit!"

"Oh, I did, when I listened to a couple of ya phone calls, nigga. I don' did my work. I made sure yo' ass was really trying to double cross me before I made any sudden moves."

"Look, Neo is about to get me out, mane, and we need to put all this behind us and get this money. I can forgive you about Rori and shit too, but just leave her—"

"I love her."

"Nigga, what?" he barked, looking me up and down as if I'd just confessed to killing his mama. "How the hell you love my bitch already! Mine! Rori is mine!"

"She not yours no more." I chuckled because I couldn't help it. He looked dumb as fuck and sounded even dumber. "She's mine. She been mine for a minute now and I love her. If you want her back you gon' have to kill me first, bruh."

He hopped up from the chair so abruptly that it fell back, and then he stormed towards the guards, leaving the phone off the hook. I calmly got up and took my ass home.

Stupid ass nigga didn't even let me say what I needed to because he was so damn worried about Rori. I was trying to let his ass know that Neo, in fact, wasn't helping him get out and that if he did get released somehow, he'd have no work or any kind of pull. But, I'd just let that shit hit him like a ton of bricks.

That Night...

I hadn't had a chance to take Rori out for getting that internship because I was busy as hell with getting that barbershop, and then this shit with Neo and Gavin. I couldn't wait to be done with them niggas and just focus on my business and my baby girl.

"You look good as hell," I commented, liking the way Rori filled out that damn dress. As usual, her deep mocha complexion was glowing and looking very lickable.

"Thank you. So do you. I didn't expect you to bring me to such a nice place. I cannot wait to dig into that steak."

"Where the fuck did you expect me to take you? To Krystal burgers?" I laughed when she nodded. "You're an asshole, mane."

"Thank you." She batted her eyelashes. "What did you do earlier while I was in class?"

"Keeping tabs on me now?"

"You're my man, so yes. If I ask, you're obligated to tell me. Unless there's a reason you don't want to."

"Calm down, ma. I cut some heads, met up with a few people, and I also saw Gavin's ass. I visited him in prison."

"You did? How was he?" She sipped her water but stopped. "Not that I care, it's just that when I went to see him, I thought he was gonna jump through that glass and kill me."

"Wait, what? When did you go see him?"

"Remember, I told you. I said that I went to tell him that you and I had been together and that I was happy with you."

"Nah, ma, you ain't say you went nowhere. You told me that you let him know about us, but I assumed he called you or some shit."

"Well no, he didn't. I felt like the least I could do was let him know in person about us, especially, since I lied when he took me out to dinner."

"I don't want you visiting him no more. You with me, and you need to cut that shit off, ma. Y'all don't have no kids together, or anything keeping y'all bonded, so end it."

"Yes, sir," she smiled. "I swear that was the only reason I went. I don't have any plans to talk to him anymore."

"I love you, ma. I really do," I told her after staring at her for a little bit. I'd never felt anything for a female like this, and the shit was overwhelming as fuck.

"I love you too, Eko. I know this all seems fast but it feels real."

"'Cause it is, ma, fuck you talking about?"

We chuckled in unison just as the waitress set down our entrees. For the rest of the dinner, thankfully, Gavin wasn't the topic of conversation at all. After we had dessert, I drove her straight to my spot, to do what I'd been thinking about doing to her ass since she'd walked out the house in that little ass dress.

We took a shower together, and then I carried her to my bedroom, leaving the lights off and allowing the moonlight to shine through my window. Lying her in the middle of the bed, I climbed between her legs and started to suck on her soft ass lips, while touching her pretty brown hair. I was a nigga that loved hair, especially when I could pull on it while hitting that shit from the back.

Trailing my lips down her face and onto her collarbone, I eventually began to suck on her nipples gently. Licking and sucking my way down her stomach, I rested her thighs on my shoulders, before kissing the inner part until I got to her clit.

"Fuck," she whispered as I started to eat her pussy like it was a pie-eating contest.

She was wet as hell in no time, and I just basked in that shit, flicking my tongue over her bud before sucking it. I spread her legs wider, and buried my face further, enjoying the taste of the orgasm she'd just let loose.

"Eko, baby," she whimpered, running her small hands through my short cut, gripping it at the end just as she released hard as hell.

I kissed her pussy for a little bit, then flipped her over onto her stomach. Sliding inside, I let out a throaty moan because it was unbelievable how good her pussy felt. As I worked my girth and length into her tight wet hole, I pinned her hands to the bed while sucking her shoulders. As she loosened up for me, I went faster, making her ass jiggle against me.

"Mmm," she whined, voice trembling as I started to beat it up from the back.

Her pussy felt like quicksand, sucking my dick in and gripping the fuck out of it. I was moaning way more than usual, and pissed at myself for already being on the verge of busting a big one.

"Shit," I grumbled, pounding her hard. Our sweaty ass skin clapped together like an audience as I kept her pinned to the bed while drilling that pussy doggy-style.

She came for what seemed to be the tenth time tonight, making me growl lowly at the feeling. I was deep sea diving in this shit right now, and I couldn't take it any longer.

"Why yo' pussy so good, Rori? Huh?" I whispered into her ear before licking it. I hadn't slowed up yet. I was still pummeling her pussy, making it gush every time I slammed in.

"Fuck," I groaned, going faster, harder, and deeper. The last stroke yanked that nut out of me so ferociously that I collapsed on top of her.

"Eko!" she cried out, and finally I was able to get up and pull out. "Don't do that! You're heavy!" she cried as she slowly turned over.

"Stop putting that good ass pussy on a nigga then shit. Almost took my ass out."

We both laughed together as she scooted over to cuddle up under me. She started sniffing my chest like she always did, making me scoff.

"Stop doing that weird shit, shorty."

"You just smell so good, babe."

"It's the same damn cologne I've *been* wearing."

"I know, and I love it." She cheesed and I looked down at her for a minute before pressing my lips against hers.

"You ready to go again?" I rolled on top of her.

"Eko, are you joking?" she frowned. I just raised my brow and let her feel that monster pressing against her opening.

Like a good girl, she spread her legs a little wider for me, as I pushed my way in.

12

YIKAYLA

I had one more hour left of work, and I couldn't wait to go home. I was feeling so sleepy, and even a little sick now. I was six weeks pregnant, so I'd been pregnant for much longer than expected. I made the doctor double check when she first told me because I just knew that was wrong. How in the hell had I been pregnant for almost two months and not know it? I hadn't gotten my period, true enough, but that always happened to me whenever I was under stress. And the past few months have been stressful as hell for me, so I chalked it up to that. I shook my head at the thought, just as Jerica entered my workroom.

"Hi, honey, I'm gonna be stepping out to lunch with my husband, but if you need anything my assistant is here. Or even call on Brynn."

Fuck Brynn.

"Yeah, okay. I'm sure I will be fine though."

"Oh, babe, this is Yikayla, my star employee I told you about." Jerica smiled and waved her husband into the room. He must have dicked her down in her office because she was never ever this happy and giddy.

Placing the steamer down, I turned it off and faced the door, ready to meet her husband. The tall guy stepped into the room, and I recognized him from somewhere. Upon seeing me, he smirked as he wrapped his arms around Jerica's waist.

"Nice to meet you…"

"Desmond." He stuck his hand out to shake mine.

That's who this nigga was. He was the extra aggressive nigga at Prive that night, who I had to throw a drink on. I swear to God, Memphis was way too small. This nigga had no business being as thirsty as he was when he had a wife, and a wife like Jerica at that. Jerica was a beautiful, successful, black woman, and here this weak ass nigga was in the club trying to fuck around.

"Nice to meet you, Desmond."

"Well, honey, I'm gonna get my purse, so why don't you pull up in front. You know I don't like to walk too far in my red bottoms." Jerica tapped his chest and walked out of the room. I expected him to do what he was told, but of course he stood there.

Not willing or wanting to hold a conversation, I turned away and cut the steamer on, ready to finish these damn dresses so I could leave.

"You gon' act like you don't know me?" His deep voice startled me a tiny bit because of how quiet it was just seconds ago.

"I *don't* know you."

"You don't remember throwing a damn drink in my face, ma?"

"Yeah, I do. However, I don't know you. But you need to go bring the car around like your wife asked you to so I can finish my business." I removed some dresses off the rack and walked them to another. I caught him smiling, nibbling on his lip like I was joking.

"Yikayla. Fine ass with a ghetto ass name."

"Okay, can you go, please?"

"Let me get yo' number," he whispered.

"Okay, Desmond, what do you think is going on here? Do you think we're flirting? Are you mistaking my annoyance of you for admiration? I hope not."

"Nah, you just like to play hard to get. I know girls like you, ma."

"Look—"

"Baby, leave Yikayla alone and go get the car." Jerica stepped into the room smiling. She must not have heard any of our conversation.

"I was just making sure she was doing her job right. You know I don't want nobody fucking up my baby's business." He leaned down to peck her, and I put my finger in my mouth to fake throwing up. That was a bad idea because I almost did actually puke with my pregnant ass.

Once they left, I went to the small break room and made myself some hot tea. Jerica had bought two Keurig machines and they were the best things ever. I told Waayil I wanted one, and he promised he would get it for me if I stopped saying he ate my ass. I didn't know if I could give that joke up, so I told him I'd think about it.

"Damn, you just can't help it, can you?" Brynn walked in, reaching up into the cabinet to grab one of the mugs.

"Brynn, I'm not in the mood for your reindeer games."

Shrugging, she replied, "Not a game I'm playing. I was just watching you flirt with Jerica's husband. First you take Roscoe from me, and now you're moving in on Desmond? You are shameless."

"You never had Roscoe, baby girl, and you never will. No matter how many times you fuck and suck him, no matter how many kids you have by him, he will never want you. He smashed you because you let him, and you just so happened to get pregnant. Where is your pride, woman? Because you're looking and sounding pitiful as hell." I chuckled before sipping more of my tea.

"You don't know shit about what me and Roscoe have! You don't know me!"

"No, I don't, but I do know Roscoe Cousins, and I can tell you right now that he was never yours, Brynn. Put it this way, that nigga got on his knees and begged me not to have another man's baby. That's just how much he loves me, and he *still* did me dirty. So what do you think he'd do to some woman he impregnated by accident?"

Her mouth opened and closed but nothing came out.

Finally, she said, "Well, I'm still gunning for Waayil."

"Good luck with that. Just don't let me catch you, or they'll have to surgically remove one of my Nikes from that ass."

I tossed the rest of the tea back, and then placed it in the sink for housekeeping to clean tonight. I then left the break room area as she stayed silent. Only reason I hadn't popped that bitch in her mouth was because I knew right now, she was just talking. She was a confused ass dummy, who was scrambling for scraps after realizing that Roscoe didn't want her ass. But as soon as I got wind of her trying to push up on my nigga, I was clocking her.

By the time I finished the last rack, it was time for me to go home, so I tidied up my workroom and then locked it up. I'd asked Jerica for a key because I didn't trust Brynn. She'd probably try to fuck my hard work up once I went home. And if that hoe did that, I'd kill her or have Waayil do it.

Speaking of Waayil, tonight I was finally gonna tell him about the baby. I'd been holding off because I didn't know how to come out and say it. Not to mention, he'd just dealt with the baby drama with Alba, and now she'd miscarried.

He seemed to be bothered by it, not too much, but just a little. It did make me a bit jealous, but instead of being childish, I comforted him the way he comforted me about Roscoe. That was what I loved about our relationship; we were best friends still to this day. A lot of couples claim they have that, but it wasn't like what Waayil and I had. We could literally tell one another anything.

When I got home, I could hear my baby Lonan talking loudly as hell. I walked towards the bedroom to see him laid out next to Waayil as Waayil played the video game. As usual, they were somehow having a full-on conversation about it. It was adorable how Lonan would stop yapping once Waayil started, as if he could honestly understand.

"I told you I don't want him watching those violent ass video games, Waayil." I set my purse on my dresser then went to pick Lonan up. "Mmm, you smell good, Lo. You already had a bath?"

"Yeah, I got him together so we could play the game," Waayil replied.

I kissed my baby's plump cheek and then gave him his pacifier so he could pass out while I went to take a bath. I soaked in some bubbles for a nice while since I didn't have to be back at work until Monday and had time to waste. Plus, I needed my skin to be buttery soft for tonight's festivities.

KNOCK! KNOCK!

Before I could say anything, Waayil was walking into the bathroom.

"Little man is knocked out. I put him in his bed, and yes, I turned on the right night lights and shit so don't ask."

Chuckling, I replied, "I'm trying to relax, Waayil. And what did you feed my baby?"

"We smoked and had some burritos."

"Seriously, fool."

"My moms brought some enchiladas over here to try to get me to talk to Wednesday. I told her ass the same thing I told punk ass Nusef; that I would do it on my own time. Anyhow, that's what he and I ate."

"Saved me some?"

"Of course." He nodded as he sat on the closed toilet top. "Baby, I wanna tell you something."

"Okay." I slunk down under the bubbles some more as I watched his handsome face. He tucked his lips in, prompting his dimples to appear, and then he looked my way with his beautiful eyes.

"Remember when you asked me how I was gettin' by with no pussy in jail?" He squinted.

If he was about to tell me some gay shit, I would have a heart attack.

"Yeah."

"Calm down, it ain't what yo' weird ass is thinking." He laughed and so did I. "But umm, I told you I had a girl coming through to give me some pussy on the regular. And in order for me to get such a privilege, I promised her father, who was locked up with me, that I would be with her. And while locked up, I kind of was."

"Why would you—"

"I thought I wasn't getting out, Kay." He shook his head with pleading eyes. "What harm could that decision do to a nigga who got life? That's how I saw it. Anyway, when I got out, her pops, and her of course, expected me to continue on with the relationship, but I wasn't with that because, now that I was free, I wanted you."

"So what's the problem?"

"The problem is I don't think either of them are just gonna go away. Now this ain't some shit you need to worry about, at all, but I wanted you to know. I don't want that snake ass bitch to try and embarrass you or some shit. I want you to be ahead of the game if she runs into you or something."

"Do I need to beat her up?"

Laughing, he replied, "Nah, I got it. I'll figure some shit out." He looked down at his hands for a moment then added, "You know she wasn't nothing to me but some pussy, right?"

"Of course."

"Just wanna make sure."

"Now leave because I wanna bathe in peace."

"Damn, I can't watch?"

"No, this is for relaxing purposes, not for you to get a free show, nigga."

"Why can't it be for both? Look what you got me looking like 'round here." He pointed to his crotch and his dick was definitely trying to burst through his basketball shorts.

"Get out, Waayil!" I grinned while snickering.

He sucked his teeth and mumbled something, before finally leaving out. I finished my bath, and after spreading my natural body butter on, I wrapped myself in a towel. I entered the bedroom to see Waayil lying back, still playing the game.

"What the fuck, Yikayla!" He hissed when I snatched the

controller and turned the TV off. "Baby, you gon' fuck my—" I shoved him back onto the bed when he tried to stand.

He was about to speak again, but I dropped my towel. His attention was elsewhere now as I straddled him. Men were too easy.

Reaching down into his bottoms, I massaged his already hardening dick, before pulling it out. Leaning down some, I sucked sloppily on the tip while looking him in the eyes.

"Fuck, Kay," he whispered, looking down at me by pressing his chin into his chest.

Once I was done with that, I rose up a little to position his dick at the opening of my pussy. I rubbed the head slowly along the length of it, since I was already wet from sucking his dick. He tucked his lips in with his fine ass, liking the way it was feeling. Finally, I pressed my pussy against his brick hard head until it made its way inside. It was a little painful, but I kept going down. I stopped for a moment to recoup, but he gripped my hips with his large hands and forced me all the way down on him slowly.

"Uhhhh," I whimpered lowly, feeling him in my damn stomach.

"Ride that shit," he demanded, smacking and gripping my ass so roughly that I came just from him sitting inside of me.

Gaining some composure, I placed my hand on his brick hard abs and began to rock my hips while slowly moving up and down. I felt my pussy adjusting to him, as he threw his head back, still groping my ass here and there. I came yet again, and he picked his head up to get a view of how much I had coated his dick.

"I want you to cum like that again."

I picked up my pace, going 'round and 'round, then up and down. I saw that look in his face, so I moved more, bouncing on it and then rocking my hips.

"Wait, Kay, fuck. Baby, slow down before I bust... ahhh, shit," he groaned, trying to take control, but I had control now.

"Shit," I cried, riding the shit out of his dick.

"Kay, wait, baby." He panted as I bounced on his dick, letting my juices drown him. The pleasure in his face gave me motivation, so I kept it up. I released again on him, but I didn't slow up for long. He was gripping the hell out of my hips and I loved it.

"No—no mo—more secrets, right?" I stammered, taking complete control of his dick. "Say it."

"No more secrets. Shit," he groaned, holding my ass cheeks tightly as hell as I rode him.

I made sure to grip his dick while bouncing on it, letting the head of his dick hit as deeply as it could. I'd lost count on how many times I'd came. Before I knew it, we were both exploding together.

Flipping me onto my back, he growled, "Don't you ever do that shit again, ma. Had me feeling like a bitch."

"You didn't like it?" I giggled, still out of breath.

"Nah, that shit was the business." He slipped his tongue into my mouth.

"Waayil, we're having a baby."

He pulled back quickly as hell and stared down into my eyes.

"We are?" He then cheesed widely. "You got my baby in your belly?"

I nodded but then laughed as he dropped down to kiss on my stomach.

"You don't think it's too much too soon?" I quizzed, looking down at him since his head was still by my stomach.

"Nah, this shit was overdue."

13

CANYON DENNIS

I was sending out some emails in my office when the assistant peeked in and told me that my appointment was here. I nodded to say it was okay for shorty to come in, and then exhaled heavily. This girl, in particular, was always trying to find ways to get out of taking certain classes and shit, but still wanted to graduate. Now, here she was a senior, but with the same amount of *countable* credits as a damn sophomore.

"Hey, Mr. Dennis." Kendra walked into the room smiling. She closed the door behind herself and slid into the seat across from me.

"Good morning, Kendra. So what's up? What kind of scheme are we about to discuss today?"

Laughing, she responded, "There is no scheme, Mr. Dennis! And I never have schemes. I simply do not agree with all of the courses this school forces upon us. Is it illegal for me to try to relieve some of the stress you guys put on me, by not taking a class or two?"

"Not illegal, but it's hindering you, Kendra. You've been here for four years and from the looks of your transcript, it looks like you've only been here for two."

"And see, that's what I wanted to talk to you about. I mean, technically, I have the credits of a senior, it's just 60% aren't the classes I need to graduate. Mr. Dennis, graduating is really about the credits and not where you got them from."

"Kendra, taking three art classes does not cancel out the need for your history, math, and geology courses, okay?" I leaned forward on my desk.

"But why not? They're all the same amount of credits!"

"Kendra, if you wanna graduate, ma—" I had to stop myself because she was bringing the hood out of me. "If you wanna graduate, you need to take the classes on this list. You cannot just take whatever you want and expect it to count towards graduation." I placed yet *another* paper in the middle of us and began circling the areas she was *still* missing. "If you wanna get out of here, just take what you need, please. You're gonna run out of financial aid assistance soon, and I'm tired of seeing your face."

"You are? I thought you liked me!"

"I do," I chuckled. "I do like you, but I'm tired of your game plans, Kendra. Take these classes and finish school."

She took the paper and sucked her teeth as she looked it over. Grunting out of frustration, she got up from her seat and stuffed it into her bag, crinkling the shit all up, which made me shake my head.

"How old are you, Mr. Dennis? You seem so young."

"Why?" I frowned, leaning back in my chair.

"Me and a couple of friends just want to know." She shrugged one shoulder.

"Y'all need to worry about graduating and not how old I am. But if you must know, I'm 27 and will be 28 this year."

"Not bad. So are you married? No, you don't have a ring. You dating anyone?" She ran around my desk and sat on the edge. "Oooh, is it someone that works here? Roselle?"

"Okay, Kendra." I moved her off my desk. "Mind ya business and go. You have a class right now."

"You are so uptight to be so young, Mr. Dennis." She walked back around my desk and ran her finger across my degrees on the wall. "Well, I may be back fairly soon, so keep an appointment open for me."

"Bye, Kendra."

When Kendra opened the door after rolling her damn eyes, she ran right into Dree's sexy ass, standing there in some tight ass jeans and a top.

"Oh, sorry," Kendra said lowly, looking Dree up and down. Dree was extremely beautiful with her perfect features and smooth dark skin, so it was normal for a person to stare. I even did the shit sometimes.

"Take a picture next time so you can look at it anytime you want. Excuse me," Dree snapped and stepped around Kendra before closing the door in her face. "Is that the kind of sluts you advise?"

"She's not a slut, ma," I chuckled. Dree's ass would call anybody a slut and sometimes the shit was hilarious because it would be way off. She'd call an old church lady a hoe in a hot minute and be dead ass serious.

"Yes she is. It's cold out and she had shorts on that were all up in her bony little cooch."

"Okay." I snickered as Dree tossed her bag into a chair. "What you doing all the way on this side of campus, Dree?" I welcomed her into my lap.

"I have a pretty lengthy break, and I wanted to come see you." She scanned my eyes and then kissed me. "Were you ever gonna tell me that you beat up Sean?"

"I have no idea what you're talking about."

"Canyon Dennis."

"Dree Goode."

"Stop it!" She whined like a little child, prompting me to laugh. "I'm serious! He's telling people some shit about a brawl outside of a liquor store."

Tittering, I responded, "That nigga? At a liquor store fighting?"

"I know it's bullshit, which made me wonder what the truth was. So did you do that to him or not, Canyon?"

"I didn't do shit to him, Dree."

I wanted to tell her, but if this shit came back to bite me, I didn't want her having to lie for me. I knew Dree would tell muthafuckas she didn't know shit without giving it a second thought, and instead of making her commit a crime by lying, I wanted what she'd say to be the truth.

"You promise?"

"Drop it. I told you I didn't do anything to that bitch ass nigga, now let's talk about something else."

"Fine," she sighed. "I wanna go salsa dancing."

"Nope. Next subject."

She burst into laughter just as my door came open. Roselle was standing there with a surprised expression.

"Hey, what's up, Roselle? This is my girlfriend, Dree. Dree, this is my co-worker, Roselle."

"Nice to meet you, Roselle," Dree replied, getting up from my lap.

"Yes... same, Dree. Uh, Canyon, can I talk to you for a moment? It's about some business." Roselle cocked her head.

"Well I better go anyway." Dree picked her messenger bag up from the chair. "See you at your place? I'm making stuffed pasta shells."

"Of course." I grinned hard as hell. I couldn't help it while looking at Dree smiling. I loved seeing her happy because that nigga Sean had her moping occasionally, and I ain't like that shit. Once Dree left, I asked Roselle, "So what did we need to talk about?"

"I'm sorry, I didn't know you had a girlfriend, Canyon." Roselle sat down across from me.

Roselle was an okay looking girl. She had light skin, dark wavy hair, a basic ass face, and a small body that you shrugged at. She reminded me of the type of bitch you smashed because it was convenient and for no other reason.

"Yeah, I do." I squinted my eyes in confusion. "So what's up?"

"I wanted to ask you how you were doing and everything, but now I'm kind of upset."

"You told me you had business to discuss."

"Yeah, I said that so I could get your little girlfriend to leave. How could you lead me on? You just used me to get that information on that student!"

"Wait, wait, hold up. Lead you on? Use you? I did none of the above, Roselle, and you know it. I asked you for a favor and you did it. When have I ever led you on?"

"Being all nice to me, smiling at me, giving me hugs in the morning, and bringing me things from Starbucks when you went sometimes."

For a moment, I stared at her completely dumbfounded. I didn't know whether to blow up on her stupid ass or feel bad as fuck for her. If she thought what I did was flirting, that meant her ass had never been flirted with in all her life.

"And you think that all of that meant I wanted to be with you? I hope you're joking, Roselle. I'm nice to you because I'm a nice guy. I smile at you because we're cool, and I'm at work. I give you hugs when I see you, because again, we're supposed to be cool. You act like I felt on ya booty or some shit when I did it. And lastly, because I thought we were cool, I offer you drinks or food from where I'm going."

"Cool? Yeah right."

"Trust me, that is it. If I wanted you or tried to lead you anywhere, I wouldn't be giving you church hugs and coffee, ma, I'd be on some other shit. Trust me." I had to get a little unprofessional for her delusional ass to understand. "So until you get the late night come through text," shaking my head, "Don't think I'm into you or coming onto you."

"Now I'm upset that I helped you."

"And I'm sorry you feel that way."

"That boy got beat up recently, and I wanna know if you had

anything to do with it. His parents are very involved financially with the school."

"Nope, nothing to do with it."

"Well you'd better make sure you didn't, because if I even think you did, I'm speaking up since you used me."

"Nah, I don't think you will. Because see, you'll lose your job for giving me his information."

"I only gave you his class schedule and nothing else! How you got his address had nothing to do with me!"

"Like I said, I didn't do shit to that nigga so I don't have his address. And regardless of what you gave me, your job requires you to keep shit confidential and you didn't. So if I lose my job, guess who else will."

"You fucking snake."

"I'll be that. Now step, I got shit to do."

"Ugh!" she growled before shooting up and yanking my door open. She neglected to close it on purpose, which irritated the fuck out of me.

Stupid ass bitch. Ain't my fault her ass don't get any male attention so she mistook my kindness for wanting to smash them flat ass cheeks. I shook my head at the thought before getting back to work.

Later That Evening...

The clock hit 3:45 p.m., and I hurriedly clocked out. I'd been here since 6:30 a.m. and I was tired as hell. When I walked out, Roselle's office door was open, so I gave her a smile and said 'bye' to her. She of course ignored me and turned her attention back to her computer. I just chuckled to myself and kept going.

By the time I made it home, Dree had texted me to let me know she was at the grocery store but would be to me soon. So I sat in my car for a bit and FaceTimed Luna so I could talk to Cade for a bit. After that, I went upstairs because I wanted to take a shower and be out by the time Dree was here and cooking, since she had a key now. Wow, a woman outside of my sister really had a whole key to my shit out here.

"Canyon!" Jupiter, my little sister, smiled when I walked into my spot.

"What's... good?" I replied, closing my front door behind me. She had some girl sitting next to her on my couch.

"This is Amaia. Remember Amaia?"

"Nah, not really, but nice to meet you, shorty." I set my bag down on my bar top and shook her hand. Amaia was cheesing hard.

"Nice to see you again, Canyon, even though you don't remember me."

I simply nodded before turning my attention towards my sister.

"What y'all doing here? I told you to call before you came by at all times, Jupiter."

"Well, we were in the neighborhood, and I wanted to drop by. Amaia has grown up a lot huh, Canyon?"

"I don' told you I don't remember shorty. Now you gotta go. I'm about to shower and Dree is about to come through."

"I like Dree, why can't we all chill together?" Jupiter folded her arms. I knew she was being funny because if anybody hated Dree, it was Jupiter.

"Come here, Jupiter." I went to the back. I heard her whispering some shit to Amaia before she followed behind me. "Look, I know what the fuck you're trying to do, and I'm telling you to stop that shit."

"What? What am I trying to do?"

"Don't play dumb, ma. Get ya friend and get up out of here so I can shower like I don' told you. If you don't want me to be with Dree, too fucking bad. It's happening and it's gon' stay that way."

"Really? A girl that doesn't even appreciate you? There are so many women that want you, Canyon, yet, you're still playing a little lovesick puppy for her!"

"And that's my business!" I palmed my chest. "If I wanna play a fucking fool for Dree for the rest of my damn life, let me do that then, Jupiter. Now get ya damn friend out my spot before I say some shit you won't like."

"Fine. Fuck you. Be happy I have to pick my son up from tee ball practice or else I wouldn't be leaving." She switched out.

"Yeah, mm hmm." I followed her and made sure she and Amaia both got the fuck out.

I really hoped Jupiter gave this shit up, because I was not trying to referee some shit between her and Dree.

14

———

RORI

I woke up in my bed feeling like I'd ran ten miles yesterday. Eko had bent my ass into a damn pretzel last night, and basically had me running out of there to get home. I wished I could have spent the night, but I knew I wouldn't get any sleep lying next to him and I needed it. Eko was always touching and feeling on me, and even though it always led to the best sex ever, sometimes a bitch needed her rest.

Today I had to be at work, or my internship if you will. So far it was pretty easy because all I had to do was make signs and help with slogans. This week, I was told would be a bit more work, and I was excited to somewhat be in the thick of things. The mayoral candidate would even be dropping by today, and I was anxious as hell to meet him.

Everyone said he was really nice, especially Scarlett, who worked with him during his last campaign when he lost. She said even though she wasn't getting college credit that time, she wanted the experience.

I hoped he won, simply because I liked a lot of the things he claimed he was gonna do. Plus, I was working for him and I'd feel like a failure if my efforts were all for not.

Getting up, I threw the covers off of my body and rolled my eyes at the sound of all the damn ruckus my mother was making in the kitchen. I just had to choose the bedroom above the kitchen when we moved in here ages ago.

My stepfather, Jasper, would be home this evening, and my mom and sisters were making a big feast. I wanted to help them, but I'd be working today. So instead, I made a cake yesterday with my baby Eko's help. He didn't do much but feel all on me and eat the leftover chocolate frosting from the bowl, but I enjoyed his company in my house.

I brushed, flossed, and rinsed with Listerine, then hopped into the shower feeling good as hell. My life was on the up and up in every aspect, so I wanted to take a moment to be thankful for it all. After putting on my lotion, I got dressed, sprayed on some perfume, sent Eko a good morning text, and then left out of the house.

"Going somewhere fairly early, I see," I heard a voice as I approached my mom's car. I looked over my shoulder to see psycho ass Jenni.

"Jenni, fuck off. And I got your little bouquet, bitch."

"Good, I'm glad," she smiled. "I've decided to give you a chance to apologize to me. If you apologize and tell Eko that you set me up, all will be forgiven."

"Like I just said, fuck off."

"Is that a no?"

"It's a hell no!"

"Very well. Then let the games begin."

"What is this, *Game of Thrones*? Girl, bye. You let the wrong game begin and I'll fuck you up."

Jenni just smiled like the crazy bitch that she was and pranced off happily. I watched her for a moment, hand still on my mother's car door handle, and then I got in. I didn't know what that bitch was trying to do, but in a minute, I was gonna go upside her damn head.

Apologize. Yeah right. I wasn't apologizing for her being a damn dummy, and I definitely wasn't gonna tell Eko that I'd set her up. I wasn't sure how he'd feel about that, and things between us were too good to fuck up over whack ass Jenni.

I made it downtown where my internship was, and parked inside of the structure connected to the building. I felt so official having to show the security my little badge so that he'd let me onto the floor that candidate, Troy Garrick, had rented out or something.

"Morning, Rori!" Scarlett called out to me as she stuffed a donut hole into her mouth.

"Hey, morning. You're here early, aren't you?" I stopped and picked up one of the raspberry Danishes. I tried to be one of those who didn't eat the food offered here, but I was getting over that shit. It looked good as hell and was free.

"Yeah, I just wanted to see if there was any extra work I could do?"

"Why? It's not like you're gonna get paid overtime or paid at all."

Scarlett looked around and then pulled me to one of the tables to sit at. The suite we were in had a big ass waiting area with couches, desks, coffee tables, relaxer chairs, and a big receptionist desk. Towards the back, walking down the hallway, were a couple of office rooms on each side; the one in the back belonging to the mayoral candidate, Troy. Only about seven of us college kids worked his campaign, along with some official campaign workers, who got paid. It was a pretty spacious area and very comfortable to work in.

"What?" I frowned once Scarlett and I were sitting on the two-seater couch in front of the coffee table.

"Remember how I told you I worked for Troy last time too?"

"Yeah." I bit down into the Danish.

"Well, he remembered me this time."

"Okay? And when did you see him? He hasn't been by since I started... well, since the both of us started."

"Well, he had a speech at a luncheon, and my mom and I attended." She scooted closer to me. "Anyway, he and I rekindled things and he was happy to know I would be working for him again now that I was in college."

"Scarlett, all I asked was why did you come early."

"I'm getting there. So the night of the luncheon, we got back really close, if you know what I mean. So I stopped by early because I was told Troy would be here early today. I was thinking we could get a quickie in."

Coughing and placing the Danish down on the plastic plate I had, I asked, "You slept with the potential mayor?"

"Shhh! But yes. I mean, it happened last time too, but once everything was over and he lost, we also lost touch. But now that I'm older, I'm excited about where this could go," she grinned.

"Scarlett, he's married with like... five kids," I whispered harshly as this guy, Boris, walked in. He was another college kid working an internship here. He put his hand up to say good morning to us, and then went to the food table.

"So what! He's bored with her. I'm young and I'm fun."

"You know he's just using you, right? If he had feelings for you, he wouldn't have gone a whole four years without speaking to you."

Shaking her head, she replied, "Nope, not true."

"Okay, Scarlett."

We didn't say another word to one another as we ate our food. By the time I'd finished and used the bathroom, it was time to get to work.

I was keeping an eye out for Troy, even though I was kind of disappointed in him. It felt good to see a fairly young black man in the position that he was in. Hearing that he'd slept with Scarlett, was just a blow to me. Hopefully, she was lying though because she seemed like the type to lie about some shit like that.

"Okay, guys, Mr. Garrick is coming up. Make sure you are working when he walks in, and only speak to him if he comes up and speaks to you. Do not, and I repeat, do not stray from your work to shake his hand," this lady who ran things named Parker explained.

We all nodded and said, 'okay' simultaneously, while continuing to work. I admit, my heart was beating really fast waiting on this man to walk through the door. Finally, a big buff guy came in and Troy came in right behind him with his wife, Tamara. A few other people walked in as well, before Parker closed the door.

"Good morning, everybody. I want to thank you all for being a part of this even though the campaign is pretty far away. I hope that this time around I do win. As you know, or as I *hope* you know," he grinned as everyone chuckled, "I have a lot of great plans for Memphis and I would love to see it all come to fruition." He brought his beautiful wife to his side, and I couldn't help but feel sympathy for her. "This is my wife, Tamara Garrick, the brains of this operation here," he joked, making us laugh before he kissed her.

I rolled my eyes on the low, then stopped myself.

Rori, Scarlett is probably lying.

Once Mr. Garrick finished his speech, he, his wife, and his crew went to the back. Parker made sure we resumed working, and about fifteen minutes later, Mr. Garrick came back to the front, but without his tuxedo jacket. He started introducing himself to everyone personally, and when he got near me, I felt my palms get sweaty.

"Nice to meet you, Mr. Garrick." I smiled shyly as I shook his hand.

"Please call me Troy. And what's your name?" he cheesed. He was extremely handsome, and if he wasn't married and I didn't have Eko, I would probably be interested. Well, maybe if I was into older niggas.

"I'm Rori, Rori Goode."

Frowning for a minute, he questioned, "Is Jasper Vaughn your stepfather?"

"Umm, yeah, how did you know that?"

"He's an old friend. I remember him mentioning his stepdaughters, and the name Rori was one of them. He said his wife's maiden name was Goode, and that her daughters had it too."

"Oh, well yes," I nodded. "Yes, Jasper is my dad."

"Great man."

"Yes, he is."

Mr. Garrick moved on, finishing up meeting everyone, and then he announced that lunch would be arriving soon before he returned to the back. Parker was on his heels of course.

"Seriously?" Scarlett rushed over to me, since overbearing ass Parker had disappeared for a minute.

"What?"

"You were flirting with him!" she growled in a whisper with her teeth clenched. Her dark long ponytail was swinging everywhere and her light face was bloodshot red.

"Are you serious right now? I wasn't doing anything but holding a conversation like a normal person. And plus, if I *was* flirting, the only person who has the right to be mad is Mrs. Garrick, his *wife*!" I spat lowly before slipping past her psycho ass.

Scarlett and I didn't talk for the rest of the workday, and once I was off, I rushed home. Eko told me he was there already, so I told him to wait outside until I arrived. I parked in the long driveway once I'd gotten to the house, and Eko got out of his car looking so fucking good that I wanted to hump his leg like a dog in heat.

He was wearing black jeans with a black, long-sleeved, polo type shirt. On his feet were some all black Nike Air Max, and he had on a nice watch and chain. He walked his tall built self over to me, deep brown caramel skin glistening under the lights in the driveway. I could tell he'd gotten a fresh haircut, which made me happy. He took meeting my father very seriously, which I found to be so sexy.

"Damn, look at me, and then look at yo' ass. Yo' pops gon' be wondering why I'm with you."

"Shut up." I threw my arms around his neck and kissed him. Smirking, I sniffed his chest because I knew he hated it. He just smelled so damn good that I couldn't help but to do it.

"Stop doing that shit, Rori." He laughed but shook his head at me like I was crazy.

"I can't help it."

"You're like a damn police dog or some shit. No wonder you cum the hardest when I'm hitting it doggy-style."

"Fuck you." I chuckled as I led him to the front door and into the house.

I smiled as I closed the door behind Eko because I could already smell my father's expensive cologne. I slipped my hand back into Eko's and then led him to the den where I could hear everyone was. When I walked in, my mom had her arm locked with my stepdad's, as he conversed with Canyon, Nusef, and Waayil.

I made my way over, and when my stepfather saw me, he smiled and said, "Rori." He hugged me tightly and kissed my forehead. "I was a little upset that you weren't here to greet me like your sisters, but when I found out why, I was happy. You know Troy Garrick and I went to high school together."

"Yeah, actually, I found that out today. I finally met him."

"Good guy, I hope he wins."

"Me too," I smiled. My stepfather smiled back, and then turned his attention to Eko. "Oh, Dad, this is my boyfriend, Eko Bennet."

"Nice to meet you, Mr. Vaughn."

"Nice to meet you, Eko. Strong grip which is a good sign." My stepfather shook his hand. "Now I ask every guy that dates my daughter this, so don't get offended," Jasper stated sternly, and Eko nodded as he slipped his hands into his pockets. "How do you earn your keep?"

"I manage a barbershop that I just actually purchased outright."

Raising a brow, Jasper responded, "So you own the place?"

"Yeah, I do."

"Where at? I may have to come by and check it out; get my hair cut or something."

"Off Highway 51."

"Well alright then. Don't be surprised when I drop by. It better be a nice place."

"Oh, it will be. And you had patients in New York this whole time right?"

"Yeah," my dad smiled, impressed. "I had three patients that I had to perform surgery on. It takes me away for a while because I have to do pre-op appointments, the surgery of course, and then the post-op care to make sure everything is okay. But three is the most out of town patients I've ever had, which is why I wanted my wife to come along but she never wants to leave Memphis," he laughed.

"But that bread is good huh?" Eko raised a brow, as the boys laughed and my father nodded.

I smiled seeing them all get along because Jasper was a tough critic. He'd met Gavin, but after Gavin couldn't tell him where he worked, because it was on the corner, and couldn't make eye contact, Jasper was off him.

"Well, I'm gonna go change and stuff, Dad, so I will be right back."

I rushed off and went upstairs to take a quick shower. I only washed off once and then got right out. As I wrapped my towel around myself to go into my bedroom, since my bathroom was within it, Eko came in.

"Let's do it right quick," he whispered.

"Eko, no, my dad is here."

"That nigga is downstairs with everybody else setting the table. And as horny as I am, I'm gon' bust quickly as hell, baby."

"No." I giggled as he moved towards me. He yanked my towel off, just as a loud knock sounded off.

I snatched my towel up and wrapped it around me as my father peeked his head in.

"Eko, come help me downstairs, young man."

"Uh, sure, yeah, no problem."

"And next time you want to sleep with my daughter, make sure it's after you meet her at the altar. Got it?" Jasper fake smiled as Eko met him at the door.

"Of course." Eko nodded, but when my dad turned his back he made a face, prompting me to chuckle before he left out.

I swear I loved him.

15

NUSEF

"What you got for me?" I asked the homie, Poe, when he got into the car.

He was a street dude that stayed in some shit, so I knew if anybody was talking about me getting shot, he'd hear about it. He was one of them nosey muthafuckas that hung around every damn body so he could know some shit. I didn't trust him with anything as far as telling him something I didn't want to get out, but if you needed some information, he was the perfect person to go to. Plus, I couldn't care less if he told the person I was coming after that I was looking for them. Either way, their asses were gonna get found.

"Nah, man, and I don't think Marquise did it." He shook his head repeatedly as if he really knew. "I been around some niggas that know him and they ain't said shit."

"Maybe it's because they know we talk."

"Nah, not even. Poe finds out every muthafuckin' thang, ya heard me?"

"Nigga, shut yo' ass up." I chuckled and shook my head.

I admit hearing for the second time that Marquise *wasn't* behind it fucked with me. Not only because I hated his ass, but it confused the fuck out of me. If it wasn't Marquise, then who the fuck was it? I clearly had an enemy I didn't fucking know about. And I'm still breathing, which means that muthafucka is losing a battle his opponent didn't even know he was in. That's some weak shit.

"Yeah, man, so I'll keep an ear out for some more information, but right now, all people are doing is saying how crazy the shit is."

"Yeah, well if you wanna keep getting this ten dollars, you better bring me something, Poe. I'm dead serious, bruh."

"I got you. I promise I do."

I sucked my teeth and shook my head as I reached into my pocket to hand him two fives. He hurriedly shoved that shit into his pocket, then dapped me up before getting out of my car. I tell you, to a crack head, ten dollars was everything.

My next tattoo session wasn't until about two hours from now, so I wanted to swing by my parents' crib and see how everybody was doing. Jonaya was in class, so I couldn't drop by there and chill with her. Shit between us had been good as fuck lately, but I noticed not having Leighton in her life bothered her a lot. I hated to be the reason for that shit, but I wasn't about to deny my damn feelings for a bitch I didn't even know like that. I mean, yeah, Leighton had some good shit between her legs, but it wasn't enough for me to lose Jonaya so they could be friends. Nah. Fuck that shit.

"How you doing, son?" my father greeted me when I came into the house.

Hugging him, I replied, "I'm good. How you holding up, old man?"

"Who the hell is old? I'm a spring chicken, little nigga."

"Yeah, aight. Where is Mama?"

"She's in the backyard looking over her garden." He sighed and shook his head.

"It's cold as hell outside. She needs to leave that garden alone until it warms up. Go make sure she ain't frozen, Pops."

"No, she'll be fine. And maybe if she freezes she'll learn her lesson." He continued to the den as I laughed.

"Is Wednesday up there?" I called after him and he nodded.

"With her girlfriend, Leighton."

I rushed up the stairs and before going to Wednesday's room, I went to Emil's. He was in there, but knocked the fuck out taking a nap. I wished I could get through to his ass, try to get him to hang out or some shit, but he acted like we made his damn skin crawl. I had enough damn problems right now, so I'd have to address his bullshit at a later date.

"Fuck y'all doing?" I burst into Wednesday's room.

"Damn, nigga! What if we were naked?" Wednesday smacked her lips as I sat down in her La-Z-Boy chair.

"Fuck would y'all be naked together for?"

Leighton rolled her eyes and Wednesday said, "Hey, you never know. I'm full of surprises."

"Trust me, I know. So what y'all got planned for the day? Since it appears y'all don't have class."

"Yeah, it's my day off, but Leighton's class got cancelled."

"Leighton, you good, ma? You look like you're about to burst or some shit?" I questioned as Leighton kept her eyes on the TV.

She didn't respond, and when I looked to Wednesday, she shrugged.

"Can Jonaya come here after school? You take up all her time." Wednesday got off the bed and limped over to me with that big black shit on her foot.

"Maybe tomorrow night." I snickered when Wednesday rolled her eyes.

"You want something from the kitchen, Leighton?" Wednesday inquired. "I'm gonna bring up some pizza rolls."

"That's fine," Leighton smiled. She was a pretty ass girl, even prettier when looking all mad and shit.

Soon as Wednesday left, I got up and sat on her bed next to Leighton.

"Look, ma, I know you don't fuck with me and that's cool, but whatever this shit is between you and Jonaya, find a way to kill it."

"Excuse me? How dare you!"

"How dare I what?" I frowned hard as hell.

"Ask me to forgive her for what she did to me, when you played a huge ass part in it! You used me! Instead of being a man and telling me you didn't like me, you led me on until Jonaya snapped her fingers and said come on."

"First off, I didn't use you. I don't know where the fuck you got that from. When I was fucking with you, it was simply because I wanted to. Did I love Jonaya at the time? Yes. Was I trying to get her to be with me? Yes. But I didn't fucking use yo' ass."

I hated to admit it, but Leighton had every right to be angry with Jonaya and me. But was I about to tell her that shit? Hell nah.

"Regardless of what your reasoning is, I don't like you and I don't like Jonaya. I don't want to be friends with her, and I wish you would get out of my face with that mediator shit."

Chuckling, I said, "Okay, so I'm gon' leave before yo' mouth gets you smacked the fuck up."

She made a face that said, 'I wish you would,' but she didn't say that shit aloud, so I let it go. Without another word, I left the room, no longer giving a fuck if Jonaya and Leighton resumed their friendship. Jonaya would get over that shit... hopefully.

I said goodbye to everybody, and then took my ass back to the shop so I could handle some desk work before my client arrived. When I got there, I saw my brother was in his office, and when we made eye contact, we didn't speak. Ever since that blow up we had about his childish ass still not speaking to Wednesday, we hadn't said shit to one another. It was weird as fuck to be honest, but I wasn't gon' fold and I knew he wasn't either, so fuck it.

Waayil left out of his office after locking it, and we walked right by one another as if we'd never met. I heard Chiara's thirsty ass saying 'bye' to him, but of course he barely responded.

"Stay yo' ass behind that counter, Chiara," I gritted when I saw her getting up. Bitch was always trying to walk Waayil to his fucking car like she was a gentleman or something.

"I was just about to sweep."

"Nah the fuck you weren't. Leave that mean ass nigga alone and realize it ain't ever gon' happen."

"I can't," she whined and smiled when I shook my head at her. "He's so handsome and when he's nice, he's nice as fuck. I just..." She shrugged. "I just like him. He's different."

"That nigga is a bitch." I started back towards my office.

"You're just saying that because y'all are beefing right now!" she laughed.

A Few Hours Later...

I'd finished doing that big ass tattoo, and now it was time to close up. Since Rebecca had the day off, I had to lock up so Chiara could get home. She claimed her damn DVR was broken and that she couldn't record some shit she'd been watching and had to see it live, so I let her go.

As I closed the blinds of the big ass window up front, someone started knocking on the door. I didn't have any heat on me because I wasn't crazy ass Waayil, so I slowly started moving towards the door to see who it was. When I did, I was floored and low-key didn't believe my fucking eyes. They had to be deceiving me. I was so caught up in my own thoughts, that them banging on the door again finally snapped me out of it.

"Mama, what the fuck?" I opened the door, surprised as hell that I even still recognized her. It didn't even feel right calling her 'mama'.

"Nusef!" She pounced on me and hugged my neck tightly as hell. "Oh I missed you." She kissed the side of my face repeatedly before I peeled her off of me.

"What are you doing... out here?"

"I got sentenced to sixteen years, love, don't you remember? It's been sixteen years and a few months now! I expected you to be counting down the days."

She looked good, even though her hair wasn't done. It was in two braids, and not long and straight like I remembered her wearing it. Seeing her in jeans and a t-shirt was weird for me, because my biological mother always dressed up when I was a kid.

The last time I saw her I was eight years old, and I couldn't believe that she pretty much looked the same physically. I didn't know how to fucking feel right now.

"Nah, I'm sorry. I got a lot going on so I wasn't keep—"

"It's fine, baby." She started to pace the lobby, tilting her head back to take in the scenery. "Where is Waayil? I thought he'd be here at the shop. You guys own it together, right?"

"Yeah, we do." I nodded. "Dana, how did you know about my tattoo shop and where it was?"

"One of your little neighborhood friends. I asked them if they knew you and Waayil, and they told me everything." She picked up one of our business cards, looked at it, and then placed it back down. "How could you let your brother go to jail, Sef?"

"Let? I didn't let him do anything. It just happened, Dana, and I—"

"Stop calling me Dana! When did I tell you that you could call me by my first name, Nusef Christian?"

"Never, but I'm having a hard time calling you 'mama'. I mean, you haven't been my mother for over a decade."

"Yeah because I was away! I knew when they told me you guys got adopted, that whatever bitch became your mother would brainwash you! And Freya's ass did just that!"

"Brainwash? No one brainwashed me. And Freya and Theo took Waayil and I to see y'all all the time! Not to mention, it's nobody's fault but yours that you did some illegal shit and got sent to jail, leaving ya kids behind."

"Yeah, whatever. And the visits from you two stopped! Talking about it was a bad influence on y'all." She laughed to herself angrily.

"Dana— I mean, Ma, I have to finish closing up, but maybe you can come by tomorrow or something and I can take you to lunch. Uh, who are you staying with?"

"A friend, since your father has a few more weeks to go. I was hoping I could stay with you though. I already told my parole officer I would be."

"Uh... yeah, sure, you can stay with me. I got an extra room you can sleep in, but it's nothing fancy. Just a bed and dresser."

"I came from a hard ass mattress on a bunk bed and having to watch my cellmate shit in front of me, so that room you have sounds like a five-star hotel right now." She slinked her arms around my waist. "Oh, baby, I missed you so much. And in a few weeks, you, me, Waayil, and your father will be a family again."

Inhaling deeply, I replied, "Can't wait."

What the fuck?

"**B**aby, you do not have to take me back across campus," I explained to Canyon who only ignored me and continued to put on his jacket.

"It's cold as fuck out, and a long ways from here, Dree. I'm going."

"Fine."

I stepped out of his office into the lobby-like area where a couple office assistants sat at their desks. There were also some students waiting, seated in the seats near the door. I felt someone burning a hole through the side of my face, and when I looked, I saw it was that Roselle woman Canyon had introduced me to last week. I put up my hand up to say hello, and she gave me a subtle smile before dropping it and turning her attention back to her computer.

Never again would I speak to that bitch. It only took one time to act that way towards me. I wasn't a nice person by nature, as I'm sure you guys know by now, so for me to go out of my way to say 'hi' to that bitch and she reply that way? Oh no. It was over with for her. I wouldn't care if I was the only person who knew the cure to a disease she had, I would never speak to that bitch again.

"Come on." Canyon came from his office, his cologne bum rushing my nose as he leaned down to kiss my temple.

Following behind him, I admired his clothing. His outfit was casual, but still very well put together and professional somehow. His long tan pea coat was fresh as hell, to the point where I had to run my hand down it just before he opened the door to let me out.

On the way to my class, Canyon and I stopped for hot chocolate with extra whipped cream the way we liked, and then continued on. It was freezing cold outside right now, but for once, I was enjoying being out here since I was with him. I smiled softly up at him as he pressed his cold lips to the back of my hand as we neared my class.

"Now who is gonna walk you back?" I pouted.

"I'm fine, ma. I'm a man."

"So what! I came all the way over there to you alone, earlier. Does that make me a man?"

"Nah, it makes you hard headed as fuck and low-key suicidal."

Laughing, I said, "It is not that cold." Sighing, I added, "I probably won't see you again until my day is over, but I want you to come over to my house. My dad has been asking about you."

"I will."

We shared a couple kisses that I couldn't help but to smile in between, and then he walked off. I watched him for a little bit, lapping up all the sexiness he oozed just from smoothly walking across the campus. When I turned to go toward the entrance of the classroom, I saw Sean there with a hating ass expression on his face.

"Excuse me," I said lowly as I slipped past him and trashed my empty hot cup.

Like a dummy, he grabbed my arm, but I shoved his ass back so hard that he fell on his ass. It'd rained a little bit earlier, so the concrete was a little damp. And to make matters worse, the area he fell in had a puddle covering it.

"Awww damn!" his friends hollered out as I continued into the class and took a seat next to Monroe and Andrea.

I tried to hold in my laughter as Sean walked past me with a drenched ass. He was mean mugging me, but it wasn't intimidating in the least.

Class seemed to fly by because we were still working in groups, and since Andrea, Monroe, and I had this shit in the bag, the majority of the class was just us talking about random things.

Once class was over, I started out behind Monroe and Andrea, but before I could get out, someone grabbed my ass roughly as hell. When I turned around to see, Derek, one of Sean's friends, I slapped him across the face. He started to come at me, but didn't make it in time because of the T.A. Tyson.

"Aye, what the hell is going on?" Tyson jumped in between us, glaring hard at Derek who knocked Tyson's hand off of him.

"That stupid bitch slapped me!"

"Watch your mouth, man," Tyson warned Derek.

"He grabbed my ass!" I shouted.

"Oh please. With your reputation, stop acting like you minded. Sean already let us know how easy you are."

"Alright, that's enough, Derek. I said that's enough, Dree!" Tyson barked down to me when I tried to go around him and strike Derek again. "Derek, please go over there for a moment, and Dree, go to your next class."

I stood there, panting heavily as my eyes scanned Derek, and then Sean and Cary who were snickering like something was funny. I couldn't deal with this shit. It was hard enough trying to suppress the memory or lack thereof of what happened between Sean and I, but him having people rub it in my face was becoming too much. Yeah, I was tough, but how long could I go on fighting these niggas off for making rude comments or touching me?

"Fuck," I mumbled to myself at my thoughts as I left the class.

Some hours later, all my classes were over, and thankfully, Derek wasn't in any of them. I'm not sure what had happened to him, but I was just happy that his ass was absent for the rest of the day.

When I got home, I almost jumped for joy seeing Yikayla's car at the house. I really wanted to talk to her, so I lucked up with the fact that she was here. It must have been because my stepfather was back. Speaking of him, I noticed his car wasn't here, which wasn't odd because he always worked long hours. Not to mention, sometimes he was on call if patients needed him for emergency reasons.

I walked inside and could smell the food my mom was cooking. Whatever it was, I planned to kill a plate of it, and I knew Canyon would too when he got here. Just as I closed the front door, someone started attacking the damn doorbell like they didn't have any damn sense.

"What the hell—" my mother spoke up.

"Buddy?" I cut my mother off as she walked up behind me to also see who it was that was acting a fool on the doorbell.

"Yeah. Natasha, let me talk to you for a minute," he all but growled when he saw my mom behind me.

"What, Buddy?" she replied as I stepped to the side so that she could get closer to the screen door. I heard Yikayla come up behind me holding Lonan, so I took him to give him a kiss.

"Can you open this screen door?" Buddy inquired, hitting it.

"No, I can't, and you need to go now. I told you what we had was over with and that I needed to move on with my life."

"You can't do this shit, Natasha! After all the shit I did for you, you just gon' throw me away?" He socked his chest.

His face was angry but tears welled up in his eyes. For the first time in... well, forever, I felt sympathy for this nigga. He was deeply hurt, and what my mom did to him was wrong. However, he knew this whole time that she was married, and I'm sure she'd told him she *wasn't* getting a divorce.

"It's complicated, but you need to go right now before I call the fucking police on your ass, and I am not joking," my mother replied sternly, placing her hand on her hip.

Shaking his head repeatedly as a lone tear traveled down his cheek, Buddy turned on his heels and went down the porch steps to leave. My mom watched him for a little bit, mumbling shit, and then slammed and locked the door before turning to face Yikayla and me.

"Mama, you need to get him together," I said, following behind her since she slipped between Yikayla and I to get back to the kitchen.

"I have him together. He just left when I told him to, didn't he? Mind your business, Dree Goode."

"Yes, ma'am." I rolled my eyes and looked at Yikayla who shook her head as we went to the den.

She had the fireplace going since it was cold as hell, which reminded me that I wanted to talk to her. I couldn't even look at a fireplace without thinking of Sean. His stupid ass always had it going, even though it was hot outside when we first started dating.

I placed Lonan to his feet, and he immediately rushed to his toy bike and hopped on it, before getting right back off to walk over to his other toy. He was the busiest baby ever, moving all over the den to tend to different things in under thirty damn seconds.

"You alright, Dree?" Yikayla asked, touching my knee.

"I have to tell you something. I'm only telling you because I want your advice. I don't want you to reprimand me or get mad at me for keeping this from you. I want you to just give me advice, and that is it, Kay."

Adjusting herself so that she was facing me more, she replied, "Yeah sure. What is it?"

"So a while back when I was still dating Sean, we went out to dinner. While out, I had a drink with my meal. It was only one drink, vodka and lemonade, and nothing else. I've had those before, even two at a time and I've been fine." I looked into her eyes and she nodded. "After dinner, we went to his home and he offered me champagne. I drank the first glass, and still, I felt okay. I had to pee a couple times back to back, which always happens when I drink liquor so that was normal. When I came back from the bathroom the second time, I had another glass of champagne. After drinking that one, I did feel a little lightheaded but I assumed it was because of the thoughts I was having at the time.

I was feeling like I had chosen the wrong man, which I had, and hearing Sean's parents bicker made me see things for what they really were as well. But once I finished that champagne glass, actually I don't know if I did, I woke up in Sean's bed... naked... and I could feel down there that I'd had sex. I ended up getting pregnant but I had an abortion. Umm... yeah, and now Sean and his friends have like... umm." I began to fidget because I was regretting telling her already. My strong older sister armor had completely vanished and I felt naked and cold.

"They what, Dree?" Yikayla's voice was soft, and her eyes were worried, almost like she was angry but sad.

"They say things..." I felt the tears coming up as I stared down at my hands because I couldn't look at her again. "They say stuff to me about what happened and they've touched me before and I just... I don't want it to keep going on. I don't know how to stop it though because I can't keep fighting them off alone, and I don't want Canyon to, because he could lose a lot over me and I've done enough to him."

"Dree, you need to tell the police." She took my hand into hers.

"What? No, I can't do that!"

"Yes, you can, and you will. You can start with letting someone on campus know, and give them time to maybe help you, but eventually, you need to go to the police."

"But why? I don't want to."

"I know, but Sean raped you and now he's antagonizing you with it. The only way to get him to shut his ass up without having Canyon do it, is to let the police get involved."

I gazed into Yikayla's eyes as she spoke. As badly as I wanted to say 'no,' I knew I had to at least give that method a try. I was sick and tired of seeing that smug smile on Sean's face, and dealing with his friends. So I guess I'd have to let the world in on my secret.

17

———————

WAAYIL

The Next Afternoon...

I was in my office looking over my calendar and appointments that Rebecca had set up. She always did a good job as far as scheduling sessions and how closely or far away they should be, but I always liked to double check just in case. As I skimmed through everything, my office phone rang, and I saw the number was from Chiara at the front desk.

"What's up, Chiara?"

"Hey, there is someone here to see you."

"See me about what?"

"A tattoo. I told them I had your email and they could converse with you through that, but she wants to talk to you in person. She said it's a pretty complicated design."

"What's her name?" I sighed, not in the mood for this. I didn't appreciate whomever the fuck this was popping up on me.

"Hold on." Chiara moved her mouth from the phone. "Okay, she said her name is Brynn."

"Aight, send her back."

I hung up the phone and then finished looking at my schedule for the rest of the week, while I waited on old girl. I heard a knock at my door soon after, so I got up to go open it for her. She walked in like she was scared or something, which I found odd since she was adamant about talking to a nigga face to face.

"How are you today, Brynn?" I gestured for her to have a seat as I made my way back behind my desk.

"I'm great, actually. I'm off today so you know how that goes."

"Nothing like an off day, right?" I smiled. She cheesed back, and her eyes kind of roamed all over my face for a moment. Shit was awkward. "So, what can I do for you? Chiara up front told me the tattoo you wanted was pretty complicated." I leaned back a little, lacing my fingers together.

"Yeah, it is." She pulled her iPhone from her purse. "I want this dragon, and with all those same colors as well. You can swipe over, there are four pictures total."

I took her phone and looked at the photo, nodding because it was nothing for me. She must have not been too familiar with my work if she thought a dragon was gon' be complicated for me. I swiped over since she said there were four pictures, but I realized there were only three, when the fourth picture was of her in her underwear and nothing else.

"Oh shit, I'm sorry." I quickly swiped back to the last dragon picture and handed her phone over. "My bad, you told me there were four and—"

"Oh shit!" she laughed. "I guess I miscounted. So, do you think that you can do that for me? I can do multiple sessions if you need it."

"Well, I don't need multiples. The only time I have a person come back is if they don't have the time, or if I squeezed them in and I don't have time to finish. But let me see what I have." I turned to look at my computer with my hand on my mouse, and I felt her watching me closely. To be sure, I glanced her way and she was definitely observing me. Her behavior was very fucking weird so I asked, "Do you know me from somewhere? Or how did you find me?"

"Oh... uh, I just was telling people I wanted this done and that I couldn't find anyone that could do it for me. Then I was referred to you."

"Okay, nice." I nodded. "Well, I have an opening in two weeks but it's on a Monday. I don't know if that's good for you. I can do the whole thing on that Monday though. Otherwise, you can come that Friday and I can do part of it."

"Friday would be best for my work schedule."

"Aight." I nodded before placing her name there. "And I just need your number and email just in case I need to contact you."

"Absolutely." She read her number off to me, as well as her email, and then I handed her one of my cards with my information. Smiling down at it, she questioned, "This cell number, is it like your real one or work?"

"Work, ma."

"Do you always answer it?"

"Mostly, unless it's late at night or something, then nah, I don't. But just hit that line before, say 8 p.m. and you should get a response."

"Okay, good. Well, thank you, Waayil. Ooh, did I pronounce it right?"

"Yeah, you did," I chuckled. My name wasn't that hard in my opinion. I believe people just overthink shit, and make it harder than it is.

"I figured since two a's make the sound of ah."

"Yeah." I nodded, ready for her to go. "Well, you have a good rest of your day, ma, and I'll see you in a couple weeks, aight?" I stood up and so did she. She acted as if she wasn't ready to go though.

We shook hands, and I escorted her to the front. As I headed back towards my office, my brother came into the shop. I ignored his bitch ass and kept it pushing, but to my surprise, he followed me in and closed the door behind himself.

"I'm telling you right now, Sef, if you're here to talk about Wednesday, we may just throw hands."

"Ma is here."

"Here? Fuck you mean she's here? To talk about Wednesday? I don't give a fuck who you bring down here, nigga, I don' told yo' ignorant ass just like I don' told her, I—"

"No, muthafucka, our *blood* mother!"

"What? When, nigga? How? And what do you mean *here?* She's in the lobby?"

"Nah, she's not here at the shop, but she's free. She's out of jail." He sat down at the same time I did. "It's been sixteen years, mane."

"Damn, it sure and the fuck has. So what... umm... what she look like? She looks okay or what?"

I was dumbfounded like a muthafucka. I planned to visit my mother and father when I turned 18, but then I got locked up and after that, I was no longer allowed to visit them because of my record. I hadn't thought about the fact that they'd be getting out, because the day I was told Nusef and I would be going into the system, their jail sentence sounded like a lifetime. By saying that, counting down the days seemed pointless.

I was almost afraid to see my mother because I knew she would feel some type of way about me having gone to jail. Nusef said when he first told her, she cried like a newborn for the rest of the damn call. I was always the levelheaded brother, and going to jail was the last thing anyone ever expected of me.

"She looks good, bruh, but shit is weird. Like, she don't want me to call her by her first name, and she's living with me—"

"Nigga, she's living with you? Bruh, what the fuck?" I laughed, happy as hell I'd dodged that bullet. Don't get me wrong, I love my mama, but I wasn't trying to have her ass living with me after not seeing her for over a decade.

"Yeah, man. I didn't know what the fuck to say when she asked. She didn't have a place to stay and she told me that she let her parole officer know that she'd be staying with her son, the one who hadn't been to jail."

This was the only time I was happy that I was an ex-con.

"You're too damn nice, Sef, that's yo' fuckin' problem."

"It's these damn hazel eyes, bruh. People take advantage of niggas with light eyes and you know it."

Laughing, I replied, "Nigga, don't no muthafucka take advantage of me. That's just yo' ass always trying to be nice and shit to any female in need. Fuck that bullshit."

It was quiet for a moment and then he said, "Aye, Yil, I'm sorry for coming at you the way I did about Wednesday. I just don't like y'all at odds because I know how badly it hurts her. But I had to realize that what she did didn't affect me as much as it affected you. Yeah, I lost my brother, which fucked me up, but I didn't do that hard time. I don't have to deal with the fact that I murdered a man for nothing. So again, I apologize, bruh."

"You good. And I knew you'd figure it out just as soon as ya nuts dropped. You was on that bullshit."

"Mane, fuck you," he chuckled. "My nuts too big to not have dropped already." He stood up.

"Aye, for as long as you fucking live, don't you ever tell me how big ya nuts are again, Sef, on God."

He threw his head back laughing as he left my office to go to his tattoo room.

"Gay ass," I mumbled as I texted Yikayla. She sent me a picture of herself, standing in the mirror in her underwear, talking about she wanted to know if I liked the color. She knew damn well that shit was gon' get my dick hard. Especially knowing she was carrying my baby because she was even sexier to me.

Me: *I'm gon' fuck yo' ass up. I got like six more hours of work and you gon' send me that shit.*

Kay Baby: *It was just a question lol.*

Me: *You could have at least let a nigga see one pussy lip or sum.*

Kay Baby: *No! Lmao!*

I pocketed my phone and then went to my tattoo room so I could get everything set for my next person. I worked nonstop for the next six hours, excluding the thirty minutes I took to eat some of the spaghetti Venus's mama brought through for us. She stayed dropping food off for everybody, and I was starting to love her ass.

I had to make Chiara go home because she wanted to stay and close up with me. I wasn't about to be in here alone with her overzealous ass because it'd be just my luck that Yikayla would drop by. Yeah, I knew she was at home with Lonan, probably making me dinner, but that's just how shit worked.

Whenever a nigga was on the up and up in his relationship, shit just happened to him to fuck it all up. A bitch you ain't talked to in fifteen years would show up on yo' wedding day, or she'd text you right when yo' girl is using yo' phone for something. The universe was against us niggas and *for* y'all females, and I don't care what y'all muthafuckas say. So I already knew that for some reason, Yikayla would show up, and Chiara and I would be here alone. So nah, fuck that. I sent that bitch on her merry way.

I locked up once I had everything together, and just as I was about to pull the handle on my car, something heavy as fuck clocked my ass over the head.

I OPENED my eyes but my vision was blurry as hell and my head was hurting badly as hell too. The smell of some sort of cologne was strong as fuck, so whoever had it on must have bathed in that bullshit. My stomach churned and my throat jumped, but I did my best not to throw up. I was so out of it that I didn't even have the time to try and figure out where the fuck I was.

As I started to come to a little more, I realized my hands were tied behind me to the chair I was seated in. I shut my eyes tightly and then shot them open. I did that a couple times until my vision became a bit clearer. It was then that I saw bitch ass, Neo, seated on the edge of a desk. We were in a nice ass office that appeared to be in a tall ass building downtown, overlooking the city.

"Finally, you're awake. For a moment, I thought you were dead." Neo and his flunky laughed.

"Neo, what the fuck, bruh? You couldn't just... you couldn't just come talk to me? Ain't nobody scared of you, my nigga, so what the fuck you got me tied up for like I'm gon' run?"

"Shut yo' ass up! I'm tired of that slick ass mouth! You got too much fucking pride, little boy!"

"Fuck you, bruh." I let my head cock a little because I was feeling too weak to hold it up steadily.

Neo chuckled, irritated that I wasn't bitching up since he had the upper hand right now. He should have known better. I wasn't the type of nigga that you could scare. That's why he fucked with me in the first place.

He nodded towards his flunky, who walked up to me with a crowbar and slammed it into my midsection. Shit hurt like a mutha-fucka, but I just bit down on my lip to keep from groaning or yowling. Neo nodded again and the nigga slammed it hard down on my back, and I just clenched my teeth, still not making too much of a sound outside of a subtle grunt. My angry eyes landed on Neo's, and I could see my resistance to fold was pissing him off.

"I told you that we had a deal, Waayil. You don't back out of deals with me and get to keep your life. So this is how things are gonna go. You and my daughter are gonna be together, and only then, will life be easy for you. Got it?"

I said nothing in response. He was leaning down in my face, and I just adjusted my position so I could stare at him back.

"Did you hear what I said, boy?" he gritted.

Again, nothing came out of my mouth.

His flunky whacked me a few more times, but I kept my groans at bay. I just kept telling myself that them niggas would see their day. I kept my mind on my girl, Lonan, and my new baby, and before I knew it, the flunky had tired out from whipping me like a damn slave.

Afterwards, they sacked me, and then rushed me out. I was thrown into what felt like the back of a van, and I heard Neo making a call as we began to move. My head was pounding so damn loudly that I could barely hear what he was saying, so I just leaned my head up against the wall to hopefully, let the pain subside. After a while, they yanked me from the van, threw me onto some wet grass, and pulled off the sack before driving off.

"Waayil?"

I looked to see Zia in her doorway, rushing down to me.

"Don't touch me!" I shouted to her as I struggled to rise to my feet.

"Baby, let me help—"

"I said get the fuck back right now! I know you were in on this shit, so quit playing before I hurt you, ma!" I grimaced, making her flinch a little.

Holding my side, I limped down the street as I patted my pants for my iPhone. When I felt it, I let out a sigh of relief and called Yikayla. I didn't want her to come out this late, but I needed her.

"Oh my gosh, baby, what happened!" Yikayla shrieked once I slid into the passenger seat groaning.

"I got into a little altercation," I responded, checking on a sleeping Lonan in his car seat in the back.

"That's obvious, Waayil Christian. Who did this to you? And I've never seen you lose a fight so did you get jumped?"

I chuckled at her statement, but then hissed at the pain in my ribs as I leaned up against the inside of the door.

"That girl that I told you about? And her father wanting me to be with her? That's all this was, but I got it."

"You do? It sure doesn't seem like it." Yikayla glanced from me to the road as she drove.

"Just a setback for a major comeback." I used the hand that wasn't clutching my aching side to pinch her chin.

"You make me sick."

"I love you too, baby." I smirked to myself at her ass. "Take me to Monarch so I can get my whip."

She didn't respond.

She was more worried than she needed to be, which was understandable. But best believe, Neo had that shit coming.

18

ALBA

Tammy and I were over Ashley's house just having some wine and food. I needed this because I hadn't been out in a long while. Ever since my miscarriage, all I did was lie in bed. I got time off from work because of it, and when I went back, all I did was work and go home.

I didn't realize how badly I wanted the baby for *me* until I'd lost it. This whole time the child was just a ploy to get Waayil, and I never once stopped to enjoy it for myself. And now that it was gone, I wished I could go back in time and just focus on my baby and nothing else.

My doctor said my stress levels were extremely high, which caused the miscarriage. She claimed it was because of my abusive relationship with my boyfriend, but I knew it was due to my constant plotting, planning, and failing. Now in the right state of mind, I felt like a complete fool for what I was attempting to pull off. I loved Waayil, but he wasn't worth all that I'd done. He wasn't worth me losing my baby. Yes, it was hard to let those years I spent with him go down the drain, but I was young and had a lot of life ahead of me. By saying that, there would be other guys, guys who actually loved me the way I wanted to be loved.

"I'm so happy you're feeling better, girl." Tammy smiled. She was happy as hell to know that I'd given up on chasing Waayil. She was never behind it, and in hindsight, I wished I'd been around her more so she could have had more influence on me. Maybe then I would have my baby.

"Yeah, me too. I didn't think I'd make it, but I'm glad that I did." I sipped my wine before dipping another tortilla chip into the salsa.

"So are you gonna date now? Or are you gonna try to make things work with Gavin?" Ashley quizzed.

Why would I try to make things work with a nigga in jail? Ashley was incredibly stupid sometimes.

"I'm gonna date, but not anytime soon. Right now, I just want to relax and enjoy my life. I wanna travel soon, maybe to Las Vegas, Miami, or Los Angeles."

"Well, I'm down." Tammy held up her wine glass before taking another sip. "I think the chicken is ready, so make a space for your plates." She got up and went to the kitchen.

As I ate some more of the chips and homemade salsa, my phone began to ring. I looked down to see it was an unknown number, and rolled my eyes.

"Who is it?" Ashley inquired.

"Gavin." I set my wine glass down and answered. I told the voice I accepted the charges, and waited for Gavin's voice to pour through.

"Alba, why you only answer for me sometimes?"

"Because we have nothing to talk about, just like I told you the last time, Gavin. You and I are over. We were never anything anyway."

"But the baby, Alba. Regardless of whether or not you wanna be with me, you got my baby inside yo' stomach, so we gon' have to get along at the least."

"It's gone, Gavin."

I hadn't told him yet because I didn't feel the need to before. I would only make small talk with him before having to get off the phone, so things never really got that far. But as of now, I was trying to move on with my life, forget about all that had transpired in the past, including me getting pregnant by him to keep another man. I was over it all, and very embarrassed to even think about it.

"Gone? What you mean? You got an abortion?"

"No, Gavin, I miscarried. I was stressed as hell, and it took its toll on the baby, so I'm not pregnant anymore." This was the first time I'd been able to say that without bursting into tears. It still had me a little, but I was getting better.

"Fuck!" He sniffled and I sat up because I was surprised. Was he really crying over the fact that I'd lost the baby?

"Gavin."

"Baby, why were you stressing? Why you ain't talk to me about it?" he cried, and I actually felt bad for him.

"How would I, Gavin? You got locked up and ... and that fucked with me so it just happened. And it's not like I can call the jail cell to speak with you."

I was suddenly feeling bad as hell for sending the police over to his trap house. I was so wrapped up in my plan to bag Waayil, that anyone who got in my way didn't matter to me. I was definitely regretting all of that shit.

"Come see me."

"No. Gavin, I cannot come see you. What we had is over now. Just stop calling me, and if you do get out, don't come looking for me, okay?" I hung up before he could say anything, and felt bad as hell.

"Dang, girl, was he crying? I could hear it through the phone." Ashley questioned with her eyes bucked.

"Yeah." I shook my head and sat back.

Tammy brought the food out, and after we ate while having some light conversation, we watched some movies. By the time the clock hit 7 p.m., I decided to go home because I wanted to take a hot bath and snuggle up in my own bed with the heater blasting while watching TV. It was Saturday, so I didn't have to be anywhere tomorrow.

After getting out of the bath, I covered myself in body oil, then put on my silk robe. Just as I tied my hair up in the mirror, I heard someone knocking. I didn't know who the hell that could be, because only two people came by my house and that was Waayil and Ashley. However, I'd just left Ashley, and Waayil would never come by these days.

"Sax?" I frowned when I opened the door. He slipped into my house as if he were invited, and I pulled my robe tighter after closing the door. "How the hell do you know where I live?"

"I followed you the last time we met at my house. You never wanted me to come by, so I had to see why."

"Okay, you need to go. I'm about to go to bed."

"I need to talk to you for a minute. Can I at least do that? All the information I gave you, the least you can do is let a nigga vent."

Still feeling weird about him finding out where I lived, I sat down on my couch next to him and waited.

"Well?"

"Alba, I wanna be with you, ma. I have for a while now, and now that it seems like you and Waayil are completely done, I was thinking that—"

"Wait." I put my hand up. "Weren't you dating Rebecca?"

"Yeah, I was, but that was only because you weren't fucking with me. You only talked to me when it was to get information on Waayil."

"Listen to me, Sax. I like you as a friend, but no, you and I will never work. You and Waayil are supposed to be friends and that wouldn't be right."

"Man, fuck him! Yeah, we cool, but I ain't gon' *not* be with you because of him. And truthfully, I don't even think he would care like that."

For a moment, I just looked at him because he was dead serious. He honestly thought we had some kind of connection, and I didn't know why. I did nothing to lead him on not once. He said it himself that the only time I talked to him was to get information on Waayil, so he was bugging for sure right now.

"Sax, I don't want to be with you."

"Why!"

"Because I just don't! I don't want to be with anybody right now! For the longest, I've been with Waayil, and then worrying about getting him back. For right now, I want to be alone."

"This is some bullshit! You and Rebecca are the same type of bitches! I do for y'all and y'all don't appreciate the shit! I go out of my fucking way to help y'all out, even when it involves other niggas, and y'all both just shit on me!" he shouted as he stood up.

"I don't know what you're talking about, Sax! You knew from the beginning that what we had wasn't more than a friendship, and that I needed you for information on Waayil. How can you expect me to just want to be with you!"

"I betrayed the homie for you, and you treat me like this? I shot at that bitch for Rebecca and she did me the same! Y'all talk or some shit?" He neared me with his face knotted up.

"Wait, shot at what bitch?" I backed away, slightly afraid.

"Jonaya Goode! And then that bitch ass nigga, Nusef, that she was hung up on got in my way, so I blasted his ass instead!"

"Wait a minute, Sax. Why would you try to shoot Jonaya?" My voice was trembling a little bit because now I was a bit afraid of him. Sax was always a nice guy, but he appeared to have gone off the deep end.

"Because Rebecca told me how she ruined shit for her and I wanted to get rid of that bitch for making my girl miserable. But it was for nothing, because her hoe ass turned on me saying the same bullshit you just said!" He started to pace my living room.

I was quiet, trying to process everything he'd just said to me, and during my silence, he looked to me.

"What?" I inquired frantically.

"You better not say shit about what I just told you, Alba!"

"I won't!"

"I swear to God if you say something I'll kill yo' ass!" He rushed me and pinned me up against the wall.

"Sax, stop!" I cried. "I'm not gonna say anyth—"

BAM! BAM!

We both went mute at the sound of someone banging on my door. Sax backed away from me with his eyes bucked, and with my eyes on him, I slowly unlocked the door. I had never been so happy to see Waayil in all of my life.

"Fuck is going on in here?" Waayil hissed upon seeing Sax. "Fuck you doing here, bruh?"

"Oh, I was just checking on her because I heard what happened. But I'll check both of y'all later." Sax quickly moved past Waayil and on his way out, he gave me a look that said I'd better not snitch.

As soon as he was outside, I closed the door and locked it.

"Checking on you? Since when did y'all become close?" Waayil questioned.

"We're not, Waayil. I don't even know how he found out where I lived. He just popped up here and said he needed to talk to me."

I was still in shock at Sax's confession, and didn't know if I should tell. I wanted to, but I was afraid. Sax was clearly off his meds at the moment, and I didn't want to be his next victim. He was obviously more about that life than I thought, so I was a bit conflicted. Plus, Waayil hadn't really been on my side lately, so who knows how he'd react to what I told him? He may kill me before Sax got a chance to, just because.

"Whatever. I just came to see how you were doing, ma, that's it."

"I'm doing better." I sat down on the couch. "Oh, I'm sorry. Did you want some water or something?"

"Nah, I'm good." He sat next to me. "Be honest with me, Alba. Was that my kid you were carrying for sure? That shit has been bothering me ever since you lost it, and I just wanna know. Were you one hundred percent sure it was mine? Were you 50/50? Or was it a lie altogether?"

"I showed you the DNA test, Waayil."

I wanted to tell him the truth, but I couldn't. I was ashamed of how far I'd gone just to keep him around. I couldn't tell him I'd slept with another man to get pregnant. I also couldn't tell him that I'd paid someone to make a false DNA test for me.

"You did, but I'm asking you right here, right now. If you're honest with me, I promise I won't hurt you. But if you lie, and I find out later, it won't be pretty."

I contemplated his offer, wondering if he was just telling me this to get me to spill the beans, or if he was being honest. I would love to get this shit off my conscience, but not if it was gonna cost me my life.

"It wasn't your baby, Waayil, and I paid someone to make up those results." I tensed up once the words left my mouth, not even believing I'd said that.

Chuckling, he nodded and then rose to his feet.

"I'm actually happy to hear that shit kind of. I wasn't there for you like a father of an unborn should have been, but now I don't feel bad about the shit because the kid wasn't mine."

I could see it in his face how happy he was. He was content right now and I must say... it kind of hurt.

"Waayil, I—"

"Thanks," was all he said before leaving my house.

I locked the door fast as hell, just in case he tried to double back and fuck me up. Leaning up against the door, I exhaled with a smile, happy that shit was out in the open and over with.

19

JONAYA

The Next Afternoon...

"**F**uck, Jonaya." Nusef grunted as he gripped my hips tightly.

He was hitting it hard, tapping my spot every time he slid inside of me. I could barely hold on as I buried my face in the pillow, grabbing at it with my freshly manicured nails. His strong hands gripped me even tighter as he beat it up, prompting my juices to gush onto his pole and wet up my inner thighs. I was sweating hard as hell, him too, so the sound of our bodies coming together was as loud as ever.

"Baby," I whined, feeling my pelvis tighten because another orgasm was on the horizon.

I bit down on my lip as Nusef hammered me into another release. Gripping my shoulder, he pounded me a few more times before he exploded in the condom, and dropped down to kiss all over my back. I was literally drenched, as if someone had dropped my ass into a pool. Sex with Nusef was always a workout, and a shower was always a must afterwards.

I called myself just stopping by before I went to the mall, but now

I would have to clean myself up. No way was I sliding back into my outfit all sticky and soaked the way that I was.

"Where you going?" Nusef whispered, yanking me back into the bed with him.

"Sef, I'm going to take a shower."

"I'm gon' come too."

"No, your mother is here and I don't want her knowing we shower together. It's weird enough fucking with her across the hall."

"That's why we had the music playing. And the shower water will cover up anything else." He smirked with his adorable self.

"Absolutely not."

I got up and grabbed some underwear from the drawer I kept over here, then put on the robe Nusef bought for me. I went to take a nice hot shower, and as I came out of the bathroom in my robe, I bumped right into Dana. It was weird as hell meeting someone other than Freya, who claimed to be Nusef's mom. Granted, I knew he was adopted, but still, it was strange as hell. I'd known Nusef for ages and Freya was always his one and only mother.

"Remind me of your name again," Dana smiled.

"Jonaya."

"Right, I'm sorry, sweetie. Us black folks always have to think out of the box with what we name our children," she joked.

"Yep. Yeah." I never saw my name as out of the box until now.

"So how long have you been dating my son? He's never mentioned you before to me." She shrugged.

"Oh, it's only been some months. But I have to be somewhere, Mrs. Christian, so can we do this another time?"

"Oh sure, of course." She looked me up and down, but when she realized what she was doing, she gave me a fake ass smile and walked off.

"You never mentioned me to your mama, nigga?" I went into Nusef's bedroom and closed the door. He was laid up with his fine ass.

"What?" he frowned.

"She just told me you've never mentioned me to her."

"I barely talked to her since I was like twelve, and the few times I did over the phone, I told her about you but you were just a friend then. Shit, maybe she forgot."

"She forgot," I repeated, staring at his ass.

"Why do Black women have to repeat your sentence back to you when they don't believe it?" He got out of the bed and pulled his boxers up, before walking out of the bedroom. I tried to grab him and ask what the fuck he was doing, but he ignored me.

"Nusef, no!"

"Ma, you don't remember me mentioning that my best friend's name was Jonaya?" He pointed to me and I wanted to punch him. Now he had me looking like some bratty ass tattletale. His mama already seemed kind of salty, and now that bitch was gon' be a whole bottle of Lawry's with my ass.

"Now that you mention it... that name did seem very familiar when I first met her. Ah, yes, now it's all coming back. He used to talk about you all the time." She looked to me with another fake smile. I could see under it though, and she was not happy about Nusef stepping to her.

"Thank you. You got her all in my shit thinking I hadn't mentioned her ass." Nusef chuckled, and so did she.

He gave me a goodbye kiss before slipping into the bathroom and turning on the shower. After looking at one another in awkward silence for a few moments, I turned around and went back to the bedroom so I could get dressed, leaving Dana in the living room alone. I'd never gotten my clothes on so quickly in my life, except the time I was trying to save Marquise from getting his ass beat.

I came out of the bedroom, and his mother was still sitting on the couch, shoving popcorn in her mouth. She was a very pretty woman, and the boys looked exactly like her except for the fact that she had a caramel complexion. Her smile was extremely reminiscent of Waayil's because she had those same deep ass dimples in her cheeks. I'm guessing their father had the dark skin and the honey colored eyes they'd inherited.

"Well, it was nice, umm... seeing you, Mrs. Christian." I walked to the door.

Pushing her long dark hair behind her ears, she turned and looked up at me with a grin before asking, "Will you be back by here tonight, Jonaya?"

"Uh, I'm not sure. I might. I have some homework to do so—"

"I'm asking because," she set down the bowl of popcorn on the coffee table and turned to face me completely, while still seated on the couch. "I want to spend some alone time with my baby, and it's kind of hard for me to do that with you all over him every second of the day."

"I see. Well, I guess I can just work on my school work for the night so you guys can have some mother-son time together."

"Thank you. You are so sweet. I hope I didn't offend you in anyway by forgetting that Nusef had mentioned you."

"No," I chuckled. "I didn't even care, I was just making conversation and he got a little bent out of shape about it. You know how he can be."

"Yeah... I do. Have a good day, love."

"You too," I cheesed. I felt a little better now that it seemed she wasn't angry with me. I guess I just didn't know her, so I took things the wrong way. She could have been one of those people who didn't know they were making certain facial expressions.

I drove to Oak Court Mall and found a park pretty quickly since it was a weekday, and it was still fairly early in the evening. I saw a car in the parking lot that looked like Leighton's, and as I bypassed it, I confirmed it was hers because of the teddy bear in her back seat. I admit, I was hopeful that I ran into her because I missed her. Even a little bit of conversation would suffice right now.

I shopped at a few stores, and even got this shirt for Nusef that I thought he would like. And as usual, I bought something for my nephew, Lonan. I knew Yikayla would blow a fuse because she always told me to stop spoiling him with clothes because he grew fast, but I couldn't help it when I saw the cutest little jeans or top.

As I was leaving, I saw a group of girls by Leighton's car. I realized it was three people, including Leighton, and when I got closer, I could hear them arguing a little bit. I slowed down my steps so I could eavesdrop for a little longer, without Leighton seeing me.

"You fucked my baby daddy, bitch!" one girl shouted in Leighton's face.

"I already told you I didn't know he had a bitch, let alone a baby mama. Go get at him because he's the one that lied!" Leighton hollered back.

"No, we're getting at you." The friend or family member stepped closer in Leighton's face.

"Get out of my face," Leighton warned.

"What the fuck are you gon' do if I don't?" she replied, just before Leighton shoved her back. The two of them started fighting, and the baby mama jumped in on Leighton too.

"Fuck," I mumbled trying to figure out where I could put my bags. But when I saw one pulling Leighton's hair, while the other punched, I said fuck it.

Dropping my merchandise, I rushed over and started fucking the one up who was doing the punching. I would have gone for the other, but she was the baby mama of some nigga, and the one who really should have been fighting, if at all.

I punched and punched on that bitch until we were up against some random person's car. She couldn't back up anymore, as I continued to wail on her ass like she'd fucked my man or killed my mama. By the time I got tired, someone had yanked me off of her, and I realized police cars were parked right by us. I frantically searched for Leighton, only to see her being restrained by an officer as well. I smiled upon seeing the girl I left her to fight, looking fucked up.

"My shopping bags!" I hollered as an officer brought me to the police car. "Please, I have some new panties in there!" I cried as he palmed my head, forcing me to duck down into the back seat.

The officer who had me cuffed was a young black guy, and after sucking his teeth and shaking his head at me, he went to snatch up my bags. His perverted ass looked into the Victoria's Secret one, before tossing them all into the back seat with me.

The officers had me and Leighton in separate cars, and as we left, I saw the ambulance coming in to tend to those girls.

Once inside the police station, we got interviewed as if we'd committed a murder or rape, and then ultimately, they decided to let us go. I didn't see Leighton until I came walking outside with my bags and phone in hand.

"You need a ride back to the mall for your car? I'm texting Rori to come get me to take me back to get my mom's," I offered, shivering a little because it was cold and windy as fuck right now in Memphis.

She looked to me and nodded, as she tied up her hair.

"Thank you for helping me, Jonaya. I know you didn't have to since I've been a bitch to you for weeks now."

"Maybe a little, but I deserved it, Leighton. What I did was fucked up, coming from someone who is supposed to have your back. I just didn't know what to do, and I didn't want to want Nusef."

"I know. You did me dirty, but I know you, and I know you would never do something like that to me purposely."

I nodded with a smile, and she gave me one back before we chuckled.

"So are we friends now? Or just associates or what?" I nudged her.

Sighing, she replied, "Well, I guess we can be friends, but only if you do something for me first. Relax, bitch, it's not that. I don't even want Nusef anymore."

"Okay, shoot."

"You have to take me to dinner, and I want it to be somewhere nice."

"Bitch, you want me to romance your ass back into this friendship?" I laughed and so did she.

"Uh, yeah, pretty much. I'm not just gonna let you have me back that easily."

"Fine." It was silent for a moment and then I said, "That bitch you fought was ugly as fuck; no wonder her baby daddy lied about her. Shit, I wouldn't want people knowing I had a baby by that albino gorilla either."

"An albino gorilla, Jonaya? Really?" she chuckled. Looking off, she added, "Her baby daddy was fine as hell though too."

"Did you know about her or were you telling the truth?"

"I honestly didn't know about her or their child, but after we fucked, I saw a toy figurine in the corner of his bedroom so I had an inkling. I asked him about it and he said they were his little brothers. His brother is nineteen." She gave me a look like 'yeah right,' making me snicker.

"Niggas," I said, shaking my head just as Rori pulled up. "I love you."

"I love you too." She smirked as we walked to the car.

20

───

EKO

I opened my eyes to see Rori topping me off with her little freaky ass. She was looking me in the eyes too, and that shit was sexy as hell in combination with the feeling. It took me only seconds to come to, and I palmed the back of her head while biting down hard on my bottom lip.

Rori turned me on because outside of her being fine as fuck, she was one of them undercover ass freaks. She was about her school shit, real fucking smart, but at home, she'd do shit like this; wake her nigga up with some good ass sloppy toppy.

"I'm about to bust," I warned her, letting my head fall back.

Her damn saliva was out of control as she deep throated my shit with no problem. For the life of me, I couldn't understand why Gavin would ever fuck around on her or dog her out the way that he did, but I was happy as fuck about it. Had he been doing what the fuck he was supposed to, Rori wouldn't be in my bed right now. The thought of that shit alone made me shudder.

"Mmm," I grunted lowly, letting loose, and Rori took it all down. My damn toes were cramped from folding them muthafuckas up the whole time to keep from screaming, so it took me a minute to get up.

Rori tried to get out of the bed, but I yanked her back in, made her face the footboard, and then killed her shit from the back. I climbed off the bed as she panted heavily, and then I went to turn the shower on. When I came back, I scooped her up to carry her, and saw she'd scratched the wood of my footboard with her nails.

"Damn, ma," I chuckled, nodding towards the damage she'd done.

"Blame yourself," she smirked.

We got in the shower to clean up, and then took turns brushing our teeth as the other busied themselves with something else. She was dressed before me since she had class, and I wanted to chill in my towel for a little bit before making some calls.

"See you later," she smiled, tying her scarf around her neck and pulling on her big ass coat.

"Bye, ma." I held my head back and she planted a kiss on me. "Let me walk you to the door."

"Umm, no, not in that damn towel."

"It's just the door."

"And I said no! That old bitch from across the street likes you, and every time you come to the door shirtless, her dried up ass be watching. I'm two seconds from cutting her Lady Eloise ass up."

"Aight, ma, chill," I laughed. "And she's only like fifty, why you gotta call her Lady Eloise?" I asked, chortling.

"Excuse me, fifty? In what, dog years? That saggy faced ass bitch is not fifty, she's more like eighty."

"Get out my crib, Rori," I snickered.

She grabbed her bag up and switched her little sexy ass out. I leaned up against the wall in the hallway just watching her, already missing her. I had shit to do though, and fucking around with Rori, I'd be in the damn house all day. Thank God she had school and that little job helping the mayor out because otherwise, the two of us would be held up in this bitch making babies.

I made a few phone calls to a couple contractors, I was referred to because I wanted some renovations done on Coney's now that I owned the place. It was an aight looking spot, but you could tell the owner was old as fuck, which Barry Coney was. I wanted to spruce shit up, which was why I was still working with Neo to save up some extra to pay for any repairs and developments. I was gon' make Coney's my own, but still keep the name, so the usuals wouldn't feel out of place.

I finally got dressed after setting up some appointments, and just as I opened the door, I saw Jenni's homegirl, Kina, about to knock on my screen door. She was wearing gray sweats, a big ass t-shirt, and her hair was covered in one of them loud ass abstract print scarves.

"Oh yeah, you scared now, nigga! Open up!" Kina hit my screen.

"Back yo' stupid ass up before I hit you with this shit," I barked, pushing the screen door open and coming out.

It was then that I saw Jenni, looking like a damn fool because she was dressed like Kina. Them hoes looked like bopsy twins, and the only difference between them right now, other than Kina being black and Jenni being white, was that Jenni looked scared as fuck, and Kina was ready to throw down.

Before I could even get a word out, Kina rushed me and started swinging.

"Jenni, help!" Kina yelled as I struggled to catch her fucking wrists.

Jenni came to her aide, and started swinging on me as well, but not as roughly. When Jenni realized they had the upper hand, that bitch took it too far and kneed me in the nuts with some Dragon Ball Z power behind it.

"Fuck!" I grunted, falling to the ground and holding myself. "Make one more fucking move and I'm shooting both of y'all bitch-es!" I roared, on the verge of crying.

Finally acting like they had some sense, they stopped in their tracks and just stared down at me. My damn stomach was on fire and hurting badly as fuck. And I swear my nuts had swollen to the size of oranges. I wanted to murk these hoes right now, but I was damn near handicapped. I didn't have asthma, but if someone offered me an inhaler right now, I'd definitely take that shit. In a minute, I was gon' need a defibrillator.

"Bitch ass nigga." Kina smacked her teeth and switched back to the car.

My damn vision was blurry as hell from that vicious ass Mortal Kombat dick kick Jenni had given me. It took so much out of me not to beg one of these bitches to call an ambulance, because a nigga felt like he was done for.

"Oh my gosh, baby, I'm so sorry! I didn't mean to hit you so hard!" Jenni knelt down and caressed my face.

"Get off me, bruh," I whispered, pressing my face into the freshly cut lawn. "Just take yo' stupid ass home before I fully recoup and shoot you, ma," I gritted. A nigga was drooling as I talked a little bit right now because of the pain.

"No, I'm gonna stay right here with you."

Picking my head up from the grass, I looked up into her pretty ass eyes and said, "Jenni, what I told you when I caught you in my house was for real, shorty. It's over with. I know before you would just pop up over here, and I'd let you suck my dick and all that shit, but that's not gon' happen no more. I'm through. I barely wanted you when I had you, now stop trying to make this shit seem like more than what it is. We weren't in love, we weren't in a real relationship, and I never had feelings for you. I need you to get the fuck up outta here and forget about me altogether, aight?"

She shook her head and opened her mouth as if she were about to speak, but nothing was said. She stood up and panted as she looked down at me somberly.

"Ah!" I shouted when she kicked me in the stomach.

"Ah!" She tried to run off, but I grabbed her ankle and made her stupid ass fall. My strength was back, so I got up to grab her by that headscarf as she attempted to crawl away.

"Next time I see you around me, I'm putting a bullet in yo' head," I whispered in her ear before letting her hair go.

Hopping to her feet, she darted to her car that Kina was already sitting in. Before I even got in my whip good, they were speeding off down my street. After taking a few deep breaths to calm down, I gave my nuts a pep talk to stay strong enough to put some kids into Rori, and then I drove to the shop.

"Ayyyye, the new boss man!" this barber, Chris, yelled as everyone clapped like some fools.

"I *been* the damn boss. I was the manager the whole time," I replied as I walked through, dapping a couple people up.

"Damn, so who the new manager now?" Robert asked, chilling with the broom next to him.

"Not yo' ass. Empty them damn trash cans, nigga," I told him and he rushed to get started.

I went to the back to put my shit up before my next head came, and heard a knock on my door. Robert peeked his head in, but before he could say anything, Neo barged his way in, almost knocking Robert over.

"Eko." Neo grinned as he sat down across from my desk.

"I got it from here, Robert. Let me know when Jeremiah comes, aight?" Robert nodded to say 'okay' and then he left out. "What you doing at my shop, Neo?" I frowned as I sat down at my desk.

I was beyond concerned because I wanted to keep my legit shit from this illegal shit. I didn't even want him to know about the shop, but Gavin had mentioned it to him once, a while back. Now that I think about it, nigga probably did that shit on purpose.

"Wanted to see what had so much of your attention since you can't seem to figure out who got my shit taken by the cops."

"Neo, I have been diligently looking for the culprit and, mane... I don't fucking know."

Honestly, I was puzzled as hell about who had set Gavin up. I was usually good as fuck at weeding out the snakes in the grass, but none of the young niggas appeared to have done it. I didn't know what to think. I wasn't sure if I was losing my touch or if the perpetrator was just that damn hard to detect, but it was pissing me off just as much as it was Neo.

I wanted to find the muthafucka, get rid of their asses, and then be done with this shit altogether. I was over this dope boy shit, on God! However, I knew if I didn't find that person, Neo would be on my head and I didn't need that. A nigga was ready to live a quiet regular life with Rori, and that was it, just as soon as I got the cash to pay for this place to get refurbished.

"I don't think you are. I think you're too busy focusing on this place, and not what's more important. Is this shop paying your rent, or is my dope paying it?"

Both were actually paying my rent, but now that I was the owner, I could live pretty well with just having the shop. After a while, I planned to open up another as well. But was I gon' tell his ass that? Hell muthafuckin' nah! I didn't want him knowing how much I made from this shop, because that would just give him ammo to fuck shit up.

"The dope," I responded.

"Good answer," he grinned. "But see, until you learn how to act, I'm bringing in some help."

"Help?"

"Yeah. I'm getting Gavin out and bringing him back on. He's angrier about the situation, so maybe he will actually find the nigga, since you're acting like the person is a needle in a haystack."

"You said you weren't gon' get his ass out and that you were done," I gritted.

"Well, I've changed my mind." He got up. "Gavin will be out on bail soon, and he'll be back working with you, while trying to figure out who snitched. I've gotten him a pretty good lawyer to beat his upcoming case."

Laughing angrily, I shook my head.

"Don't do this shit, Neo, because you gon' regret it."

"I didn't do shit, Eko. You did it to yourself."

"I got work to do, so see yaself out, mane."

Neo nodded and then left my office and establishment. I didn't feel like dealing with Gavin's ass, because not only would we be competing on the low, but also, I knew this situation with Rori had him on some bullshit. I didn't need anything getting in the way of me earning these last few dollars I needed to bow out. But it was cool. I'd just take that nigga out like I had planned, and hopefully come out with my cash. Only thing that changed, was that now Neo was on my hit list too.

21

______

YIKAYLA

"Smells good," Waayil walked into the kitchen looking and smelling good, as I set a plate of food in front of him. "Crepes? I ate that pussy good last night, huh?" He grinned with his adorable self.

"No, boy, I just felt like making them. Plus, Lonan loves them."

"I can tell." He nodded towards my baby, who had completely unfolded the crepe and was holding it up in the air as he fed it to himself.

I sat down at the table to have breakfast with my family, and once Waayil was done, he kissed us both goodbye. I was already dressed, so I got Lonan in his clothes after a warm bath and brushing his little teeth.

Today, he was going to his father's house for a few days, and I did not want to let him go. Those three days without my baby were always the worst. I knew Miss Laughton took good care of him, but I felt like no one could look after my baby better than I could. Plus, he learned new things every day and I hated when I got him back and he could say a new word already.

Once Lonan was dressed and I had his things packed, we left to my parents' home. Roscoe and I agreed to meet there to exchange Lonan because him coming over here just wasn't a good idea. I was dreading meeting him, not only because I was selfish with Lonan, but also because shit had been very awkward ever since he got on his knees and begged me not to have Waayil's child. I think it was weird between us now because he was ashamed of his actions, and I was ashamed *for* him.

"Come here, man," Roscoe cooed to Lonan who turned his back on his father and hugged my neck tightly.

"Lo, I thought we were over this," I said to him. The past few times he'd gone to Roscoe with no problem.

I peeled his little arms from around my neck and was about to hand him over until he cried in his little voice, "Mommy, no!" with tears sliding down his plump cheeks. That was his first complete sentence and it was just too much at one time.

"Give him here!" Roscoe barked when I hugged Lonan back against my body.

"No, I can't, Roscoe. We can try tomorrow and I'll just come over here early to make sure that he's asleep."

"Nah, you just doing this shit because you wanna keep him! Give his ass here. He's a fucking boy, Yikayla, you gotta stop babying his ass!"

"Roscoe, stop! Give me a second to at least calm him down and talk to him. If you grab at him again, I'm gonna kick your nuts up into your stomach, nigga." I moved a little ways away from Roscoe, and I noticed when Lonan thought he wasn't going with him anymore, his crying turned to light sniffles. "You wanna stay with Mommy?" I asked him, rubbing his baby soft, curly hair back.

He nodded his head 'yes' as he kept it laid on my shoulder, and I just couldn't let Roscoe take him. I knew what Roscoe was saying was partially true about me babying Lonan, but how could he expect me to let him take him like this? I did have to be at work, but Jerica would just have to let me bring Lonan.

"What's good?" Roscoe yelled in an irritated fashion, as I started back towards him.

"Roscoe, I can't. But tomorrow, I will make sure he's asleep and then I will bring him to you."

"He's only acting like that because you got that nigga around him all the fucking time!"

"No, you need to stop being so rough and mean to him! He is a one year old, Roscoe! He is going to touch things, he is going to talk a lot, he is going to be a busy body, walking around the house every-where. You can't yell at him or wanna spank him because he won't sit there like a fucking statue!"

Inhaling and exhaling sharply, he replied, "You right. I'm just used to my other kids who are older and they—"

"I don't really care to hear about the babies you had on me at the moment, Roscoe. But just meet me here tomorrow around 7:30am."

Hearing him say the words 'my other kids' still made me cringe. For the last year or so, I'd been under the impression that Lonan was *both* of our only child. Shit was just so weird for me right now.

"Yikayla, I wanted to say I'm sorry for the way I acted when I saw that pregnancy test. It's just the thought of you having a baby by another nigga kills me. And to make shit worse, it's by *that* nigga. Of all the muthafuckas you could have gotten pregnant by, it had to be him. The nigga I don' had issues with since I met you and before I'd even seen his ass in person."

"Get over your jealousy issues, Roscoe. And you're not the only one who can have babies by other people, okay? Don't touch me." I snatched back when he tried to take my hand into his. "See you tomorrow."

He watched me as I went into my parents' home. I wanted to tell my mother that I had stopped by since I thought it was awkward to meet outside of her home and not say 'hi' or anything.

"Hey, Ma," I smiled.

"Yikayla!" She looked way too happy to see me. "Come here." She kissed Lonan's cheek, and then took my hand to lead me to the downstairs bathroom.

"What, Ma?" I frowned when she closed the door.

"Your father is getting suspicious." She fidgeted.

"Suspicious about what?"

"About the things I do when he's away. I don't know who said anything or— did you or Dree say anything to him?"

"Ma, of course not! I know for sure I didn't, and Dree has her own stuff to deal with, so I know she didn't either."

I'd never seen my mom look so concerned. But as reckless as she was with her lovers, a bum on the street could have told Jasper.

"Well, someone planted something in his head and now he's saying all these threatening things, like if he finds out I've been unfaithful, he's divorcing me immediately."

"Ma... I mean, I don't know what to say. What did you think would happen? Every time he leaves, you parade a new boyfriend all over Memphis, like you don't have a well-known husband."

"Well, he shouldn't leave so much! I don't like being alone, and he needs to spend more time with me instead of always running off to work when they want him to!"

"Mama, seriously? Yes, I understand that you want him around more, but he spends every minute of his free time with you! And he is a successful man who makes a lot of money, and to make a lot of money, you have to sacrifice time. You don't make the kind of cash he does, sitting around and you know it. You wanted to be with him because of who he was and what he had, so don't cry about it now." I walked past her so I could leave the bathroom.

"Yikayla, I just ask that if he comes to you about this, you back me up on it and say you don't know anything. Okay?"

I couldn't even respond, so I just shook my head. My mother had been doing what she did with Buddy for years, and it always bothered me. I didn't say anything for reasons I've previously explained, but I'll admit that it was getting under my skin.

Women prayed to God at church every Sunday to have a man like Jasper, and she acted as if it was nothing. I understood she needed more attention, but when she first got with Jasper, he was like this. I remember when I was just five years old, how he would have to travel a lot or leave in the middle of dinner because his pager was beeping.

I guess, I just hated when people overlooked things, just to complain about it later. Don't marry a cheating ass nigga, only to complain and act shocked when he cheats on you down the line. You knew what type of nigga he was.

I left the house fairly quickly with my baby in tow because I had to start work soon. It was early in the week, usually when Jerica, for some reason, had a lot of dresses. Her being able to sew as quickly as she could was still baffling to say the least.

"Good morning." Brynn smiled when I entered. Her eyes landed on Lonan as I kissed him and ignored her ass, continuing to my room.

"Okay, Lonan, eat these." I placed him on the soft couch in my workroom, and handed him his snacks and placed his sippy cup next to him. I chuckled when he just stared up at me as I walked over to the first rack I needed to steam. "Relax, baby." I laughed because he was so stiff.

Eventually, he laid back some and started talking in baby talk while shoving his Graduates into his mouth. An hour had passed, and he was surprisingly behaving himself, but I guess that was because I brought his baby iPad with me. It kept his attention, even though he didn't know how to use it. I was angry when Waayil first bought it for him, but now that little shit was a lifesaver. Whenever I needed some time to handle business, I threw Lonan that iPad.

I heard a knock on my workroom door, and before I could say 'come in,' Jerica entered. I was stuck for a minute because I'd forgotten to text and tell her Lonan would be here. That talk with my mom threw me off.

"Well, who is this?" she cooed.

"This is my baby, Lonan. I'm sorry I didn't tell you, I just—"

"No, it's perfectly fine, Yikayla. He's so well behaved. How old is he?" She neared him.

"He's one year old."

"Adorable."

"Thank you." I smirked at Lonan, who was eyeing Jerica for a moment. It's true when they say every parent thinks their child is perfect because I definitely felt that way about my baby.

"So, Yikayla, I wanted to talk to you for a moment about the sketches in your book that you had me look at."

"Oh yeah, okay." I cut the steamer off and sat at the short coffee table in the room.

I was nervous as hell to hear what she had to say. Everyone claimed what I sketched was really good, but I wanted to get the opinion of someone like Jerica. Plus, Waayil would say anything to get between my legs some nights.

I'd told Jerica that I wanted to start getting some of my dresses made, and selling one of a kind pieces on a website. But I wanted her to tell me her thoughts before I started staying up late, sewing a bunch of potential garbage.

"So, I see you have a lot of talent in choosing fabric, but a lot of the dresses you have here, I can't really see anyone wearing. Namely this one." She tapped her finger on it.

My heart sank into the pit of my stomach when she said that, because I'd never heard anything like it before.

"Oh, I see," I nodded, feeling sick.

"Your drawing is great, but it's just the designing part."

Bitch, that's the main part of the job! What do you mean *just* the designing part?

"Oh, okay, well thank you. Do you have any suggestions for me? Like what I should do to improve?"

"Well, designing should come naturally to you, but maybe you should look into fashion classes. I'd be happy to alter your schedule as needed so you could still steam dresses for me while in school."

"Wow, I'm sorry. I'm just a bit caught off guard. But thank you for being honest with me about it."

"No problem. Fashion is a lot of hard work, honey." She got up. "Well, I will let you get back to work." She handed me my sketchbook, said 'goodbye' to Lonan, and then walked out.

I went to sit next to my baby, and pulled him into my lap before opening my sketchbook back up. I wasn't in the mood to do anything right now, especially steam dresses that I'd probably never be able to make.

22

———————

CANYON

I was on my computer working, when Dree knocked on my door and then came in. I swear her ass came by every damn day, but I wasn't mad about the shit. I admit when we first got back together, I was kind of waiting for her to pull some bullshit again so I could wring her neck, but so far, she'd been on her best behavior.

I smirked, watching her close my door and come around to sit on my lap. She smelled good as fuck like always, so I nuzzled my nose into her neck as I locked my arms around her waist.

"What you doing here, ma?"

"What do you think? I have a break in between classes."

"Ain't this ya time to eat and shit? Not be in here up under me. You ain't catching feelings or nothing, right? I ain't got time for a girlfriend."

"Oh, you don't?" she raised a brow. "Well that's too fucking bad because I got time enough for the both of us."

"What the fuck?" I laughed. "How the hell do you have enough time for the both of us?"

"Because I do. So now you don't have an excuse." She leaned down to peck me while I squeezed her ass. She had on some tights, and I loved that shit. It was the closest thing to feeling her skin. "I wanna tell you something but I don't want you to get upset, okay?"

"It depends."

"Canyon, I need you to be calm when I tell you this."

"Just say the shit, Dree."

I was frowning a little bit because you just never knew with Dree. For the small time that I'd been back in her life, so much shit had transpired that I didn't know what the fuck was coming next. From leaving a nigga over dumb shit, to getting drugged, to getting an abortion, it was no telling what else Dree had to tell me.

"Sean has been kind of harassing me, almost making fun of what he did to me, so I'm gonna tell the Dean of Students over our department this week."

"Harassing you like how?" The scowl on my face was so deep that I could feel it. "And when did this shit happen? How fucking long—"

"Canyon," she exhaled. "Just calm down. I'm gonna talk to the dean and see what she can do about it. I tried to just put them in their place, but that wasn't working so well for me."

"Them?"

"Yeah, he and his friends. Actually, he's putting the battery in his friends' backs, and they're doing shit."

"Get up."

"Canyon—"

"Get up!"

"No! I won't let you do anything to them because you have a lot to lose and I wouldn't be able to live with myself knowing you jeopardized everything to defend me. I appreciate what you've done so far, baby, but at this point, Sean needs to be handled legally, not physically."

I was fuming from hearing this shit and wanted to go beat that bitch nigga's ass, mask off this time. However, as much as I loved

Dree, I had worked way too hard to get to where I was in my life. The Black man already had to do twice the work of a white one, so I couldn't lose everything behind that nigga Sean. Yeah, it was gon' fuck with me, but at least I'd beaten his ass once and well. Also, I agreed with the fact that the nigga needed to be held accountable for what he'd done to my shorty.

"Aight, I'll fall back, but if that nigga does anything else, Dree—"

"I know, I know." She got off my lap. "I just want you to remember that he's not worth losing all of this." She moved her hands around, gesturing to my office. "And you worked hard for these." She ran her small hands across my degrees on the wall.

I nodded, feeling myself calm down a bit.

Dree and I talked for a little more, and then I walked her hard-headed ass back to the other side of campus. That shit was far as hell, and it was way too damn nippy outside for the shit she was trying to do. Instead of walking, I jogged my way back to my work building, and when I came into my office, I saw my supervisor in there looking around like he was waiting for me.

"Hey, Ennis, you need something?" I took my coat off and hung it up on the wooden coatrack in my office, before rounding my desk.

"Yeah, actually." He closed my door and then sat down across from me. "I wanted to talk to you about a student named Sean Ike."

"What about him?"

"Well, he was assaulted some time ago, and he reported it to the police. In his report, he mentioned that he'd been threatened by *you* prior to being beaten."

"And?"

"So you threatened him?"

"I didn't threaten him, I tried to have a conversation with him about a personal matter, and he got heated for no reason," I quickly lied.

I knew I couldn't deny having talked to his snitching ass, but no way was I about to admit to threatening any fucking body. And if the little bitch he was with wanted to jump on the snitching campaign,

I'd have her ass smoked while I was sleeping peacefully next to Dree. Only reason I hadn't done that shit to Sean, was because he and his family were too well connected. If he went missing, the damn U.S. President would be trying to find out who did it.

"I see, and what was the personal matter?"

"It's personal, like I just said." I leaned back in my chair. "The most I can tell you is that it had something to do with a friend of mine that he'd wronged. He got defensive about it, and that was the end. No threats were made."

Exhaling sharply, Ennis responded, "I understand. Well, he implied that you might have had something to do with it. Now, Canyon, I understand that this person you were defending is close to you, but if you want to keep your job, you need to leave Sean Ike alone."

I chuckled out of anger for a little bit.

"So because I talked to him, I could lose my job? That's what you're saying, right?"

He leaned in a little bit, and placed his hands on the edge of my desk before speaking.

"Canyon, what I'm saying is that Sean and his family have a lot invested in this school, so anything that could possibly jeopardize their contributions will be eliminated. I would never fire you, but it won't be up to me at that point. Whatever Sean did to your friend, let them handle it if you like working here. That's all I'm saying," he whispered.

"I hear you," I sighed.

"I know it's frustrating, but sometimes, you have to make sacrifices in order to keep life steady. There are many students whose necks I wanted to wring, but I couldn't because I have a family depending on me to bring home the money."

"You're right," I nodded.

"I'm glad we had this conversation." He half smiled as he got up to leave.

For a little while, I just stared at the door, soaking up everything

Ennis had said. Sometimes, I struggled with trying to keep the old Canyon tied up and locked away. Muthafuckas seemed to try me more now that a nigga had a good job with benefits and shit.

After calming myself down, I got back to work and before I knew it, I was off. Shit was awkward now at work with Roselle, but I really didn't give a fuck. She'd mean mug me here and there, and I wouldn't even return the fucking gesture. She wasn't worth it, and I still slept soundly at night. Didn't even think about the bitch once I stepped out of this muthafucka. I'd have to have some sort of feelings invested to be mad, honestly.

The whole way to my car, Luna was blowing me up back to back like a fucking fool. I swear her ass was touched. I was picking up my son soon, so I had no idea why she was calling me. A part of me wondered if it was an emergency, but knowing Luna, it was some dumb shit. The worrisome part got the best of me though, so when I got in my car I answered.

"Where are you?"

"Work, Luna. Fuck you keep calling me for, shorty?" I was frowning so fucking hard that it was difficult as hell to change my expression as I waved bye to one of my co-workers.

"You get off work at 3:45, nigga!"

"It's 3:55pm, Luna! What the fuck, ma! I get *off* at 3:45! Off! Which means up until then, my ass is still at work and working!"

"It's been ten minutes!"

"So what! Can I gather my shit and walk to my car? Or do you just want me to *I Dream of Jeannie* my ass to yo' spot?"

"Whatever, Canyon, you just hurry up!" She hung up.

I didn't know what had crawled up her ass today, but I wasn't in the mood for it. She was gon' find herself rotting in a damn ditch somewhere fucking around with me. I sped out of the parking lot on two wheels, more irritated than I was before.

When I got to Luna's, I hopped out the whip fast as hell, and banged on her damn door as roughly as I could.

"What!" She opened it.

Lord... please lend me your spirit.

"Fuck do you mean what! I'm here to get Cade! Did you not just call me and go the fuck off? I swear you're out yo' damn mind, Luna. I'm starting to think ya name is short for lunatic."

"Shut up." She unlocked the screen and pushed it out to let me in. "Why are you with Dree Goode!"

"You need to bring yo' voice down like ten octaves first off. Secondly, don't question me about who I'm with."

"If you're gonna have my son around her, then I have a right to know. I don't like her and neither does Jupiter, so y'all need to break up."

After looking at her like she was crazy for a minute, I couldn't help but to laugh and clap my hands.

"This ain't no damn electoral college. You and Jupiter's big mouthed ass don't decide who I fuck with. Shit, Jupiter barely likes yo' ass, so what the fuck y'all banding together for?"

"For the interests of Cade. I don't want him around that privileged ass bitch. He needs to know what it's like to struggle sometimes, and she won't show him that."

"Don't call her a bitch, ma. And every time he visits you, he'll get a reminder of what it's like to struggle, in this hot box that ain't never clean. And you don't know shit about Dree."

"I know her daddy is a surgeon and they have money."

"And?"

"And she's a hoe!"

"Fuck I just say about all that name calling?" I moved in on Luna with my teeth clenched.

"You said I couldn't call her a bitch," she whimpered. She was so damn ignorant that all I could do was close my eyes and exhale.

"Cade! Come on, son!" I shouted.

Before I could even finish my sentence, he came running to the front. I shook my head seeing he needed a haircut because Luna swore she'd take him to get one.

"I need to go see the man with the cape and the clippy things," Cade told me as he walked up on me, picking at his kinky curls.

"Yeah, I know. Yo' mama got yo' head looking rough as hell."

"I want him to have braids, I said." Luna sucked her teeth.

"And I told you he ain't gettin' no damn braids. You— nah, let me get the fuck up outta here before I say something else." I moved Cade towards the door and followed behind him.

"Ugh, I hate you and I hate that bitch, Dree!" Luna growled.

"Mommy, I told you I don't like when you start being a hater," Cade pouted. Luna's eyes widened, and as hard as I tried, I couldn't hold in my laughter. I think what made it funnier was that Cade was real life sad that his mama was being a hater.

"Cade, you don't talk to me like that! I am your mother—"

I slammed her screen door in her face and took my son to the car. From Luna's, we went straight to the ice cream parlor so I could reward my kid for getting on his mama. I just wish I had recorded that shit.

23

RORI

I was exhausted as hell leaving my last class, and I just wanted to go home, eat, take a good nap, and then see Eko. However, life wasn't on my side right now, and I had to be at work for the potential mayor. I didn't know why we had to do this shit so damn early anyways, when he wasn't running until later this year, but whatever. I was just mentally complaining because I was dead tired right now from staying up watching *The Walking Dead* all night with Eko. He'd told me to take my ass to bed, but I was too comfortable cuddled up with him, and the show was surprisingly good as hell.

"Hey, Rori, are you coming to the party tonight?" Carissa ran up to me and handed me some flyer.

"Absolutely not." I handed it back to her.

"Well, why not? It's gonna be really fun and I don't have anyone to go with. Plus, you know all the cute guys."

Stopping in my tracks, I said, "Carissa, I am a busy woman. What that means is that I'm also tired. I appreciate you wanting to hang with me at the party, but I cannot tonight. I am beat as it is and I have to be at work."

"Yeah, okay. Maybe next time."

"Maybe."

I made my way to my stepdad's car, and drove straight downtown where I worked. I wanted to stop for food, but I was sure they had a nice lunch at work that I could dig into for free.

Once I made it there, I parked inside of the structure, and grabbed out my makeup bag so I could put some lipgloss on.

KNOCK! KNOCK!

Someone knocking on my car door window jarred me from my seating position, almost making my head hit the ceiling. Looking over, I saw busted ass Jenni desperately pleading for me to get out of the car. I don't even know how she got inside the damn structure and all the way up in here on this level, but then again, this bitch was crazy.

Shoving my shit back into my purse, I opened the door and got out.

"What!" I shouted, slamming my door back and hitting the alarm.

"How is Eko doing?"

"Did you seriously follow me here to ask me about *my* man? The man you and your friend tried to beat up?" I hissed.

Granted, I couldn't stop laughing when Eko asked me later that night to take him to the emergency to get his nuts checked, but this bitch didn't need to know that. Plus, *I* could laugh about it.

"I didn't want to. I— I only did it because my best friend, Kina, said we should and I was angry with him."

"Jenni, now is not the time. Just forget about Eko. That's all you have to do. He doesn't want you, so get over it."

Almost like she was turning into a different person, her soft expression turned hard immediately.

"You think I've forgotten about making your life a living hell, Rori? Well I haven't! I went easy on you because I thought I still had a chance with Eko, but now that it appears that I don't, it's over for you."

"Blah blah blah. Yeah right, bitch. You've been singing that same old tired song for weeks now. I think you know better and you're too scared of getting that ass beat."

"Oh please!"

"Bye, Jenni!"

I started off, a bit in a rush because I only had twenty minutes left before I had to start, and I wanted to eat something. I didn't have time to be out here going back and forth with that deluded ass bitch.

I was cursing her to myself, and when I stepped onto the elevator, I realized this bitch was getting on as well.

"Jenni, get off!"

"No!"

"You cannot follow me in here anyway, so I don't care if you ride up. You're just gonna have to leave and look dumb." I folded my arms, trying not to let her get to me.

She declined to respond, and when the elevator opened on the floor Mr. Garrick had completely taken over, Jenni and I both stepped off. This big buff guy approached me, asking to see my badge, but before I could answer, this hoe Jenni started acting a fucking fool.

"Baby, don't do this to me!" she shouted, hugging me tightly from behind as the elevator doors closed behind us.

"Get off me! What the hell is wrong with you!" I barked, trying to get her arms from around my body without whooping her ass in front of Mr. Garrick's security.

"I don't wanna break up with you! I love you, Rori!" she cried.

Oooh okay, I saw what this bitch was doing. I was gonna fucking murder her stupid ass.

"You two are gonna have to go." The security guard pressed the down button to call the elevator back up to get us.

"No! I work on this floor! I'm helping out with the campaign for Troy Garrick!" I yelled, fumbling with my purse to pull out my badge as Jenni bear hugged me from behind. Was this really happening?

"All I ever wanted was to be with you!" Jenni cried as she got down on her knees and begged me.

"We can't have all this up here, you need to go!" the security guard barked.

"No, I can't leave! I have to be here! I don't even know her or why she's acting this way, I swear!" I continued rummaging through my purse for my badge as Jenni hugged my waist from the front now.

"Rori Goode, how dare you deny me? I refuse to leave until you forgive me. I never did anything! I even kept my mouth shut when you slept with *all* those other girls," Jenni whimpered, making my eyes widen in horror since Troy had hit the corner along with Parker.

"What is going on here, Rori?" Parker questioned, frowning at the scene in front of her.

"You know this girl?" the security asked and Parker nodded.

"I'll just see you at home, hopefully. Just know that I love you and won't stop fighting for you and our love." Jenni rose to her feet, and shot me a discreet smirk before getting on the elevator, which had just arrived.

I was mortified, floored, ashamed, and furious as I stood there with Troy, Parker, and the security guy in silence. For the first time in months, I was entirely speechless.

"I am so sorry, I—"

"Rori, come back to the suite so I can have a word with you." Parker glared at me.

"Actually, Parker, you go on ahead to that meeting," Troy interrupted. "I will have a talk with Miss Goode."

"Are you sure, Mr. Garrick?"

"Yeah, they don't need me at this one. All of this stuff is preliminary right now. Just take some good notes for me, okay?"

"Yes of course," Parker blushed. I'd never seen her ass show interest or any kind of emotion because she was always so serious. She must have had a little thing for Troy.

I watched Parker eye me as she got onto the extra elevator, and I knew she wanted to kill me for the scene I'd just caused. However, I was more afraid of having to be reprimanded by Troy. I would much rather endure Parker's wrath because she wasn't really anybody. Troy was a big deal, and I didn't know what his plans were for me. I needed this internship.

"Follow me, Miss Goode," Troy said to me and then nodded towards the security to let him know everything was fine.

As I followed Troy, inhaling his mature cologne, I couldn't help but think murderous thoughts about Jenni. Had I not been in my place of 'business,' I would have mopped the floor with that bitch. I tell you what, if she cost me this internship, I was dedicating the rest of the semester to finding that bitch and butchering her like cattle.

When Troy and I entered the suite, I continued to follow him towards the back and I felt Scarlett's eyes on me. She apologized for her behavior prior, but I'm sure now she was all riled up again. If she came at me today, I just might slap her ass because between her and Jenni, I was gonna have a damn meltdown.

"Have a seat," Troy gestured for me to take a seat on the couch in his office once we got inside.

"I'm really sorry, Mr. Garrick. I—"

"Who was that young lady?" he sat back, crossing his legs, and staring at me.

"She— she's an ex of my current boyfriend, and right now, she's having a hard time letting him go. She tried to purposely embarrass me."

"I see." He sat up. "Rori, you know when you walk into this building... actually, when you pull into the parking structure, that all personal matters should be left at the door, right?"

"Yes, I know that and I never bring personal business here. She followed me and then surprised me. I—"

"You need to decide whether your career or your relationship with your boyfriend is more important right now."

"Well, Mr. Garrick—"

"Troy."

"Troy," I half smiled. "Both are important to me. They can both coexist; it's just her that is the problem. And she's not even really a problem because this is the very first time that she's done anything," I pleaded. I felt like he was judging Eko and it was annoying me. He didn't even know him!

Smiling softly, he inhaled and said, "What would your father think of all of this? I mean you have a very promising future from what Parker showed me, and it'd be a terrible thing for you to get caught up in childish drama."

"My father would be disappointed yes, but I promise nothing like this will ever happen again, Mr.— Troy. I have been on my best behavior this whole time, so please do not let this one incident ruin this opportunity for me."

He stared at me for a moment, before smiling a little.

"You know you're a very smart girl, Rori, and I think you've chosen the right career path. You have a very convincing nature about you because had anyone else caused a scene like you just did, I would have let them go," he laughed. "I think when the time comes, you'll be able to get people to vote for you with no problem."

"Thank you," I chuckled breathily, feeling at ease suddenly. I just knew he was about to fire me, and I'd be going straight to Jenni's place... wherever that was.

"I could help you get really far in the political world. I mean if that's something you're interested in. I have a lot of faith in you, and your father, as I've told you before, is a good old friend."

"I am! I plan to go to grad school once I finish college this semester, but I am very eager to be hands on while in school."

"I figured as much. I have a couple things that I'd like you to do, but I want to get them in order first. Write down your email for me." He placed a Post-It pad with a pen in front of me. Parker had my email on file, but I wasn't gonna tell him to go get it.

I wrote my email down, and he looked at it before taking the single sheet off the pad.

"Thank you for being understanding, Troy."

"Of course. Look out for an email from me, okay?"

"Yeah, I will."

We both stood up, and I was feeling very anxious about what he had for me. What if he planned to give me a job like what Parker had? I would be in heaven. I'm not sure how I'd be able to monitor that while being in school, but I would sure and the fuck figure it out.

I left Troy's office and got right to work since I didn't have time to get a snack, and was even fifteen minutes late.

"What was that about?" Scarlett walked over to me.

"Nothing. Something happened outside and Troy just wanted to make sure it didn't happen again."

Looking me up and down, suspiciously, she replied, "Oh. Okay."

After talking with Troy just a minute ago, I really felt like Scarlett had lied on him. I had my reservations about her story before, but after conversing with him I was convinced. He didn't seem like the type to mess around on his wife, especially with a low-level bitch like Scarlett.

Shaking my head at her, I focused my attention back on my work, excited about what was to come and anxious to fuck Jenni up.

24

———

NUSEF

"When are you coming home, Nusef?"

"Dana, I'm gonna be there in a couple hours. I told you to go get ya nails done or some shit because I was gon' be busy," I huffed, clutching my office phone with one hand and massaging the bridge of my nose with the other.

"I already did that. I'm trying to have some fun before your dad gets here because you know we're gonna be cooped up for a minute," she giggled.

"I really don't need to hear that. And did you speak to ya parole officer about you getting your own spot? I can pay for it for a little bit. Waayil even agreed to do half."

"Speaking of that little nigga, why hasn't he been by to see me? I refuse to drop by that shop unannounced like some side chick, when he is my son! I changed his damn diapers for God's sake!"

"Yes, Dana, we know. I told you he has to get up with his parole officer. Y'all are both ex-cons and you know y'all ain't supposed to be together like that."

"But he's my kid."

"And that's why he's gonna see what he can do. See if there is some way around it, Dana. But look, I'm at work, and I need to be focused so you can't keep calling up here."

"You don't answer your cell."

"If I don't answer it's because I'm busy. Listen, stop calling the shop. If you need something that bad, hit my cellphone and I will get to it eventually."

"Fine. Oh, Nusef?"

"Yes, Dana?" I punched the air and frowned.

"Can we go out to dinner tonight? I'm tired of fast food and your cooking isn't as good as it should be."

"Why can't you cook then?"

"Because I want to go to dinner."

Yes, we can go out. If that will stop you from calling my place of business all day, then yes, Dana, we can go to dinner."

"Thank you. Bye, sweetie!"

"Bye." I quickly hung that damn phone up in fear that she would try to keep shit going.

I shutdown my computer as I stood up, and gulped down some of my water since talking to my mother had my damn mouth dry. As I started out of my office, I heard Rebecca, Chiara, and Venus laughing up in the front. I made my way up there since I wanted to remind myself of who my next client was, and when I got to the lobby, I saw some nigga up there grinning.

"Oh, Nusef, this is Zaire," Rebecca introduced me. "Zaire, this is one of the owners of the shop, Nusef."

"Nice to meet you." He reached out and I shook his hand.

"Likewise. So you here getting a tattoo?" I questioned as Chiara handed me the clipboard I'd gestured for.

"Oh, nah, I just came to check on shorty. I didn't mean to intrude or anything on her job, I just missed her." He hugged Rebecca from behind as she laughed like a little ass kid.

Nodding slowly because I was starting to catch on, I said, "Oh, so y'all are together or something?"

"No, we're not." Rebecca rolled her eyes with a smile. I knew that face and she was feeling this nigga.

"She's right, we're not, but I'm definitely trying to get there."

I didn't know if I was jealous or what, but I'd be lying if I said I didn't feel a certain way seeing this nigga all in Rebecca's grill. I guess the shit was just weird for me. I was used to her being mine, and now she wasn't and was moving on as well. It was a fear of mine, which was why I never wanted to let her go in the past, but when it came down to it, Jonaya had my heart. I would give up every damn thing to be with that crazy ass girl, and Rebecca was one of those things.

"That's dope," I nodded again and looked Rebecca's way.

"Okay, so I will see you later, Zaire. I have to get back to work now." She turned to him and he leaned down to kiss her lips. Shit bothered me a little, but it wasn't as bad as seeing Marquise all over Jonaya.

I caught myself watching, but then snapped out of it when I realized Venus and Chiara were giving me looks.

"What?" I hissed when Rebecca and Zaire left out the shop.

"You're jealous," Chiara smiled.

"No, I'm not jealous. Fuck would I be jealous for when I'm the one that broke up what we had?"

"I don't think you're jealous, because you definitely love Jonaya, but you *are* a little salty." Venus chuckled as she put her pointer finger close to her thumb to show how little salty I was.

"Yeah, a little salty but I'm good." I looked down at the clipboard. "Aye, where the fuck is Sax? Nigga, got like three appointments on here, and one is in about five minutes." Right when I said that, his client walked in with Rebecca right behind him.

"I can call him," Chiara offered.

"Nah, I got it." I went back to my office and dialed Sax's cell number. The first time it went to voicemail, but the second time he picked up.

"What's good?" he answered, blowing out smoke. I could hear it in his voice.

"Nigga, you're supposed to be here at work! You got three sessions today, and one of them is here right now looking for you!"

"Oh fuck, I totally forgot, mane," he coughed.

"You forgot? You forgot? Nigga, how long you been tattooing and you talking about you forgot? How the fuck you forget?" I was so baffled I couldn't stop saying the shit.

"Because I did, aight? And why does it matter to you when they're my clients!"

"Because this is my muthafuckin' shop, nigga! That's why! What you do reflects negatively on the whole fucking company, dummy!"

"Dummy? Nigga, who the fuck you getting tough with? You been acting real hard now that ya brother is back."

I pulled the phone away and looked at it for a minute as if it were that nigga.

Bringing it back to my face, I hissed, "I don't act like shit, and don't bring Waayil into nothing. Get yo' ass down here so you can do these damn tattoos, or let ya clients know to reschedule."

"I'm just stating that you're starting to jump bad a lot now that you got Waayil here to hold you down."

"Be here to handle ya business or let ya customers know. If another person shows up looking for you, don't come back, aight?"

"Nusef—"

I hung up the phone and plopped down in my chair to take a breather. I knew when I woke up today it was gon' be a horrible ass fucking day. As soon as I climbed out of bed and accidentally stepped on one of Jonaya's hair accessories, I knew it'd be downhill from there.

I pulled out my iPhone and when I got ready to dial Jonaya, Rebecca came into my office. She looked happy even though she wasn't smiling really. Whatever that nigga was doing, he was doing the shit right because she was damn near floating like a ghost around this bitch.

"You need something?" I inquired.

"No not really, I just wanted to apologize for Zaire being here. I know I'm not supposed to be hanging out on the clock, but he'd literally only been here for like five minutes."

"As long as nothing gets left undone then it's cool." She nodded and turned to leave but I added, "So is he what you were looking for?"

"What do you mean?" she turned back to face me.

"You told me you wanted to find somebody who felt a certain way about you, so I'm asking if it's him. You obviously felt like Sax wasn't the one."

"Yeah, I think he is. I really like him, but I'm pacing everything to be sure. I don't want to become too invested in something that won't last. I can't do that again."

"Is that a dig at ya boy?"

"Just a little bit," she grinned. "But don't get me wrong, Nusef, I loved being with you and don't regret the good times. Things with Zaire are just easier because we want the same thing."

"Well, I enjoyed being with you too... at times."

Laughing she said, "You just had to ruin it with that *at times* bullshit. Typical Nusef."

"Well you look good, shorty. I like to see you happy, even if it ain't with me."

"Likewise," she smiled. "So is Sax coming or not? This guy seems a little impatient."

"Uh, offer him another artist. Moses is almost done with the girl he's working on now, so see if he can hook old boy up and then see if dude is aight with it. If not, tell him we couldn't get in contact with Sax and he can try himself."

"Okay."

Once Rebecca left my office, I took a moment to myself to collect my damn thoughts. I didn't know what the fuck had gotten into Sax, but that nigga was tripping. Trying to play me like I was a bitch before Waayil got released. I was starting the think that muthafucka had an early case of dementia or some shit. But sick in the head or not, he wasn't gon' keep coming at me foul and not face the repercussions.

Picking my phone back up, I dialed my girl to get some peace of mind.

~

Some Odd Hours Later...

I was finally off, and not in any mood whatsoever to be out in this cold ass weather, but I wasn't gon' back out of taking Dana to dinner. I even felt a little bad that she had to ask, but I'd been busy as hell with running the shop, doing tattoos, and trying to find out who the fuck shot me. So, regardless of how I felt right now, I was gon' take her ass out.

When I got to the front, I was surprised to see Dana in the lobby dressed up with her coat on. She was laughing and talking with Chiara.

"Dana, I was coming home to get you."

"I know, but I decided to save time and just come here to meet you. Plus, I wanted to make sure you weren't gonna flake on me."

"How did you even get here?"

"Your neighbor drove me."

Turning my lip up in irritation I asked, "What neighbor? I don't even talk to my damn neighbors, so how do you even know one well enough to get a damn ride?"

"Watch your tone and language with me, boy! I let enough of your cursing slide! And I'm at the damn house all day, so I *do* meet people when I get out for fresh air."

"Whatever, let's just go. You know where you wanna eat?"

"Somewhere nice that has ribs." She turned her back to me and started out of the shop as Chiara laughed her ass off. She had a lot of ass too, so imagine how hard she was laughing for me to say that.

I left out, following Dana to my car, and then I opened the passenger side door for her. Once I got in, I plugged my iPhone up to the charger while I thought about where I could take her that was nice and had ribs with her bougie ass. Hadn't been out of jail a month and was trying to be on some Master P shit.

"You know that Chiara girl is so sweet and cute." Dana turned on the heater as I put my seatbelt on.

"Yeah, she's cool."

"And she has the biggest crush on Waayil. I wanna get them together. Since I couldn't pick your woman out, I want to pick Waayil's."

"Dana, Waayil has a girlfriend. One that he's very much in love with." I backed out, trying my hardest to pay attention and not shake my head at her meddling ass.

"Who?"

"Her name is Yikayla. She's Jonaya's older sister actually."

"Ha! That little tramp he used to be best friends with when he was a boy? Oh please. I like that Chiara girl and that's who I want him with. We already hit it off. You should always be with a woman that your mother likes, Nusef," she stated matter-of-factly.

"You've never even met Yikayla, only heard about her when we visited you in jail ages ago."

"I heard enough to know that she isn't the one for him."

"She was like ten at the time, she's a woman now. Plus, all he said back then was that she was his best friend." My brows dipped, annoyed by the nonsense she was speaking.

"I don't care! I know a trifling woman when I see one, even if she's a *little girl* at the time, as you say."

"But you've never seen her."

"You know what the fuck I mean, boy! I want him with Chiara and that's final. Waayil will listen to his mother. Maybe you should do the same."

I just shook my head as I kept driving.

Dana hadn't seen us since we were thirteen years old, so she had no idea what type of personalities we had. If she thought, for a second, that she was about to make decisions in Waayil's love life, she was in for a rude ass awakening.

25

DREE

Today was the day that I'd finally get to speak with the Dean of Students. For a minute, I wasn't going to, and only planned to go to the police, but I wanted to notify the school as well because they would be in the mix of everything. Plus Sean and his family were deeply involved with the school, so I'm sure they'd want to know what was going on with their star student. I rolled my eyes hard at the thought as I sat in the lobby of the Dean's office.

"Dree, Mrs. Pordrey is ready for you now."

"Great, thank you." I got up and followed the assistant into Mrs. Pordrey's office, but she wasn't in there.

"Have a seat and she'll be in, in just a moment."

I sat down and just surveyed the office as I waited. I ran through everything that I planned to say in my mind, and prayed this didn't go left. Canyon told me about his little meeting he'd had with his supervisor, so I was a bit wary that this Dean would be going to bat for Sean. In the end, this was only a courtesy I was doing them because the rape didn't happen on campus.

"Sorry about that, Miss Goode, I had a family emergency that I needed to tend to." Mrs. Pordrey walked in and closed her office door.

"Oh, no problem." I stood up to shake her hand.

"Okay, let me just sit down here, and then we can get to talking." She got some water from the big water cooler dispenser, and after offering me a cup, she sat down. "Alright, so what did you want to speak with me about today, Miss Goode?"

"Well, I had an incident with a student a little while ago, and I wanted to inform you of it, since I will be pressing charges."

Frowning slightly, she cocked her head and asked, "Pressing charges? Of what nature was the incident, Miss Goode? Because if you're pressing charges then that means it was something very serious."

"Yes, it was very serious..." I paused and she raised a brow. "It was a rape." I quickly spit it out before clearing my throat. I hated saying it, but I'd better get used to it if I wanted to have Sean punished.

"A rape? Wow. I'm extremely sorry to hear that, Miss Goode. Who is the student that did this?" She pulled out a pen and pad. "And this was on... campus?"

"It was Sean Ike and no it was at his home in Belle Meade."

My heart began to race when I saw her pause for a moment and then place the pen back down. She intertwined her fingers, and then looked at me with squinted eyes.

"Sean Ike is the one who raped you?" she quizzed skeptically.

"Yes."

"And you're sure."

"Excuse me? Yes, I'm sure, and I don't know what you're trying to imply by asking me such a thing."

"I'm not trying to offend you, Miss Goode, but what you're accusing Mr. Ike of is... out of his character is all." She sat back in her office chair.

"Yeah because you don't know him. Have you ever hung out at his home with him? Went to dinner with him? Had a conversation with him?"

"No, but I *have* spoken and dealt with his parents on many occasions."

"That wasn't the question. His parents didn't rape me, he did. The person we're discussing is Sean Ike and no one else, Mrs. Pordrey."

"What exactly happened, Dree?" she sighed as if she were over it, and picked her pen back up.

"Why should I even tell you? It's obvious that you don't believe me." I was so furious that I wanted to slap her beady-eyed ass.

"Please, just tell me what happened. I'm not trying to judge, I'm just... surprised if you will."

"He put something in my drink, and I woke up in his bed without my clothes on."

"And how much did you drink, Miss Goode? I mean, I understand that sometimes, as women, we make bad decisions and sleep with men, only to find out that was all they wanted. But you can't cry rape because a man doesn't call you back. Or sometimes, we drink too much and make a bad decision, but you cannot accuse someone of rape because you slept with them in a drunken state and regret it now." She chuckled as if my claim was preposterous.

"I would never do something like that, first of all. Secondly, any man I sleep with will definitely keep calling so that has never been a problem with me. Sean Ike took advantage of me and there is no other way around it!"

"Miss Goode, think about this for a moment. You don't want to start something that you may not even be ready to finish. Sean and his family are very well-established people, and this could end badly for you."

"End badly for me how? Would it be worse than waking up in a man's bed that I didn't wanna sleep with, and having no memory of it? Or worse than me finding out that I was pregnant and getting an abortion? You let me know."

I could see the astonishment in her facial expression as she looked at me.

"I am really sorry about all of that, if it did in fact happen. But what I am saying to you, is only to help you. If this was just some drunken night gone wrong, or you feeling like he wronged you by not wanting more from the relationship, don't do this," she pleaded.

"You know what, I'm *not* doing *this*." I stood up. "It didn't even happen on campus, so technically, I don't even have to be here. I just wanted to give you guys a heads up that I was pressing charges against one of my fellow students."

"Miss Goode!"

I ignored her and continued out the door. I wasn't going to lie; the stuff she was saying had really gotten under my skin. I could tell she didn't believe a word I'd said, and thought I was just some woman scorned trying to get revenge. Dree Goode never had to do some shit like that because every man I wanted, I got! Not to mention, ever since I started drinking, I was never that girl who got pissy drunk!

And now, that bitch had ruined my whole mood and the rest of my day. The same thing I used to want Sean for, his potential success and connections, I now hated him for possessing such things. These people acted like he was the King of France or something.

I calmed myself down, then cranked up the car so I could head over to the police station to report to them. Hopefully, things would go a little better there.

About an Hour and a Half Later...

"Dree, baby, what's wrong with you?" Canyon got into the passenger side of my car as I sat parked at the police station.

I was damn near hyperventilating after talking with that stupid ass detective in the police station. I didn't think they could be worse than Mrs. Pordrey, but they definitely were.

Just like her, the man ripped me apart with questions as if he didn't believe me. Eventually, I broke down, which only fed into his belief that I was lying. I didn't know what the hell he had against me. At least with Mrs. Pordrey, I knew she was trying to take up for Sean because his parents contributed a lot to the school, but what was this fucker's excuse?

"They di-didn't believe me," I cried.

Canyon sucked his teeth and got back out of the car. He came around to my side, opened the door, and then he pulled me out. Taking a seat where I originally was, he pulled me down into his lap, and we sat there with the door open.

"Relax, ma, and tell me what happened."

"I explained to the girl up front that I wanted to report a rape and this detective took me to a room and began asking me questions like who it was, how it happened, and when. Then when I guess he didn't like my answers, he started doing the same thing Mrs. Pordrey did earlier. Just asking me leading questions, trying to imply that I was lying for some reason. Then he asked me how many men had I slept with and all this stuff," I sniffled, lying on Canyon's broad shoulder.

"Who asked you that?"

"His name was Bronson. Ted Bronson, one of the detective workers."

Canyon tapped me to get off of his lap, and once he got out the car as well, he closed my door and started leading me back inside. I didn't know what the hell we were going back inside for, but I could tell by how briskly Canyon was walking, that someone was about to get an earful.

"May I help you, sir?" the same girl who'd helped me asked Canyon.

"Yeah, where the fuck is Ted Bronson?"

"Canyon!" I shouted in a whisper.

The girl opened her mouth but no sound came out for a couple seconds, "Oh, let me call his desk."

"Yeah, do that."

"Canyon, what are you doing? Let's just go."

He ignored me, still holding my hand, and a few moments later, the girl told us we could go to the back. When we walked up, Ted Bronson was by his desk with a confused expression.

"May I help you, sir?" He rose up. His face changed when he saw Canyon was holding my hand. If I wasn't mistaken, I'd say he looked a bit intimidated.

"Yeah, I need you to take her report over; but this time, keep your questions respectful, bruh."

Chuckling, Ted slipped his hands into his cheap slacks and replied, "I asked her the same things I ask everyone who reports that type of crime."

"You ask every person who reports a rape how many niggas they've fucked?" Canyon squinted his eyes suspiciously.

"Well in a sense, sir, yes I do."

"Well, we gon' skip that part of her interview." Canyon looked to me and added, "Sit down, shorty."

Even though I wanted to run out of there, I knew right now was the wrong time to try Canyon, so I sat my ass down. Canyon sat with me, and Ted hesitantly pulled his notepad out. He began to question me, and this time, he was much gentler; I noticed. Anything that Canyon didn't like, Canyon spoke up and told him to move on, and Ted's ass did what he was told too. It was somewhat comical, yet, shocking to see how differently Ted was treating me with this big black man, covered in tattoos sitting here. In no time, we were done, and I actually felt a lot better, surprisingly.

As we all stood up, Detective Bronson said, "I'm sorry if I made you feel any kind of way, Miss Goode."

"It's okay," I nodded.

"You two enjoy the rest of your evening," he smiled up at Canyon.

"Yeah, aight, you too," Canyon replied before leading me back out.

"I can't believe you did that!" I giggled. I was so turned on by him right now. I just loved that he could be both an educated and about his business type man, and then a thug in the next split second. I honestly don't know what I was thinking trying to be with Sean.

"I had to. You think I'm gon' let some other muthafucka make you cry? Fuck outta here," he hissed as we made it to my car.

"Well, thank you. I do feel better."

"Good." We kissed a few times as we leaned up against my car, and then he went to his so we could meet each other at his place.

Before going to Canyon's, I stopped at my house to get some clothes and things because I wanted to spend the night over there. After that, I went by the store for a few things so I could make us dinner, dessert, and then breakfast in the morning, since I had no classes.

When I got to Canyon's place and parked, I saw his sister Jupiter a few spaces down. She was standing by her car, in a heated conversation with some guy. Getting out, I grabbed my two grocery bags and started off, moving past them. When I did, I realized the man was her baby's father, Neil, just as he slapped the dog shit out of her and then snatched her up by her neck.

"Hey!" I shouted.

"You mind your own fucking business, bitch!" Jupiter barked at me. Her child's father looked to me smirking, eyes filled with lust, making me want to throw the hell up.

I stood there, wanting to say more, but Jupiter was looking at me like she was disgusted, so I said fuck it. I'd just let Canyon handle this nigga. I continued on my route to Canyon's, and when I got inside, he was coming from the back.

"Baby, I need to talk to you—"

"Dree!" Cade come running out of the bathroom.

"Aye aye! Did you wash yo' damn hands?" Canyon grabbed his little forearm to stop him from touching me.

"Yes," he smiled.

"I didn't hear any water running. You been with ya auntie and cousin all day and don' forgot how to act. Go wash ya hands, Cade."

"Okay, don't leave, Dree!" he shouted before rushing off.

"I won't," I laughed.

"What did you need to talk to me about?"

"I saw Neil slap and choke Jupiter," I said just as Jupiter walked back into the apartment.

"Hey, Canyon, Neil just took Taj for the rest of the week, so I'm heading home, okay?" she smiled.

"That nigga put his hands on you?" Canyon's brows furrowed. Jupiter immediately looked at me, fury all throughout her face.

"I told you to mind your damn business!"

"Don't yell at her because you wanna let some nigga put his hands on you! You wait until I see that nigga!"

"I'm back, Dree!" Cade hugged my waist and I lightly hugged him back, trying to awkwardly pretend like Canyon and Jupiter weren't arguing in front of us.

"Come help me in the kitchen, Cade." I took his little hand and led him to the kitchen.

"In the midst of telling *my* business, did that bitch tell you that she fucked my baby daddy!" Jupiter yelled, and I swear it felt like someone had shot me in the chest. It felt even worse when I didn't hear Canyon respond.

"What do I do first, Dree?" Cade interrupted my thoughts, as I tried to listen for a response from Canyon... but still nothing. He was silent, which scared me.

"Uh... umm... Well let's clean our hands again, Cade." I pulled his stool to the sink so he could stand on it.

The front door closed, so I guess Jupiter left, and I could feel Canyon coming into the kitchen. He seemed so much taller and muscular right now, and I was literally shaking as I washed Cade's hands with mine.

"Aye, you need to go home for the night," he spoke softly.

Cutting the water off and turning to him as I dried my hands, I replied, "Canyon, I did not sleep with him."

"So she made it up," he stated doubtfully, instead of asking.

I swallowed a big ass lump in my throat.

"No, she didn't make it up, but—"

"Then go."

"But I didn't have sex-sex with him! He went down on me and that was it, I swear! I was about to but I couldn't and... I left, I promise."

"Dree, I'm not gon' ask you again, shorty. Leave."

"Canyon." I felt the tears welling up. I wanted to stomp and cry like a baby right now. He just stared down at me as Cade sat at the table, trying to figure out what was happening. "Canyon, don't do this, that was a long time ago." I moved closer to him and snaked my arms around his torso.

He said nothing, he just looked down at me and I knew what it meant.

Backing away, I went to get my purse from the counter and my duffle bag that I'd placed on the floor.

"You can keep the groceries and stuff if you want to cook."

Again, he declined to respond as he went to his front door and opened it. Stepping out, I looked back at him and he just closed the door in my face.

26

WAAYIL

That Same Evening...

Today when I woke up earlier, I felt like I could finally get at Wednesday's ass. I was still angry with her, but it didn't run as deeply as before. See a couple weeks ago, a nigga wanted to murder her ass, but now, I just wanted to slap her muthafuckin' ass around a bit; so to me that was a major improvement.

I had to take all day to make sure though, so I went to work, did some tattoos and shit, and made sure my mental was alright before I rolled up over here.

Parking in my parents' long ass driveway, I took a deep breath as I stared up at what was Wednesday's window. I kept asking myself if I was truly ready, and to be sure, I didn't do anything else, I locked my gun up in my glove compartment so I wouldn't blast her ass again. I knew it was highly unlikely that I would put my hands on her, but if I had my piece, ain't no telling what I'd do.

Getting out, I made my way up to the door and rang the doorbell. I never had my damn key when I came over here anymore, and I knew that shit was irritating as hell to my parents. When the door came open, my mama stood there with a smile on her face because I'd told her why I was coming over here. I couldn't do shit but shake my head at how hard she was cheesing, before I started to smile myself.

"You are so rough sometimes, but have the most adorable innocent smile with those big ass dimples," she laughed as she hugged and kissed me.

"I ain't rough, Mama."

"Boy, please." She let me go. "Wednesday is in the den eating, so you can go in there. Did you want some food?"

"Nah, I'm good."

My mom walked off towards the kitchen so I headed to the den where she said Wednesday was. I spotted her watching one of them reality shows on TV with her feet propped up, with a plate of spaghetti in front of her. Nusef told me she had a big ass black thing on her foot, but I noticed it was gone now and she just had a small white patch to cover the wound.

"What's up?" I spoke to her as I walked in front of the television to get a seat next to her.

With her mouth open for a moment, she sat up straighter and said, "Hey, Waayil." I could see a little bit of fear in her eyes as they darted all over my face.

"Relax, I ain't here to hurt you, and I wanna apologize for shooting you in the foot, baby. I was just angry as hell, and I wanted you to back up off me but I couldn't hit you."

"I know, I understand."

It got quiet when she paused the show and set the remote back down on the couch cushion in between us.

"Wednesday, what you did to me, shorty... not only pissed me off because I went to jail and murdered somebody, but it hurt me to know that my life could mean so little to you. You know how much a nigga loves you? And for you to lie to me, and then cause all this bullshit to happen in my life like it was nothing, broke me down." I shook my head as I looked off. "I felt like I didn't know who the fuck you were anymore, and it was just too much for a nigga at the time. But you told me he threatened you, threatened to tell me about what was in your diary, was that all? Was that really all that happened for you to stir up all this shit?" I frowned and turned to her.

Tears were rolling down her cheeks in an abundance, but she quickly wiped them away.

"He told me he was gonna tell you, but if I did some stuff with him, then he would keep it a secret. I was just gonna do what he wanted, but when I saw you with Yikayla, I got angry. I thought if I told you that lie, you would just hurt Uncle Harry a little to make him shut up, and then you would get in trouble and not be able to see Yikayla."

"Wednesday, why didn't you just come tell me the truth, baby? Had you have told me that he was asking you to come to his bed, but hadn't actually touched you, I *would* have whooped his muthafuckin' ass in a hot minute. I wouldn't have even needed details. But telling me he'd raped you? What the hell did you think I was gon' do to that nigga?"

Hearing that Harry, in some way, did try to have a sexual relationship with Wednesday made me feel a little bit better about killing that perverted ass nigga. But the fact remains that he died under false pretenses. However, if I wanted a relationship with my little sister, which for some sick ass fucking reason I did, I would have to get over that shit.

"I wasn't thinking, Waayil. I swear to God, I thought you were just gonna beat him up. That's what you always did when people made you angry."

I couldn't help but to chuckle because she was dead ass serious about what she'd just said. The shit was dumb as fuck, but I guess I understood to an extent where she was coming from. Not to mention, she was only thirteen years old at the time. Maybe I was making excuses for her because I loved her, I didn't really know, but I knew I didn't want our shit to be broken like this.

Everything in my life right now was shit I used to wish for while being locked up. I was with the woman of my fuckin' dreams, literally, and she was having my baby. Lonan wasn't part of the plan, but I couldn't see my life without that little nigga. I owned a tattoo shop, and overall, life was damn near perfect. Being mad at Wednesday just felt like it was keeping everything from jelling together, and I didn't like that feeling at all.

"Come over here." I nodded to my right so she could scoot towards me.

She was hesitant, but she slid down some, until she was close enough for me to drape my arm around her.

"I'm sorry, Waayil, I really am. I swear if I knew you would have done what you did, I wouldn't have said anything."

"But I'm happy you did, kind of."

"You are?" she looked up at me.

"Yeah because you were about to let that man take advantage of you, Wednesday. So in a way, you lying to me did save you and I can live with that a little bit. I love you so I don't want anything happening to you. And I hope you learned from that shit, not to let a man blackmail you or threaten you for sex. I don't give a fuck what he's holding over you, you protect ya body at all costs, aight? As long as it's not another person's freedom and sanity."

She nodded with a smile before I turned a little more so I could hug her.

"Thank you for saving me, Waayil."

"Always."

"I love you."

"I love you more." When she pulled away I asked, "You ain't in love with a nigga still, are you?" I smirked when she turned her lip up in disgust.

"Ugh! Hell no! You? Yuck!"

"Aye, kill all the facial expressions and shit talking. All you had to say was 'no,' you ain't got to kill a nigga's self-esteem and shit," I laughed as I stood up.

"I'm just saying. The thought of me liking you at one point of my life is not only embarrassing but disturbing, Waayil," she chuckled.

"Yeah, I agree, but I'm a handsome ass nigga."

"Please leave before I throw up my food that I haven't even finished."

"Fuck you." I stared down at her for a moment, contemplating on whether or not I should give her the bracelet. Finally, I reached into my pocket and said, "Here."

"What is this, Yil?" she took it and lifted the top of the velvet box.

"I got it for ya birthday, and planned to put it in ya shoebox."

"That's why you were in my closet," she giggled as she removed it. I helped her put it on, and she held her arm out to admire it. "Thank you, bro."

"You're welcome."

I hadn't forgotten, so after reprimanding Wednesday about that short ass dress she had on while I was hiding out in her closet, I left the den to find my parents. I found them in the dining room, slow dancing to "Love TKO" by Teddy Pendergrass.

"Let's stop this now before it leads somewhere else." I sat at the table.

"Waayil, this is my song so don't interrupt," my mother replied, smiling.

"Where is Emil?" I quizzed.

"He's out at the movies with his friend, Mooney," my dad responded.

I nodded then said, "Nah but for real, I wanna talk to y'all about something really quickly before I go."

"Did you and Wednesday make up?" my mother cut the music off.

"We did, but y'all sit down for a moment." Once they sat at the table with me I added, "So Dana is out of jail and Count will be too, pretty soon."

"Your biological parents?" my mom frowned.

"Yeah, Dana has been here, and tonight she's coming over to have dinner with Yikayla, Lonan, and me. But Nusef wants to set something up where she and Count can eat with all of us, including y'all, Wednesday, and Emil."

My parents looked at one another before turning their attention back to me.

"Yeah, son, if that's what you guys want then we can all get together over here," my father sighed.

"Yeah, I do want it. But aye, don't think that Nusef and I are gon' be all up their asses and forgetting about y'all because that's not gon' happen. *Y'all* are our parents, and always will be."

Seeing my mom and pops beam at my words, made a nigga feel good inside. I loved them both a lot, and appreciated everything that they'd done for me, so I didn't want them to think for one second, that now that Dana and Count were here, I was gon' push them to the side. Hell nah.

That Night...

"Waayil!" Dana beamed as she walked into my crib and threw her arms around my neck, forcing me to bend down.

"Hey, Dana." I hugged her back.

She finally let me go and said, "I have missed you so much! I'm so happy I get to see you!"

"Me too," I gestured for Yikayla and Lonan to come closer. "Dana, this is my girlfriend, Yikayla, and her son, Lonan."

"Oh," my mom's smile sort of faded and was only hanging on by a fucking thread. "Nice to meet you, Yikayla. I see your mother is a fan of odd names."

"Huh?" Yikayla cocked her head, adjusting Lonan on her hip.

"Your sister's name is Jonaya, right? I was just mentioning that you both have very odd or unique names, I guess."

"Yeah," Yikayla nodded and then gave me a look.

"So, what's for dinner tonight?" Dana dropped her purse on the couch and sauntered into the kitchen, with Yikayla and I on her heels.

"I have pork chops, mashed potatoes, greens, yams, and a German chocolate cake for dessert. We also have some champagne if you'd like something alcoholic to drink," Yikayla went through the menu as she placed Lonan in his high chair.

"Uh huh." Dana sat down after washing her hands. "And did you cook this or is it take out?"

"I cooked it, Mrs. Christian."

Dana nodded and after Yikayla and I both washed our hands, Yikayla made a plate for everyone, including Lonan. We prayed over the food, and Dana smashed the plate like she was still in jail or some shit. She even had seconds along with me, before Yikayla cut everyone a piece of cake.

"So, Yuh... kayla?" Dana's brows dipped.

"Yes, but you can just call me Kay."

"Nah, she knows how to say it." I gave Dana a look. She was doing this shit on purpose and I wasn't having it.

"Yikayla, what do you do?" Dana quizzed.

"I want to be a fashion designer, but right now I work for a fashion house where I assist a designer named Jerica Rose."

"I see. May I ask what you were doing while Waayil was in jail? You guys couldn't have been together because you have a baby that isn't my son's."

"We weren't together while I was in jail, Dana. Let's keep this shit respectful, aight? I know you got more sense than what you're acting like right now," I stated sternly, sipping my drink.

"No, it's okay, Waayil." Yikayla placed her hand on my knee. I picked it up and kissed the back of it, making her smile softly.

The rest of the dinner went aight because Dana heeded to my muthafuckin' warning and stopped trying to come for my girl. I honestly didn't know what the fuck her beef was with Yikayla, but she needed to know that if she wanted to be around me, she'd have to check that shit at the fucking door. Yikayla and Lonan were my priorities and wasn't no damn body gon' be mistreating them on my watch.

As Yikayla cleaned up, I went to Lonan's room to pull out his nightclothes because I knew she was gonna give him a bath next. As I was doing so, Dana walked in grinning.

"I see you liked the food," I said.

"Yeah, she's a very good cook. I admit, I didn't think she could throw down because of how she looks, but I was wrong."

"Because of how she looks?"

"All pretty and stuff, like she doesn't like to get dirty."

"Wow." I shook my head and chuckled at her stupidity.

"You know who I really like for you, that Chiara girl that works the front at the shop. She was really sweet and looks like she knows how to treat a man."

"Well, the nigga that gets her will be in luck then, right?"

"I mean yeah, but *you* could be that man."

"Did you not just have dinner with my girl. What the fuck are you even talking about right now? What the fuck are you trying to say?"

"Nothing, I just—"

"Nah because it sounds like you're trying to tell me to leave my girl to go be with a bitch you don't even fucking know. But I hope that's not what the fuck you're saying."

"Waayil, I am your mother and I have a sixth sense with things like this. I know Chiara is a good woman for you. And she doesn't already have a baby like this one," she whispered the last part with a frown, but Yikayla was standing there, behind her holding Lonan, so she'd heard it all.

"Excuse me, Mrs. Christian, I need to get by so I can get my baby's pajamas." Yikayla acted like she didn't hear, but I knew her and her face told me she had.

Dana moved out the way, while looking like a deer in headlights, as Yikayla slipped past her into the bedroom.

"Baby," I tried to grab her arm but she moved it.

"No it's fine, Waayil," she spoke lowly, snatching Lonan's stuff from me and leaving back out to the bathroom.

I turned to Dana, glaring down at her ass hard as hell. If she hadn't been my mother for eight years of my life, I probably would have smacked the shit out of her.

"When she comes out you gon' apologize. And after this bullshit ass stunt you pulled, you can't come back around here until I say so and ain't no telling when that's gon' be."

"I ain't apologizing for speaking my mind, boy!" Dana folded her arms.

"Oh, yes the fuck you are." I moved closer to her. "And as a matter of fact, you gon' do the shit right now instead of waiting until she's done," I gritted.

"Or what?"

"You'll see."

"Are you threatening me? Your mother?"

"I'm not threatening you, I'm warning you of unfortunate events to come. Now go apologize."

"So you do this to me, over her?" she pointed to the closed bathroom door as we stood in the archway of Lonan's bedroom.

"Exactly. Everybody should know by now that I don't let people fuck with the ones I love."

"Oh you don't, huh?"

"Nah, I don't. What you thought, I went to jail from emptying the clip of a BB gun? Nah, so march yo' disrespectful ass in there and apologize," I hissed.

"I am your mother and—"

"Nah, you not! And if you had any plans on becoming close to me at all again, you wouldn't be acting like this to the woman I don' told you I loved! Now go!" I roared so loudly that she jumped back a little.

She darted to the bathroom door, knocked, and once Yikayla gave her the okay to come in, she entered.

"Yikayla, honey, I'm sorry for the things I said earlier. I was just talking. All I want is for my son to be happy, and I see that he's happy with you, so I'm happy too."

Yikayla simply nodded, and then turned her attention back to Lonan in the bath. Dana closed the door, and I escorted her ass right out. I didn't have shit else to say to her, and right now, she was lucky she'd gotten out still breathing. I didn't play about Yikayla and muthafuckas needed to understand, comprehend, and grasp that concept and do so promptly.

Once Dana was gone, I went into the bathroom where Yikayla was taking Lonan out of the tub and drying him off. I hugged her body from behind, and kissed the side of her face roughly because I knew she hated that. She tried to hide it, but I peeped the smile tugging at her lips.

Looking at her through the mirror as she put a diaper on Lonan, I said, "Don't let that shit get to you, ma. You know nobody can convince me that you're not the most perfect thing in the world." I brushed my hand up under her shirt to touch her flat stomach. Knowing my kid was in there did something to a nigga.

"Stop making me blush." She pulled Lonan's onesie down over his head. "I just don't want your mother's dislike of me to break us up."

"Nothing can break us up. Not jail, fuck ass baby daddy's, or fake ass pregnancies."

"Fake ass pregnancies? Who had a fake pregnancy?" she turned to face me as I took Lonan from her.

"Alba lied to me. She was pregnant, but it wasn't mine."

"That bitch ass hoe!"

"A bitch ass hoe, Kay? For real?" We walked out of the bathroom. Lonan was already dozing on my shoulder, so we just went to his room.

"Yep. I'm gonna beat her ass."

"Don't. Not while you're pregnant with my shorty, aight?" She didn't say anything in response, so after I laid Lonan down, I looked her way and repeated, "Aight?"

She tried to walk off, but I picked her up from behind, carrying her out, and making her shriek with laughter.

"Okay, I won't!"

I kissed her neck, then tossed her gently onto the bed. She propped herself up to watch me, as I started to tug her panties down from under her skirt.

27

———

ALBA

I'd just finished having a nice big dinner that I'd cooked for myself, and taken a nice hot bubble bath, so now I was 'bout to light some candles and relax in front of the television.

These days, I'd become accustomed to spending my days alone, meaning without a man. It actually felt like a relief to not be worried about a nigga and what he was doing. I was sleeping so much better, and I hadn't cried in I don't know how long. I was feeling so good that I was way too scared to enter into another relationship, fearing I would become borderline obsessed like I was with Waayil. However, even though I was feeling better, thoughts of my miscarriage still plagued my mind at times. That was one thing about the 'old me' that I did miss; my baby.

As I sat down on my couch with my feet propped up on the ottoman, I began to flip through Netflix to see what I wanted to watch, when someone rang my doorbell. Rolling my eyes, I set my glass of red wine down and tightened my robe as I went to the door. Looking through the peephole, I had to blink a couple times because I couldn't believe my damn eyes.

"Gavin, what... how?" I exclaimed when I opened the door. This nigga was not only out of jail, but he was standing before me dressed like he'd been living the good life. His hair was cut, and even his facial hair was lined up. And he smelled like he actually had some good credit.

"I told you I was gon' get out, ma," he smiled, looking kind of sexy. He sat down on the couch and squinted his eyes at the TV.

"I know but... I guess, I just wasn't expecting it to be so soon." I closed the door and came to sit next to him.

"Ain't you happy to see me, Alba?"

"Gavin, just because you're out of jail, doesn't mean things have changed. I don't wanna be with you and I mean that."

"Why, ma? We were good together until you started bugging out and tripping on me. I know I should have been here to help you out with the baby and shit, and I'm sorry for that."

"I didn't need your help or anyone's help. And don't bring up the baby please, I would appreciate it."

"But, Alba, baby, I got a plan this time. I mean for real. I'm not gon' be that nigga monitoring traps, doing the small shit. My name is gon' mean something around Memphis and I want you by my side."

"You want me by your side while you rise to the throne of some kingpin? Gavin, I do not want that life. I want a man who clocks in somewhere or owns a business making *legit* money." I stood up.

"I'm gon' have that too. I ain't gon' do this shit forever, baby, just for a little bit, and then I'm gon' retire and we can live the good life." He got up as well, nearing me.

"Gavin, I said no. I don't want that and I don't want this. We only started this because I was lonely while my nigga was in jail. Stop trying to make this become more than it needs to be."

I would be lying if I said I didn't develop feelings for Gavin over the time we'd spent together, but he could never amount to the man that Waayil was, so I never let myself go there. I told him what he wanted to hear because I needed him at one point, but right now, I was over it and trying to throw out everything that was a part of my past life. Gavin, along with Waayil, were at the top of that damn list.

"I think you're just saying that, Alba, because you're scared, ma. We made a damn baby together, so I know you gotta feel something for me."

"No, because the whole time I was psyching myself out, telling myself that it was Waayil's baby," I half lied.

Yes, I was trying to convince myself that it was Waayil's, but that was only after I realized that I was starting to contemplate having a family with my baby's *actual* father. Gavin was right in the sense that carrying his child inside of me did make my feelings for him a bit stronger, but that shit was over with.

Wrapping his arms around my body, he pulled me into him and leaned down to kiss me. His lips were so soft, just like I remembered. I moaned softly when he gripped my ass in his hands, before trailing his lips down to my neck.

"Gavin, no," I whispered, feeling the river flow between my legs already.

"Relax, Alba."

Trying to think of something to get him to stop, since I felt my knees weakening and my panties melting away, I damn near yelled, "I snitched on you, Gavin!"

"What?" he picked his head up from kissing on my neck. We stared one another in the eyes, and for a moment, I regretted what I'd said. "What'd you just say?"

"I told the police where the trap was that day because I knew you would be there. I did it because you were trying to come between Waayil and me."

"Alba." He let me go.

I was afraid now, so I said, "I'm sorry! I was messed up then and only worried about how I was going to keep Waayil in my life. I'm so sorry, Gavin."

He turned his back to me and exhaled heavily. I saw a gun locked in his waist earlier, but didn't remember it until now. This was not how I saw my life ending; childless, with no rich husband, and at the hands of some guy who was just a fuck buddy.

"Why the fuck would you do some shit like that!" he turned to me abruptly. "That nigga means that much to yo' ass?"

"No! Well he did, but not anymore! I don't know what I was thinking, but I'm sorry! I was just desperate at the time! Forgive me, please." I didn't know what the hell I was thinking by telling this nigga I'd snitched. I'd broken all kinds of codes, and by street law, he was *supposed* to kill me.

The room fell silent, and the only thing I could hear was my beating heart and the slowness of my breath as my chest heaved up and down. I was sweating bullets right now, and pondered on whether or not I should leap for his gun.

"You know niggas get smoked for that type of shit, Alba." He finally spoke. His voice was low though, which scared me. "I'm supposed to kill you right now for what you did to me."

"I know but I swear I won't do anything like that again. I'll do whatever you want, go talk to whomever I need to, if you keep me alive."

Smirking, Gavin moved closer to me and brushed his hand down my cheek. He looked down at my body, admiring what he remembered since it was covered by a robe, then he pulled on the belt of it so that it would come open.

"I think we can work something out." He picked his head up to make eye contact with me, before leading me back to my bedroom.

As badly as I didn't want to have sex with anyone right now, if this would keep me from lying in a casket, then I was gonna do it.

I was just happy that for the second time, I had escaped the wrath of a crazy nigga; first with Waayil, and secondly with Gavin.

The Next Morning...

I woke up in bed next to Gavin and surprisingly, I felt pretty good. I guess my pussy was craving a little attention because I had a burst of energy. Gavin really put in work last night, from eating my pussy until I came three times, to fucking me in all kinds of positions. However, I still had no interest in being in a relationship with his ass. I wasn't the ride or die, dope boy's girl like Rori Goode. I was meant to be with a man who did legit shit, and legit shit only.

I went to brush, floss, and rinse with mouthwash and then hopped into the shower. Today, Ashley, Tammy, and I were going to have breakfast out, and I couldn't wait for some reason. I was enjoying spending time with my girls after having such a stressful period in my life.

"Where you going?" Gavin quizzed as he brushed his teeth at my sink. I didn't even know he was in here until I'd stepped out of the shower.

"Where did you find that spare toothbrush?" I wrapped myself in a towel. This nigga was all in my shit and I didn't even know it.

"Cabinet under the sink, shorty." He rinsed his mouth and then used a cup to pour some Listerine into. "I asked where you were going?"

"Oh, just to breakfast with my friends. I won't be back for a while."

"Neither will I, but I *will* be back for sure." He spit the mouthwash out before he spoke, and then kissed my lips. When I felt chills rush through my body, I quickly pulled away. I didn't want to have feelings for any nigga.

I got dressed while Gavin was in the shower, and then headed to see my friends. When I arrived to the restaurant and parked, I saw Tammy and Ashley had already put our name on the list and were waiting to be called, which I was ecstatic about since I was hungry as hell.

"Damn, girl, you got a glow. I hope you ain't pregnant again." Tammy hugged me.

"Absolutely not. But I did get some unexpected dick last night, so I think that's what's doing the trick."

"From who?" Ashley inquired.

"Just some nigga I met a couple weeks ago. We hung out and shit just happened." I didn't want to mention Gavin after having given a speech about leaving my old niggas in the past. Alba was a lot of things, but a hypocrite I was not. Well... most of the time, I wasn't. Plus, Gavin and I would never ever be. He was a means to an end at one point and nothing else.

"Well, we need to celebrate Waayil not killing your ass after you told him the truth, so as soon as we sit down, I'm ordering some champagne and orange juice." Tammy smirked before we hi-fived each other.

I let out a sigh of relief at the mere thought of Waayil letting me go.

Still smiling, I looked down the street and saw Yikayla walking with her sister, Rori. They were laughing and talking, which made me roll my eyes. I may have been over the drama, but I still didn't like those two. They both got closer, ready to pass us, when Yikayla stopped right in front of me. I admit, for a girl who shopped at thrift stores, she was always somehow well put together.

"Can I help you?" I frowned.

WHAM! WHAM! WHAM!

"Ah!" some people screamed when I fell on top of their table, sending it collapsing to the ground. Yikayla had punched me three good times, back to back before I could even process what was going on.

A few of the restaurant staff rushed out to see what was going on, and start cleaning the mess.

"You stupid bitch!" I shouted, not liking the feeling of some hot ass coffee covering my ass and drenching my underwear.

I hopped up and tried to rush her, but Tammy and Ashley got in the middle of us. Yikayla was standing there, smiling right along with Rori, and sending my blood boiling to a high ass temperature.

"The next time you wanna lie about who your baby daddy is, remember that three piece and a biscuit I just gave you, hoe." Yikayla smirked as a couple of dudes who were seated outside laughed and commented on what had just happened. And they were fine too. Why the fuck did I have to get embarrassed in front of a bunch of fine niggas? This was a bad bitch's nightmare.

"Fine as fuck *and* a little crazy. Aye y'all twins?" one of the sexy guys hollered to Yikayla and Rori, but they ignored him.

"Shut up!" was all I could say back to Yikayla finally.

"I bet you thought you'd gotten off easy," Rori added as she and Yikayla continued down the street to wherever the fuck they were going.

"Let me go!" I shouted to my friends, when they grabbed me up, thinking I was about to try and hit one of the Goode girls.

"Alba, where are you going?" Ashley yelled to me.

"Home!" I was too ashamed to sit here and eat, not to mention, that coffee all over my bottom half wasn't the most comfortable or great smelling. Also, my face was throbbing and I felt blood building up in my nose and mouth. I definitely needed to be in someone's doctor's office and not at breakfast.

"Aye, baby, I'll clean yo' pretty ass up!" one of the fine niggas shouted, but I just kept it going to my car.

As mad as I was, and as badly as my face hurt, I knew I'd deserved what Yikayla had just given me. That was for her and for Rori.

28

JONAYA

That Night...

"David Alan Grier does not get enough credit as a comedian," my stepfather shook his head as he sipped some of his cognac.

Him, my mom, Nusef, and I were in the living room watching *The Carmichael Show*, just relaxing. I'd missed my stepdad a lot, so anytime he didn't have to work I was always excited like a little kid. Since I was three years old, he'd been the only father I knew, and I couldn't have asked for a better one. I never found myself wondering where my real father was, because Jasper was more than enough.

"I said the same thing the other day when Jo and I were watching *Boomerang*, but she acted like she didn't know what I was talking about," Nusef replied.

"You are such a suck up!" I laughed.

Jasper had thankfully taken a liking to Nusef, after he grilled him like a hamburger on the fourth of July. Once he saw Nusef and I were friends for a long time, like Yikayla and Waayil, and that Nusef co-owned a tattoo shop, it was uphill from there. I didn't even want to mention Marquise, and I told everyone else not to either.

Speaking of Marquise, he would still text message and call me here and there, but it wasn't on a consistent basis per say. He would message me all day for like three days straight, then leave me alone for two weeks and so on.

I admit, I still replied just to keep it friendly because I didn't want to have any hard feelings between us. Like Leighton, Marquise, too, got caught in the crossfire of Nusef's and my love. So if I was gonna have sympathy for Leighton, Marquise should get it too... just from afar.

"Here are the chips and the queso dip. Remember the rules boys, no double dipping because that's nasty as hell," my mom said as she set the platter on the coffee table in front of us. "And it's hot, so be careful." She refilled my stepfather's glass.

"Thank you for saying that, Mama," I nodded. I hated sharing shit with Nusef because he always did nasty shit like double dipping, and didn't understand how it was nasty. Talking about I suck his dick so it shouldn't matter.

We continued watching Netflix while eating the dip, and my parents even let me taste a little pink champagne. My mom didn't want to drink the whole mini bottle alone, and after I gave my speech about how I was only a couple months away from drinking age, my dad agreed.

The doorbell sounded off, so my dad got up to answer it since it was pretty late in the evening and he was the man of the house. That was a rule he always had when he was home. I paused the TV show and continued snacking, as Nusef stole kisses from me while my mom shook her head at us.

"Natasha, come here," my dad turned to look at us. When he did that, he pulled the wooden door open a little more, and through the screen I could see Buddy standing there.

"Oh shit," Nusef mumbled.

"Who is this nigga?" I heard my stepfather ask my mom lowly. He never used the N-word, so he must have been upset.

"I—" she shrugged and turned her attention from Buddy back up to my father.

Buddy and I locked eyes before he yelled, "Jonaya! Jonaya, tell him who I am! Tell him how I've been living here for months!"

My father looked to me as if he were waiting on an answer, and my mom turned around as well, but with a pleading expression. The love I had for my stepfather made me want to be honest with him, but I couldn't do that to my mother. She did love Jasper she was just... well... stupid.

"Jonaya, do you know him?" my dad inquired because I hadn't answered yet. Nusef squeezed my hand a little, almost like he was telling me to hurry and say something.

Shaking my head, I replied, "I— no, no, I haven't ever seen him before I don't think." My mom discreetly sighed out of relief, as my father nodded.

Buddy and I regained eye contact, and I knew what I'd said hurt him. But I didn't care about him, or what he felt, I gave a fuck about my parents and their marriage. Plus, Buddy knew what he'd signed up for. Everyone from here to Mississippi knew who Jasper Vaughn was and that my mother was his wife. Not to mention, the plethora of family pictures all over the damn house, and the Armani, Gucci, and Kiton suits in the closet of the bedroom my dad shared with my mother. So right now, Buddy was that side chick that knew she was smashing a married man so I didn't feel one bit of remorse for what I'd just done.

"Jonaya, come on," Buddy pleaded.

"You need to go," Jasper stated sternly before closing the wooden door. I could still faintly hear Buddy on the other side going off.

"I don't know what the hell that was about," my mom said. "I'm gonna go check on the food. I will be right back."

My father watched as she left the living room, and then he sat back down. Only this time, he didn't sit next to me, he sat adjacent and looked me dead in the eyes.

"Baby girl, how did he know your name?"

"I—"

"Didn't you tell me you'd seen him somewhere before?" Nusef interjected, trying to help me.

Looking his way briefly, before turning back to my dad, I replied, "Yeah, yeah; I did. That's how he knows me. He was at a barbecue party and Mama came to pick me up. He's been smitten ever since it seems."

"With Natasha?"

"Yes." I nodded.

Jasper looked me in my eyes for a little bit, and then a soft smile graced his face as he shook his head to say 'okay.' He got back in his original seat next to me, and for some reason, I just felt the need to lie on his shoulder. He kissed my forehead just as I pressed play for *The Carmichael Show* to resume.

That was a close ass call just now, and I never wanted to be put on the spot like that again. The next time my dad left town, my mother would have to get a hobby or get more involved with the waffle house because, I was not about to keep lying for her and betraying my father.

My mom brought back the dinner and we all ate in peace, almost forgetting about the little charade Buddy had put on. Once it got to be around midnight, Nusef went home, my parents went to bed, and I went upstairs to take a hot shower before getting into my own warm bed. I had only just dozed off when my phone buzzed, and I picked it up to see Marquise had texted me.

Marquise: *I miss you.*

Me: *I told you to stop this, Marquise. We can be friends but nothing else. You're about to make me take that off the table as well though.*

Marquise: *I know I'm sorry ma. I just miss you.*

He sent a pic of him chilling along with it, and as cute as he was, he was no Nusef. I wish Marquise would realize that there was nothing he could do to get me back. Nusef was better than him in every sense of the word. My baby looked better, had better stroke, head game, and fatter pockets. Not to mention, I loved the way he treated me. Marquise was just at a loss here.

I rolled my eyes and placed my iPhone back on the dresser, just as the doorbell rang again. My eyes shot open, hoping like hell Marquise hadn't popped his ass up over here again. I climbed out of bed and walked to my bedroom door.

"I got it, baby," my father told me when he saw me step out of my bedroom. It was then that I remembered Marquise had just sent me a picture of himself in his bedroom, so there was no way he could get here that quickly unless he had some sort of powers.

"Look, I told you to get out of here. Don't make me come from behind this screen door!" I heard my father bark loudly just as my mom floated through the hallway and down the stairs in her black silk robe.

"Jasper!" she called out.

Slipping my feet into my house shoes, I rushed down after my mother so I could see what was going on. This was the one time I wished my sisters weren't laid up with their significant others, but here at home with me.

"How you gon' lie on me, Tasha!" Buddy screamed at the top of his lungs when I got down there.

"Alright, that's it," Jasper stated, pushing the screen door out and stepping onto the porch.

Now Buddy was no small guy, maybe around six-foot-one and a nice build. My stepfather was six-foot-four though and had a nice amount of muscle to him. He looked a lot like an older, taller version of Ghost from *Power*, with a few gray hairs sprinkled on his head and in his facial hair.

"Jasper!" my mom called out again and was about to come out of the house until my stepfather gave her a look.

"I told yo' ass to get away from 'round here, and I mean it. I don't wanna have to beat yo' ass," Jasper gritted. I had never in my life heard him curse so I was appalled, yet, scared as hell. My mom always said Jasper had two sides, and for the first time, I was seeing it.

"Aye, get back, man, I just wanted to talk," Buddy's voice shook like a leaf on a tree in the Fall, making me roll my eyes. I even gave my mom a quick side eye for choosing such a whack ass nigga.

"Get off my damn porch," Jasper gritted down into Buddy's face and stepped forward some more.

POP! POP! POP!

"Noooo!" my mother and I screamed together as my dad collapsed to the floor, clutching his abdomen. Buddy had let off three shots into his torso and ran his ass off.

"Oh my God, honey, you're gonna be okay." My mom had dropped down onto the porch and cradled my father's head. Thankfully, he was still awake, but blood was soaking his wife beater and he wasn't responding verbally, unless you count the groaning.

I rushed inside to grab the house phone, and quickly dialed 911. I gave them our address and let them know it was urgent, before hanging up and rushing upstairs to get my cellphone. I texted my sisters within a group text, and by the time I put on an Adidas sweat suit and my sneakers, my phone was being blown up and sirens could be heard speeding down our street. There was rarely ever crime on the street that we lived on in Midtown. We were surrounded by other big houses on the street, aka rich folks. So, I knew the sound of sirens would bring everyone from their houses, just like the morning Waayil was arrested.

When I got downstairs, they were putting my stepfather on the stretcher and then they covered his nose and mouth with a mask. I heard some of the EMT's frantically trying to keep him above water because they recognized him.

He was so still, and it scared me to death. I allowed my mom to get in the ambulance with Jasper, and I got in her car to follow behind. My sisters were calling and even though I was too frantic to be driving and talking on the phone, I answered because I knew they were worried.

"On our way to Methodist Hospital!" was all I yelled out to Rori before hanging up and answering the next call from Dree, and then Yikayla.

By the time I got to the hospital, the ambulance had already wheeled my father inside. I was allowed to sit in the waiting room, and after about six or so minutes, my mom came out from the back. She scanned the area, and when she saw me, she came and sat down next to me.

"Is he okay?" I inquired.

"He still had a pulse. They have him in surgery right now, so I'm hoping that he comes out fine." She exhaled, tears pooled in her eyes.

Looking down at the hospital floor, and inhaling the smell of it that I hated, I whispered, "Mama, you have to stop."

"I know," she sighed and sniffled. "I know."

29

———

EKO

Rori was at the hospital for hours last night to make sure her pops was okay, and still right now, we didn't know. He was in a medically induced coma, but doctors said things looked good for him. I didn't trust them muthafuckas, but I wouldn't dare say that shit aloud to Rori.

When we finally left the hospital, she wanted to go home so I slept there with her. I couldn't leave her the way she was. This morning she had to go to work for that mayor nigga, and she claimed she was good, so I decided to continue on with my regular plans for the day as well.

I had an appointment with Waayil to get a tattoo, and since I'd been wanting that shit for the longest, I was excited as hell that the day had come.

"What's up, mane?" I dapped Waayil up when I walked into the shop.

"What's good?" he grinned.

I nodded towards Chiara who had her eyes locked hard on my

boy. He had to have messed with her ass because she was looking like Alba right now.

"Fuck you be doing to these bitches, Yil?" I questioned lowly as we started towards the back.

"What you mean? Shorty at the front desk?"

"You knew what the fuck I meant that's why you answered yo' own damn question."

Chuckling, he pushed his tattoo room door open for me and said, "Oh that shit was a long ass time ago. I'm talking not even a full week out of jail. I dealt with her once and never again." He closed the door behind us.

"Pussy was whack?"

"Nah, I don't even know. Got some top and that shit had a nigga lifted, but she too damn thirsty for me. And I had my eyes on Yikayla at the time."

"When have you not had yo' eyes on Kay?"

Shaking his head, he responded, "Shit, can't even remember."

We laughed in unison as he started to wash his hands and put on his gloves to get started.

KNOCK! KNOCK!

I got up to answer it, and saw some pretty, thick bitch standing there. She was smiling, but when she saw me, it faded.

"Oh, I was looking for Waayil." Her brows dipped in confusion as she looked at his name on the door.

"What, Brynn?" Waayil stepped up so I went to sit back down in the tattoo chair. "I'm working."

"Oh, I just wanted to stop by and say hi. I cooked some chicken and brought you some." she giggled, making me raise my brows.

"Give it to Chiara." Was all his evil ass said before closing the door in shorty's face, not giving her a chance to respond.

"Damn another one?" I laughed.

Sighing, he said, "Nigga, I don't know what her damn problem is. She's been acting suspect since I met her. And nah, I haven't touched her, unless you count the tattoo I'm doing for her."

"Sucks to be you, bruh," I laughed.

"Don't I know it."

"Aye but that shit with Mr. And Mrs. Vaughn? I can't believe that bullshit, mane," I sucked my teeth and shook my head.

"I know, right. Imagine getting blasted because ya bitch been fucking around on you." Waayil shook his head as he started to take his equipment out. "I wouldn't know whose ass to whoop first," he added before we both roared with laughter.

"Who the fuck you telling, nigga? I don't hit women but some shit like that'll get yo' muthafuckin' head knocked off."

"Ah fuck!" Waayil hissed when he reached up into the cabinet. I watched as he slowly gripped his ribcage and held it for a minute.

"You good, Yil?"

"Fuck. Yeah, I'm good. Got a little injury going on." He grabbed the shit from the cabinet that he needed.

"Little? That don't seem like no little injury to me, my nigga."

"I got some shit going on with this nigga I was locked up with named Neo. I gotta get rid of his stupid ass and ASAP."

"Neo?" I frowned. "Neo Sanders?"

"Yeah, you know him?"

"Hell yeah, I know that nigga but that shouldn't be surprising considering the fact that I sell drugs. But you ain't into that shit, so what dealings you got with that nigga now that you're out of prison?"

I was interested as fuck to know what beef Waayil had with Neo's bitch ass since I had a beef of my own. I was all for letting Neo live and just bowing out once I had all the funds I needed, but after he pulled that stunt on me, saying he planned to get Gavin out of jail and put him back on, I was done with him. Both of them niggas had to go.

"Mane, look, I started fucking with his daughter heavily while locked up and I made some promises. But now that a nigga is out..."

"You don't want that shit no more. You talking about Zia? That's his little pride and joy, nigga."

"Trust me, I know, which is why I don't even understand why

he'd give her to me like that. No muthafuckin' way I'd offer my daughter up to a nigga serving a life sentence. Shit, I wouldn't want my baby girl with a nigga serving two years. Fuck that shit."

"I hear you." I placed my arm on the rest since that's where he was putting the tattoo.

"Anyway, the nigga had me kidnapped from outside of here, took me to some weird ass location that I was sure was downtown, and then had his flunky beat my ass like a runaway slave." He sat down by me.

Chortling, I replied, "Damn, nigga. Well you know I got my own shit with him. He fucked me over so now, not only do I have to get rid of Gavin, but his ass too. You remember Gavin? My old homie, and he was dating Rori for a minute too."

"It's a small fuckin' world, mane. I ain't know Gavin well, but the nigga called me from jail telling me how he got Alba pregnant."

"The fuck?" I bucked my eyes.

I knew Gavin had some side bitch that he was two seconds from leaving Rori for, but I had no idea it was Alba. But the shit made sense now on why he was so secretive about who the fuck she was. Low-key, I thought maybe his ass was fucking with a tranny or into some gay shit so he didn't wanna say, but now I know why. Nigga never mentioned a pregnancy though, so maybe he was in on Alba lying about it being Waayil's. But then again, Gavin was too lovesick and had too much pride to go along with some scheme like that, so I don't know what the fuck happened.

"You ain't know? That's yo' homie, right?" Waayil inquired.

"Yeah, but he was always mum as fuck on who the bitch was that he was fucking with. Had his ass all in love and shit while he was with Rori." I couldn't stop shaking my head as I thought back to all the conversations Gavin and I'd had about his sidepiece. This whole time it was Alba.

"Well, now the nigga ain't so mum. And Alba finally came clean about me not being the dad and her faking the DNA. I wanted to choke her ass until she stopped breathing, but I realized it wasn't even worth it. She wasn't worth me catching another muthafuckin' case, when I just beat one by the grace of God."

"Amen. You got off that Harry shit by the skin of ya damn teeth."

"Exactly. Killing Neo is one thing due to his background, but Alba is too squeaky clean to just end up dead. And Gavin, I honestly don't give a fuck enough." He exhaled as he started to draw on me. "Kay served Alba's ass though. I knew she was gon' do that shit, even though I told her not to," he chuckled and so did I.

"Kay's ass is always doing whatever the fuck she wanna do. How you deal with that shit?" I grinned when he frowned like 'nigga please.'

Raising his brow as he reached for another drawing utensil, he said, "She acts tough and shit for y'all niggas but when she get home, she know who the fuck is in charge. Kay don't run shit but her mouth and you know how a nigga shuts that up."

We chortled in unison as he continued to set the blueprint for the tattoo on my skin.

I just stared off for a minute, still flabbergasted by the information he'd just dropped on a nigga. You'd think it was only six or seven bitches in Memphis with the way muthafuckas were getting recycled and refurbished.

"What you think about us getting Neo together?" I looked at him as an evil smirk spread across his face.

JUST TWO NIGHTS LATER... AROUND **11:22 p.m....**

I'd originally planned to wait until Gavin got out of jail to murder his ass and *then* get at Neo, but when I thought about that shit... I realized it was dumb. I could kill two birds with one fucking stone if I just murked Neo. If he was dead, there was no way he could get Gavin out.

The only thing that was holding me back from killing Neo, prior to right now, was the fact that I needed more time to stack a little more bread, and I needed to figure out how to pull that shit off by myself. But now that I had my cash, and an accomplice in Waayil, I was more than ready to rid Tennessee of this nigga. It's just funny how shit works because Waayil was struggling with one of my two problems as well; figuring out how to murk Neo, his flunkies, and anyone else he had around him, all by himself.

Just two days ago, Waayil and I decided we would go in on this shit together, and during the last 48 hours we'd been planning. We both took turns following Neo around, catching onto his habits. Nigga was way too predictable to be some kingpin; at least, he appeared to be predictable as fuck from the two days we'd trailed him.

For the past two nights around midnight, Neo would come 'home' to this nice ass spot in Germantown on Dogwood Road. It was a nice ways away from the spot he had his meetings at, but still in Germantown. Nigga was living good as hell, which wasn't surprising.

"You ready? This nigga gon' be here around 11:36pm if he does the same shit he's been doing," I said as Waayil stared out the window of the dark black truck we'd gotten from this dude I knew from high school. Nigga was a crooked mechanic, but that's a story for another day.

"Yep."

As Waayil twisted the silencer onto his heat, some bright ass headlights blinded us, before the car turned into Neo's driveway. I tapped Waayil so he could see, and we immediately hopped our asses out of the car since we wanted to get at Neo before he got out of his. The nigga was a little early but it was perfectly fine.

Letting another vehicle speed by us, Waayil and I rushed across the street and came up to the big ass tree that was in a portion of his front yard, on the outer part of his driveway.

We crept around the tree, and saw the driver's side door of Neo's whip slightly cracked with his leg out. His windows were tinted so we couldn't see what he was doing, but it was now or never.

"Aye, Neo," Waayil walked up closer.

PHEW! PHEW! PHEW!

Waayil and I lit that nigga up with bullets before he could even realize what was going on. His body shook and gyrated as we silently took every last breath he had in his body. He fell back, riddled with bullets and covered in dark ass blood. The only sound heard was of his window shattering when I let off into him and nothing else.

Suddenly about four niggas started coming from different directions with guns, so Waayil and I let off into them niggas as well. Once they'd dropped, we saw another one of his flunkies book it since, I guess he was too scared, but Waayil was able to pop him. It looked like someone had killed a bunch of roaches in a kitchen with all these dark bodies laid out.

We rushed right back to the car, ready to get out of there.

"Nigga's eyes were wide as hell," Waayil laughed referring to Neo, once we got back into the vehicle we had.

"For real? I didn't even see the nigga's face, I just started shooting."

Laughing, Waayil said, "I can't wait until they find his ass like that."

"What about Zia though?" I glanced from the road to him as I got ready for this half an hour drive back home.

"No fucking idea, but if I have to get rid of her ass too, then I will. A part of me feels like she didn't want the shit as badly as Neo did. I think it fucked with her ego a little bit, seeing that Neo was trying to force me to be with her instead of me willingly wanting to be. And once she saw I wasn't feeling it, she started to feel differently."

"Makes sense. Zia's ass is fine as hell, so I'm sure she don't wanna spend her time running after a nigga that don't want her."

"My thoughts exactly, but we'll see."

"We will."

"Good job tonight, bruh." He dapped me up just as I hopped onto Interstate 240.

I dropped Waayil at home, took this truck back to the homie, and then I drove to Rori's parents' spot in my car. Dree answered the door for me looking sad as hell, and rightfully so. I did expect her to be laid up with Canyon or some shit, getting comforted like her sisters, but that nigga hadn't been seen lately. As much as he loved shorty, that was unlike him to not be around in her time of need.

"She up there?" I asked Dree.

"Yep." She nodded as she went to the den, adjusting the blanket she had thrown over her back.

I went up to Rori's bedroom, and saw she was in the bed, in the dark, with the television on. She looked over her shoulder at me when she heard me closing her door.

"Is it aight if I keep you company?" I leaned against it. I didn't care what she said, I was staying regardless.

She half smiled and peeled the covers back, so I undressed down to my boxers and climbed in bed behind her. Hugging her back into my chest, I kissed the nape of her neck and inhaled the scent of whatever she'd put on it.

"Thank you, baby," she whispered.

I just hugged her body tighter, and soon enough, we'd both drifted off to sleep.

30

———————

YIKAYLA

Waayil and I had just gotten out of the shower, and since Lonan was knocked out, we could finally lay up. We'd been at the park all day, and my baby had so much energy. He got his little Jordan VIIs dirty as hell, but of course in Waayil's eyes, he could do no wrong so he spent an hour cleaning them for him.

"Why you put that fucking gown on?" Waayil inquired, coming into the bedroom and dropping his towel.

He walked closer to the bed slowly, looking like a god dipped in dark chocolate. The tattoos on his body gave him that thug appeal, and his muscles protruded perfectly. My eyes locked on his third leg as he immediately started yanking my nightgown over my head with a serious expression. His lips were tucked in, and his dimples were on display, while his honey colored eyes surveyed me.

He lied down on the bed, and guided me to sit on his face in the frontal position so that I could see him. I leaned back some, using his muscular chest for leverage, as he feasted on my pussy. I slowly wound my hips against his mouth, as his big hands grabbed at my ass cheeks. I felt myself on the verge of cumming already, but I didn't want to because I didn't want him to stop.

"Waayil," I whimpered, scraping my nails against his fresh fade as I rode his face.

I glanced down at him, looking relaxed, as he ate my pussy like it was a full course meal. My body shivered when I released, and he forced me onto my back, pressing my thighs into my stomach. Again, he flicked his tongue over my bud, before letting his soft lips collapse around it, sending a tingling sensation through my body. He moaned softly, his voice vibrating against my clit, which felt so fucking good. His mouth and my pussy stayed connected as if they were magnets, just as another orgasm ripped through me.

"Baby," I whined, as he kept eating me. My pussy was soaked, and very sensitive so I came a third time, fast as hell.

"Mmm," he mumbled against it, lapping up my juices before standing up on his knees.

He lowered himself between my legs, and pressed the head of his thick dick at my opening. I grasped the sheets in my hands as he applied pressure, barging his way inside of my sopping wet walls. My pussy hugged him as he pumped me slowly, forcing me to take all of him. My teeth sank down into my bottom lip as he filled me up, and my expression must have amused him because he gave me a sexy smirk before biting his own lip, while stroking me.

"Fuck," he grumbled, opening me up more, making it easier for him to glide in and out.

He held my legs by the back of my knees, and started to slowly fuck me. Every time he slid out extra slow, my body trembled because of how good it felt. Slamming in, pulling out slowly was how he was working me right now and it felt so good, that the only thing I could do, was grab the sheets again.

"Look at you about to cum for me," he spoke lowly, before nibbling on his lip. He kept strong eye contact with me as he slipped in and out of me, and just like he'd predicted, I gushed all over his long thick pole.

Coming out of me, he bent down to taste my nectar, before flipping me onto my stomach. Spreading my legs some, he got between them and pushed his way back inside of me from behind. I loved doggy-style, but it was always better when he had me flat on my stomach.

"Shit," he whispered, beating it up from the back, while holding my ass cheeks apart.

He was hitting it so hard and good that the only thing I could do was hold my mouth open and snivel every now and again. Hearing him moan, in combination with him fucking the shit out of me, only made me cum harder.

"Fuck, ma." He gripped my shoulder and pounded into me hard and fast until he filled me up with his seeds.

For a moment, we both sat there panting heavily, and after he slid out, he planted soft kisses down my sweaty back. I couldn't move. I was tired as hell and just wanted to go to sleep in the position that I was in. Sex with Waayil was like a drug; literally, in the sense that afterwards, I would always wanna pass out.

I felt him get out of the bed, and seconds later it seemed, he was wiping between my legs with a perfectly warm towel. He moved me back to the head of the bed, and then I felt him get in next to me.

"Baby," he nudged me.

"Huh?" I whined, feeling tired as hell.

"You want yo' bonnet?"

"Nigga, I don't wear a bonnet. I wore one, *one* damn night. I have a silk pillow." I patted my pillow as he chuckled.

"Damn, a nigga is just trying to make sure that when you wake up that yo' shit is right," he laughed.

I was irritated that he'd woken me from my semi sleep for that, but I still chuckled at his stupid ass.

"Goodnight, asshole." I turned my back to him and he snuggled up behind me. I could feel that he had his boxers on, so I sat up to grab my nightie from the floor and slipped it over my head.

"Let me have another kiss since I'm gon' be gone before you wake up."

"What? Why so early?"

"This girl wants me to finish her tattoo tomorrow morning before she goes into work." He kissed my shoulder.

"What girl?"

"Some female named Brynn. I've been working on her for a while."

"Oh, okay." I laid my head back down on the pillow and stared at the wall for a bit. That bitch wanted to make good on her threats, then so the fuck was I. She was gon' leave Monarch with not only a tattoo, but a foot broken off in her ass.

The Next Morning...

Waayil left about an hour ago, and I'd just finished showering and brushing my teeth. I got dressed in some Nike tights, a compression top, and some Nike sneakers, before tying my hair up and getting my baby ready.

"You're going to be with Grandma and Hrandpa for a little bit, Lonan." I kissed his cheek after buckling him into his car seat.

My stepfather thankfully made it out of the hospital alive, despite losing a lot of blood. The bullets, surprisingly didn't damage too much, and since he was in stellar health, all was well. All was well health wise because he wasn't fucking with my mama.

I admit, I did blame my mother because if she hadn't have been fucking around with Buddy the way that she was, none of this would have happened. My sisters and I all made a promise that the next time Jasper had to leave town, we'd make sure our mother was on her best behavior. The only good thing about Jasper getting shot was that now he was on bed rest for a couple weeks, so we got to have him around constantly.

I made it to my parents' house, and after checking on my dad and talking with my mom a little bit, I left Lonan there. I was on a time limit because I wanted to catch Brynn's ass while she was still at the shop.

When I made it to Monarch, I saw Brynn's car parked outside, and had a mind to bust the windows out of that shit. Only reason I didn't was because I didn't have a bat or anything to do so.

"What's good, ma?" Some dude waiting in the lobby of Monarch smirked at me, looking me up and down. "Who you mad at?"

I walked right by him and that bitch, Chiara, who was watching me like a hawk. Depending on how I felt after beating Brynn's ass, I just might give her ass the business too.

I went right up to Waayil's door, and twisted the knob, allowing it to swing open. Waayil had just finished covering her tattoo and she was talking his ear off in a flirty tone that I didn't like. When Waayil saw me, he frowned hard as fuck, and for a minute, I'd regretted my actions.

"Yikayla!" Brynn shrieked.

"Come outside," I said.

"Yikayla, what the fuck you doing?" Waayil inquired, rising to his feet and trying to step between me and Brynn.

"Come outside, Brynn!" I snatched from Waayil when he tried to grab my arm, and started back outside to wait. Waayil followed me out to talk, but I ignored him, waiting on Brynn.

I watched as Brynn came to the front, paid, and got a receipt from Chiara before coming outside.

"Yikayla," Waayil called my name, but I stayed mute.

"I'm here, so what did you want—"

WHAM!

I cut Brynn off in the middle of her sentence with a punch to the jaw. She screamed loudly as hell, before charging me like a wild banshee. I continued to land punch after punch on her face, and when she couldn't take it anymore, she dropped down and vagina punched me. I was too angry to react to her hit, so I kept going in, bashing her head with my fists as she continuously socked me in the vagina like a dummy. I immediately thought about my baby, so I socked her head harder, weakening her punches even more.

"Yikayla!" Waayil roared, and right when he snatched me up, Brynn's stupid ass fell to the gravel crying. "What the fuck is wrong with you, huh!" Waayil barked. His face was twisted up but I could barely look at him because I was still glaring at Brynn, and panting like a raging bull. I wanted more of that bitch.

"She did this shit on purpose! She's trying to get with you and I ain't having it!" I shouted back up at Waayil as Brynn cried like a newborn baby. In a minute, he was gon' get the works too.

"Come on, girl, get up." Chiara came outside and helped Brynn to her feet then to her car. That irritated me for some reason.

"How the fuck do you even know her?" Waayil asked.

"She's yet another one of Roscoe's baby mamas that I told you about! The bitch I work with! Brynn! Remember? He has two others outside of me, and this bitch has the nerve to accuse *me* of stealing him! Then she tries to push up on you? No! No! I am not having it!" I hollered loudly as fuck.

Waayil's once angry expression softened as he cocked his head a little bit. Finally, he pulled me into his chest and hugged me tightly.

"It's okay, Yikayla. Regardless of whether she was trying to get at me or not, you know I wouldn't fuck with another woman."

"I know," I whimpered as I started to cry.

I closed my eyes, enjoying the feeling of Waayil's embrace and the scent of his cologne, that wasn't too overbearing, but just right. We hugged for what felt like an eternity, before I picked my head up off of his chest, and tilted it back so he could kiss me. He thumbed the few tears that had cascaded down my cheeks, and then pecked my lips gently but passionately.

"I love you, Waayil."

"I love you too, baby. You feeling aight? I don't wanna have to kill shorty for fucking with my seed."

"I'm fine, I promise." I chuckled. "Her punches weren't really punches at all."

"Good." He grinned and kissed my forehead.

"She just hit my vagina." I frowned up at him, thinking about how dumb Brynn was.

"I'd rather her hit you in the face than hit my pussy. Let me check and see—"

"Stop, boy!" I giggled and slapped his hand when he pulled on the waistband of my tights to look down my pants.

I felt someone watching us, and when I looked over, I spotted Chiara talking to some guy, but peeping on Waayil and I through her peripheral.

Getting out of Waayil's embrace, I walked over to her, as Waayil followed behind me. Without saying a word, I backhanded the shit out of her, and she fell into the dude she was talking to.

"Ooh shit!" the man yelled, gripping Chiara's shoulders as she crashed into him. "You aight, shorty?" he bucked his eyes so widely, I'd thought they'd pop out.

"Are you serious?" Chiara screamed but didn't bust a move. I knew she was a punk. All bark and no bite.

"Aight, you gotta go home." Waayil picked me up and walked me to my car. "I don't know if I wanna be mad at you or fuck you right now. Maybe both." He placed me down and looked at my body while nibbling on his lip.

"Well, I'll be at home, so let me know." I smirked as I opened the door and got in the car. Chiara had stormed by and went back into the shop.

"Let me calm her down, and I'll meet you there."

"Don't calm her down with any sympathy dick, Waayil." He gave me a face that said, 'get the fuck outta here,' so I laughed.

As I watched his sexy ass walk back into the shop, I cranked my car up. My phone chimed letting me know that I had a DM on Instagram, and when I checked it, I saw it was from this rapper named Tame's fiancée. Tame was an up and coming rapper, who hailed from

Memphis, so he was a pretty big deal around here. He was dating this beautiful girl named Shanna.

Opening the DM, I scanned her Instagram name about one hundred times to make sure it was actually her and not some perpetrator. When I confirmed it was, in fact her, I almost jumped out of my skin at the message.

ShannaRene: *Hey, Yikayla. I saw some of your designs that you were wearing on your profile after my best friend pointed them out to me. I don't know if you sew, but one of your designs I wanted to be made into bridesmaid dresses. The wedding is in 10 months, so I hope that is enough time to make three dresses. Let me know if you can help me, and what your pricing is like. Money is not an object, because Tame will pay whatever. Lol. Thank you.*

I read the message a couple more times before taking a screenshot and sending it to my sisters. I'd told them what Jerica said and how it had me feeling low, but seeing this message from Shanna, definitely gave me a boost. It gave me hope again that I could be a designer.

After quickly responding to her, I sped home so I could be ready for that angry dick down Waayil had promised me.

31

———————

CANYON

I hadn't talked to Dree in a minute, ever since I found out she fucked with my nephew, Taj's, dad. That shit killed me to be honest. It was different than her just fucking with some random. She just had to fuck with a nigga that I knew and used to be like a brother to. Not to mention, he was Jupiter's boyfriend at the time and I know this because me nor Dree knew that nigga until Jupiter brought him around.

What makes matters worse was that now, I couldn't stand the air that nigga breathed, and to know he'd had my girl before, made me sick to my stomach. Not to mention, it had me wanting to strangle his ass. Yeah, the shit was old, and a long ass time ago, but still. Thoughts off all the times that nigga used to compliment Dree and say how good she looked, seemed to circle my brain constantly. No wonder Jupiter couldn't stand Dree's ass; it was for me, and for her damn self too.

I heard someone ring my doorbell, so I got up off the couch and went to see who it was. I wasn't in the fucking mood to deal with Dree, so if it was her, I wasn't gon' even open the damn door. When I saw it was my sister, I sighed heavily before unlocking and pulling the door open for her.

"Hey, how are you?" She half smiled as she stepped into my spot. I closed the door behind her and went to sit back down on the couch without giving her a response. "Canyon, I wanna talk to you about what happened with Dree." Jupiter sat down.

"I don't; so, if that's all you have for conversation, then you can go."

"I want to apologize for blurting that out only because I was mad. I should have told you a long time ago, like right when it happened."

"Yeah, you should have. Fuck was the point in keeping that bullshit a secret anyway, Jupiter?"

"Back when it happened, I was angry at Dree for what she did and I only saw how it affected me, not you. You guys weren't dating, only friends, and you were pretty much with Luna. I never expected for you two to come back together and be so damn hot and heavy like this."

"Well... shit is a wrap now. I'm sure yo' ass is happy about that."

"Surprisingly, no I'm not." She turned on the couch some more so that she could face me. "Canyon, back then, Dree was acting out because she wanted to be with you but you went and got Luna pregnant."

"I already know that bullshit, so keep that." I waved her off with a frown as I focused my eyes on the paused television show. "And that's Dree's fault. I wanted to be with her but she acted like she didn't feel the same so I moved on."

"Right and she was being reckless back then, so she did what she did with Neil, and it broke us up as friends. That's what she wanted since she'd pushed you into the arms of another girl. I was just a constant reminder of you, especially because of how excited I was when Luna got pregnant with Cade."

"Jupiter, I don't need a fucking recap, ma."

"What I'm saying to you, Canyon, is that you love Dree, and as badly as I don't want to admit it, she loves you too. This thing with

Neil is old as hell, and didn't even go that far. Was it wrong? Hell yeah, it was, since she and I were close, but she didn't belong to you then, Canyon. I know you're mad because of who it was, but you don't have the right to be, only I do."

"I appreciate you coming here to talk on her behalf, but I'm done with Dree. Shit ain't meant. Every time it's going good, a wrench is thrown into the mix and I'm done. I'm tired of waiting to see who or how our shit is gon' get fucked up."

"If that's how you feel."

"It is how I feel."

"Okay." Jupiter sat back and grabbed the bowl of chips from the coffee table, as I hit play on what I was watching.

For the next couple of hours, my sister and I just watched TV and relaxed. I hadn't done this shit with her in a while, mainly because she hated Dree and I was with Dree a lot. It made me miss the days when the three of us could kick it together, but that shit was over with.

Around 8pm, Jupiter left to go get my nephew from his dad and to get Cade from Luna since they wanted to have a sleepover at Jupiter's. Without my son, and without Dree, I needed some shit to do because watching TV and playing my video game wasn't enough anymore. Plus, I was all caught up on my work, so wasn't shit to keep me occupied over that way.

Getting up, I went to hop in the shower again, and then brush, floss, and rinse my teeth with mouthwash. I slipped into a simple fit; a Ralph Lauren Polo, some jeans, and my new Yeezy Powerphase Adidas. After spraying on some cologne, I fastened my watch around my wrist and left out the door.

I ended up at this little junt downtown that was like a bar slash eatery, which was exactly what I needed.

I was doing aight, kind of, regarding this shit with Dree, until my sister brought her ass over to me advocating for her. Now a nigga felt like he was bugging but could you blame me? I may have not been the most thugged out ass muthafucka, but I was territorial as hell when it came to a bitch that was supposed to be my girl. And knowing Dree even let that nigga smell the pussy before me, had me beyond tight.

As I sat at the bar, drinking and waiting on the burger I'd ordered, my phone started to ring. I looked down to see it was Jupiter's ass again, so I answered angrily as fuck.

"Jupiter, shorty, please. I'm just trying to relax tonight."

"Did you hear about Dree's dad?" she inquired, completely ignoring my hostile tone of voice.

"Nah, what happened to him?" I nodded to the bartender who set down my food as I waited for Jupiter's answer.

"He got shot three times. He lived, but he's like on bed rest now, I heard," she sighed.

"Shot? Who the fuck shot him? That nigga is a damn surgeon."

"It was their mom's little fuck buddy she had while he was away. I mean, she always has one when he leaves, but I guess this one got a little too attached. They arrested him the next day though."

"Wow." I exhaled, shoving a fry into my mouth.

"Sooooo... you should call her and make sure she's okay, Canyon."

"Dree is strong like a bull," I replied, making Jupiter laugh. "I'm serious as fuck." I chuckled along, even though I wasn't in the mood to.

"It doesn't matter. You love her, and you should be there for her."

"I will think about it."

"Canyon."

"Goodnight, Jupiter. Make sure my son and nephew ain't into some shit instead of calling me about my relationship."

"Fine. Goodnight, nigga."

I slipped my phone into my jean pocket, and started to go in on this good ass barbecue brisket burger. A nigga had never heard of no shit like that, but it was good as fuck. As I ate the last bite of the burger, the smell of some feminine perfume invaded my nostrils, prompting me to look to my left to see who it was coming from.

"Wow." I laughed out of pure disbelief at the sight of Jodi.

"Are you not happy to see me?"

Shaking my head because I was still floored, I replied, "Uh, happy? I can't say that. I'm happy you stopped hitting me up constantly though."

Dree was right about the fact that she could get Jodi to stop contacting me, because after she popped up on shorty, she hadn't said shit to me. Her being here was slightly alarming, but she lived in Memphis too, so it was nothing to run into her.

"Sorry about that, I was going a little crazy."

"What, you stop taking ya meds or some shit?" I frowned, feeling like her explanation wasn't enough in the slightest bit. Her behavior was outrageous.

Laughing, she said, "No. I really liked you, and I just thought if I kept at it, you would eventually give in. You know how y'all niggas do us women sometimes."

I nodded.

"Yeah, but you shouldn't have to do that. And as you can see, it doesn't help. I don't know too many niggas that got the woman of their dreams by sweating her constantly, unless she was already interested."

"Well, I thought you were. I mean we did..." she bucked her eyes, referring to our sexcapade.

"Can I get you something to drink or to snack on, ma'am?" the bartender approached.

"A Long Island Iced Tea and whatever burger he had."

The bartender nodded as he refilled my beer, and then placed it back in front of me before starting to make Jodi's drink.

"You sure you can eat what I had? That's a man's burger." I raised a brow with a smile. Shorty was looking good as fuck in that tight ass skirt and a top that had her stomach out. Her hair was pulled up, which I liked to see on women because it brought out their features more, versus when it was down.

"Negro, please. I may look small, but I can throw down with the best of them. You would have known that had you not tried to play me."

"Play you? I'm not that type. I ain't try to play you. I thought us smashing that one time was understood to be a *one*-time thing between the both of us."

"Well no, it wasn't. I wouldn't have given you my number if it was a one night stand, and you shouldn't have asked."

"You right." I nodded as I sipped my beer again. "I apologize for that."

"And for not telling me that you were dating Queen Bee, Dree." She rolled her eyes. "That's when I decided to give up. I cannot believe you're into the bougie uppity types."

I chortled for a little bit at her dig at Dree. I hated that bougie shit too, but a lot times, I found it to be sexy. Too many women didn't have enough pride or high enough standards, but not Dree Goode. Boosted a nigga's ego a little bit to have a woman like her on my arm because Dree wasn't gon' just fuck with anybody.

"I usually don't, but Dree ain't always like that. And in my defense, when I got with you in my car, she wasn't my girl."

"Sure," she smiled.

Jodi and I talked for the next hour and a half, and the next thing I knew, I was pulling into her driveway behind her, and coming into her house.

Taking my hand into hers, she led me to the back where her bedroom was, and pushed me down onto the bed. Straddling me, she began to unbuckle my jeans as I ran my hands up her skirt. Suddenly it hit me though that I needed to be somewhere with Dree, and not here in this shit with Jodi, so I gently moved her off of me and stood up.

"What?" her brows dipped.

"Jodi, we already did this shit and it didn't end well, so I'm not trying to do that shit again, ma. And you don't deserve it."

Her frown dissipated and she sat up, adjusting her skirt.

"Well, thanks for saying something this time." She half smiled. I leaned down to kiss her cheek, and then she followed me to the door to see me out.

I don't know what the fuck I was thinking just a minute ago. Shit. I had just gotten the bitch to stop hitting me up, and my dumb ass was about to smash again. I shook my head as I started towards Dree's parents' home. When I got there, I called her up to tell her to come open the door for me.

"What are you doing here?" she pushed the screen out so I could step in.

"I heard about ya pops and I wanted to come check on you, Dree."

"At this time of night?" she folded her arms and then scanned me. "You need to go back to whomever you were just with."

"I wasn't with nobody!" I lied.

"Then did you just pee in the grass outside or something? Because your pants are unbuckled, fool!" she tugged on my belt and then pushed me.

Fuck.

"Dree—"

"No, I need you to go. You didn't let me explain and I'm not gonna let you. So goodbye."

"Dree, I didn't —"

"Leave, before you wake up my father!" she hollered, eyes glazed over so I knew she was about to cry at any second.

"Dree—"

"Go!" she roared and shoved me hard as fuck again. I only budged a little because of the beers I'd had.

Not wanting to start any shit this late and with her pops here, I turned around and left. Just that quickly, I'd gone from the good guy to the bad one, but I wasn't gon' let Dree go and I'm sure once her ass calmed down, she'd feel the same.

32

RORI

I was finally off of work, and very excited about it because tomorrow, I didn't have class or work. I wanted to catch up on some homework, and relax with Eko without discussing my parents' drama for a change.

Ever since Jasper had gotten shot, it seemed to be all I could think about. People died every day in Memphis, but you don't really think too much on it until it hits close to home. The feeling I felt when I got that text from Jonaya was one I never wanted to feel again. I'd never prayed so hard in my damn life, but I was happy I did because the Lord definitely came through for me.

"Rori, can I speak with you for a moment?" Troy came into the lobby.

Scarlett's eyes were on him hard, but he paid her no mind. I was starting to think that she didn't even know him as well as she'd said. I never caught him looking her way, or smiling too hard at her, and he wasn't avoiding her either. I didn't know the hoe well, but I was starting to confirm my suspicions of her being a liar.

"Sure," I replied once I'd handed Parker my timecard.

Throwing my bag over my shoulder, I followed Troy to the back, where his office was and I saw his wife Tamara sitting in there.

"Hi again, Rori. So, honey, I'm gonna go file these and then I will be back, okay?" She looked to Troy who nodded before they shared a kiss.

Once she left, Troy smoothed his tie down and then gestured for me to have a seat as he sat behind his desk.

"So tonight, my team and I are gonna be in here doing a little extra work, and I was wondering if you wanted to help out? This wouldn't be a part of your internship, so I will compensate you, and there will be food, of course."

"Wow, yeah, I would like that." I was excited about spending my night with Eko, but I was sure he'd understand. This was for the betterment of my career. "What time should I come back?"

"We're gonna start around 7:30pm, so it'd be best to show up by that time or 7:45pm at the latest. We shouldn't be here long at all, so if you have other plans, don't worry."

"Great, well thank you for this, Troy." I rose to my feet. I still felt weird calling him Troy, but whatever.

He smiled and I passed his wife as she came walking back in. Leaving out, I pulled my phone from my purse since it'd been locked up in there all day. I usually kept my phone with me, but it was so busy today that I didn't want any distractions.

When I looked down at my iPhone screen, I saw I had a whole bunch of missed calls from a number that wasn't stored in my phone. Just as I was about to Google it, the number was calling me again.

"Hello?" I answered, lip turned up as I stepped off of the elevator.

"What are you doing, bitch?"

"Who the fuck is this?" I stopped in my tracks, so I was now standing in the lobby of the big ass building.

"Jenni."

"Jenni, we can get this shit over with now. You can meet me at

Eko's or send me your address, and I will whoop your ass because that's clearly what you want!" I ran off as I started back walking to the parking structure where my car was.

"Maybe I do, maybe I don't. But for now, I just like messing with your ass."

"Mess with me in person, Jenni, please."

"I don't like fighting so maybe another time. I may see you the next time you go to work, which is in a couple days. I know you don't work tomorrow, according to the schedule I have here."

"Schedule? Bitch, how long have you been watching me!"

"Long enough."

"Ugh!" I growled angrily as I got inside of my father's car. I wanted to mop the floor with this bitch, but from the sound of it, I wouldn't be able to get my hands on her for a long while. "I swear to God if I see you out, Jenni, it's over for you hoe."

"You just need to apologize, Rori, and all of this will end. How hard is it to say you're sorry for barging your way into my life and taking my man?"

"I didn't take shit from you, Jenni! Eko never wanted you! What don't you get! He and I had been friends for a minute, and we'd been unknowingly feeling each other the whole time! A man cannot be taken, aight! He wanted this pussy and I wanted to give it to him!"

"Ah!" she screamed and it sounded like she was stomping her feet. "Don't you ever talk to me like that again! Say you're sorry, Rori!"

"No!"

"Say it, got damnit!"

"No! And get off my fucking phone!" I hung up and blocked that number, which I had a feeling was a burner, but was hoping it was her real number.

I shook my head at the fact that this bitch really had me on the phone sounding like a damn toddler.

Once I'd finally gained some composure, I pulled out of my parking spot, and drove straight over to Eko's house. I'd texted him on the way and thankfully, he said he was there, but only for a little bit since he had to meet these people at the barbershop.

When I pulled up, he was in the driver's side of his car, blasting some rap song with his leg hanging out. The freshness of his all white Nike's damn near blinded me as I came up closer to him. When he saw me, a smile spread across his handsome face as he bobbed his head to the music.

Turning it down, he asked, "Why you frowning, sexy?"

"I will tell you once you let me inside the house. It's cold as fuck out here, Eko."

He turned the music back up loud as ever and started rapping along to irritate me, but when I punched his arm, he cut the music off while laughing hard as fuck.

"You're so uptight, ma," he chuckled, getting out.

"And you're so fucking ignorant! Open this damn door before I turn into an icicle, nigga!"

"I'll melt yo' sexy chocolate ass."

I rolled my eyes and tried to hide my smile as I brushed passed him to get into the house. He closed and locked the door, then plopped down onto the couch. I tried to keep standing, but he pulled me down into his lap and kissed me. That quickly I'd forgotten about Jenni, and was focused on how good of a kisser Eko was.

"Wait, Eko. You need to talk to Jenni. I want you to beat her ass or tie her up in a basement out in Nashville or something. Maybe burn her with a crack pipe like Rick James."

He laughed and frowned before asking, "Jenni? Fuck you bringing Jenni up for?"

"Because she came to my job and made a scene! She made my supervisor and the potential mayor think I was in a lesbian relationship with her, begging me to forgive her, and get back together! Then she called me—"

Eko burst into laughter, tossing his head back. As fine as he was when he smiled, I wanted to slap the shit out of him.

"Aight, that's not funny. This shit happened today?"

"No some weeks ago, but today, she called me forty damn times, and the forty-first time, I answered and we got into it. I'm tired of her Eko, and if I can't beat her ass, then I need you to handle it."

"Why you can't beat her ass?"

"Because she said she doesn't like fighting and won't come around me anymore. However, she's going to continue to fuck with me from afar." I squinted my eyes and glared into Eko's face because I could see a hint of laughter threatening to burst through. "Why are you laughing!" I whined when he started to crack up.

"Because you looking at a nigga all suspiciously. But I got you, ma, I'm gon' handle her ass. I ain't know she was crazy like that."

"It's because I told her to make a spare key to your house and to sneak in and cook for you half naked," I admitted somberly. Eko's laughter in response caught me off guard though.

"I swear that sweet shit is just a role for you. Yo' ass is sneaky as fuck, shorty, but that kind of makes my dick hard." He kissed my shoulder, and then stood up to carry me to his bedroom.

"Eko, no," I giggled as he laid me down and started to unbuckle my jeans. "I thought you had to be somewhere?"

He said nothing as he yanked my pants down my thighs along with my panties. Pulling me to the edge of the bed, he buried his face between my hips and began feasting on my pussy. Enjoying the feeling way too much, I laid back and let him go to work.

～

LATER THAT EVENING...

I'd made it back downtown where my job was and hoped like hell tonight moved fast like Troy had promised. I loved being in this environment, but I wanted to get back to Eko.

I didn't even ask how much Troy would pay me, and I guess it didn't matter, because money was money in this case. I was just happy to be getting compensated for doing something that I loved.

When I made it up to the suite we worked out of, no one was in the lobby just yet. That was expected since it was around 7:29pm. I wanted to be prompt, and I felt like if I came on time, I could leave a little earlier.

"Oh, Rori, you're here," Troy came in and startled me a little since I was getting some of the cheese and crackers.

"Yeah, hey. I'm not used to it being so quiet up here. It's always some conversation going on, a printer shooting out millions of copies, or phones ringing," I laughed and so did he.

"Yeah, exactly why I like to come in and work a little bit in the evenings. Being around all that noise can sometimes distract me."

"I bet." I sat down with my plate and put my purse on the low coffee table in front of the couch I was on. "So what all am I gonna be doing tonight?"

"Well," he sat down next to me. "Mainly, we're gonna be discussing my image and how I want to be portrayed this time. My main thing is that I want to feel closer to everyone, because I think the distance is what made me lose last time. I really need to appeal to the younger kids, you know? Like people your age."

"Right, yeah, I understand. A lot of my peers don't really care about voting, especially with something like the mayor. Oh! No I didn't mean it like that, but it's just you can't expect much from people who barely even show up to the polls to vote for President."

"No, I know what you meant," he smiled. "Wow, Jasper sure does have a beautiful daughter on his hands. I don't know if I can deal with it when my daughters grow up."

"I'm sure they'll be focused, so you won't need to worry."

Placing his hand on my leg, he said, "Rori, you know you have a lot of potential, right?" he began to brush his thumb slowly across my knee as he stared deeply into my eyes.

"Uh, wh—where is everyone else?" I looked over my shoulder at the door as if people would magically appear or start walking through it.

Turning me to face him by my chin, he said, "I think we could help each other out a lot, Rori; you with my campaign and me with your political career. I can take you under my wing."

I didn't say anything, so he pressed his lips against mine, causing me to gasp lowly.

"Mr. Garrick." I shot up from my seat, as he stared up at me with a confused expression. "I don't.... I have a boyfriend and you have a wife. Not to mention, I don't want this."

"I— I'm sorry, Rori, I guess I got the wrong impression from you. I thought we—"

"Yeah, I think I'm gonna pass on tonight, but thank you for the offer." I snatched my shit up quickly.

"Wait, I still want you to take your payment!" he called after me.

"No! No, it's okay!" I hollered back, slipping out of the door and racing to the elevator as if he were chasing me. "Ughck!" I wiped my mouth.

Inside the elevator, my heart damn near beat out of my chest at the thought of what had just happened. I had so much hope for that man, and hope for the fact that Scarlett was lying. He was disgusting, and I'm sure he only offered these internships to prey on young college girls. Suddenly, I felt bad as hell for Scarlett.

When I got to my stepdad's car, I drove it right back to Eko's place. I used my key to get in, but since I felt nasty, I got into the shower instead of climbing right into the bed to cuddle. When I came into Eko's bedroom wearing a towel, he sat up and paused the television show or movie that he was watching.

"Fuck you going straight to the shower for, Rori?" his brows dipped.

"I just felt dirty from the day. Can I have a shirt?"

He got up to get me one, then said, "You need to leave some shit here, ma. Fucking up all my good shit because you like to come over here bum style."

"Fuck off, Eko." I chuckled as I slipped it over my head. "Eko, that Scarlett girl was right."

He was still smiling from our interaction before, but it quickly faded.

"He touched you?"

"No, baby, he... well he kissed me but I stopped it— Eko! No!" I grabbed his arm when he snatched his keys off the dresser. His feet were already in his Nike slides that fast. "Not until I get my credit, please."

"So what you just gon' keep working for his ass?"

"It's only two months left before I graduate, and I won't do any side work. He doesn't try anything during the day when we work. I promise when I finish, you can say or do whatever, but don't ruin this for me, baby, please."

I knew what I was asking was a lot, but I was almost at the finish line. And it wasn't like Troy was gonna be harassing me at work or anything, so I needed Eko to chill until further notice.

"Aight, but as soon as you get that fucking credit, I'm coming for that nigga's head." He slammed his keys onto the dresser and kicked his slides off.

Thank you, God!

"Thank you," I replied, climbing into the bed where he was now, and laying my head on him.

He was tense at first, but over time, he loosened up and calmed down as we watched TV. He got even calmer when I gave him some head though.

33

———————

NUSEF

"How do you feel about tonight?" Jonaya asked me as she sat down on my bed.

Tonight, my biological parents were meeting my other parents and I didn't know how the shit was gonna go. My pops, Count, got out a couple days ago, and Dana hadn't been staying with me since. Only time she'd show up was when her parole officer was coming.

I didn't know where my dad was staying or why that nigga hadn't stopped by. It'd been sixteen fucking years since he's seen Waayil and me, and the nigga didn't have any interest in coming through? It was shit like that, that made me thankful for being raised by Freya and Theo.

"I don't even know if them niggas are gon' show up."

"I hope so. I was scared to come, but I'm happy to know Kay will be there with me in case some drama pops off." Jonaya cheesed.

"Drama? What kind of drama could pop off between my peoples?"

"I don't know, Sef, but Dana is a little feisty. Freya, on the other hand, is pretty calm and nice, but if you tick her off..."

"I know. But shit, I'm praying that everything goes smoothly as fuck because I don't have time for that bullshit. I'm not in the mood to be breaking up brawls and shit."

Jonaya chuckled as she checked herself out in the mirror. Once I pocketed my phone and keys, we were both out the door and on our way to my parents' crib. Upon arriving, I didn't see Waayil's car yet, so I shot his ass a text to make sure he didn't flake. No way was I about to attend this shit alone, and I'm sure Jonaya wanted Yikayla there for company as well. When Waayil let me know he was en route, Jonaya and I got out of the car and went inside.

"Hey, I'm glad you guys dressed up because I had a feeling I might be doing too much," my mother smiled as she hugged both Jonaya and me. "Come to the dining room, that's where everything is."

We followed my mom to the dining room, but before we even got there, I heard Waayil coming in. I also heard Yikayla's ass giggling, which made Jonaya smile at the fact that her sister was here. I pulled Jonaya's chair out so she could sit, and by that time, my brother and Yikayla were entering the dining room and hugging my mother.

"What's good, mane? You ready?" I grinned as I dapped Waayil up. He just exhaled and shook his head before pulling a chair out for Yikayla. After I leaned down to hug and kiss her, I took my seat as well.

"I hope Dana is on her best behavior tonight, Waayil, because you know she doesn't like me." Yikayla bucked her eyes.

"You either? I swear she doesn't like me, but Nusef says different. Some days, she's nice though, so it makes me wonder." Jonaya frowned.

"Well, I only got the pleasure of meeting her once and it was a mess," Yikayla replied.

"Alright, these are some breadsticks if you guys want to snack on something. Your father will be coming down at any moment, as well as Wednesday and..." my mom looked down at her watch. "Emil should be home soon as well. I told him about tonight and he said he'd come."

I shook my head at the thought of Emil. I'd given up on his ass. If he didn't wanna associate with me then that was aight. Of course, Waayil's bullheaded ass wasn't having it, and stayed trying to be close again with that nigga, but I was done. I had enough shit on my plate.

"Hey, everybody," my pops walked in and kissed my mother before greeting everyone. Just then, the doorbell rang, and everyone fell quiet as if it were doomsday or some shit. Because of everybody's reaction, we all tittered lightly.

"I will get that. Honey, go get Wednesday and have her help you bring some of the dishes out from the kitchen, please," my mom spoke to my dad before leaving the den to get the door.

Waayil and I made eye contact, and a few moments later, we heard my mom greeting our biological parents before closing the door. As their footsteps got closer to the dining room, I touched Jonaya's leg to stop it from bouncing so wildly.

"Well hello, everyone!" my biological mother, Dana, greeted the room as she walked in.

She looked nice as hell in a red dress that looked like it cost way too damn much. It reminded me to check my credit card statement.

My mother slipped in behind her, and for a moment, I thought my biological dad, Count, had flaked until he appeared with a boredom filled expression. Nigga was still tall as hell and dark as the midnight sky, with those piercing ass eyes he'd passed down to us. Suddenly, the memories of when I was a kid and scared as hell of him flowed through my mind. He was a good father, though from what I could remember.

We all replied to Dana simultaneously as everyone sat down. Soon, Wednesday appeared and sat down as well. I glanced at Waayil, and I knew we were thinking the same thing. How could this nigga not even say shit?

"Count." Waayil nodded to our biological father.

"Waayil," he replied dryly. He looked my way briefly, but then, turned his attention back to the cellphone he was typing on.

"So umm, how does it feel to be home?" my mom smiled.

"It feels a lot better than being locked up, I tell you that. I haven't known how to act really, but I think I'm calming down," Dana responded.

"Good. Well I know the boys are happy to have you back home, and I'm sure you're happy to be here, so you can see them," my father added.

"Yeah, too bad we haven't seen them for eleven years," Count scoffed and shook his head.

"Yeah, that is unfortunate, but they are still fairly young, so you have a lot of time to still spend with them," my mother said.

"Okay, everybody, it looks like Emil is running late, so why don't we go ahead and say grace then we can eat," my dad announced.

Everyone around the table held hands, but I noticed Dana refused to hold my mother's hand. Shaking my head, I dropped it and closed my eyes as my pops said a prayer over the food. As soon as 'Amen' left our lips, we began passing dishes around and filling our plates up.

Once the passing of dishes slowed down, Dana said, "I don't mean to dwell on things, but why haven't we seen our children for eleven years?" She was wearing that fake ass smile that she constantly wore these days.

"Because you were in jail," my mom replied, sipping her wine.

"No, I was in jail for sixteen and you brought them to see us from the time they were eight until they were about thirteen years old. After that, it just stopped."

"Well, Dana, as I explained the last day that they were there, I didn't want the boys coming anymore, because they were getting older and they didn't need to be in that environment so much."

"How can you say what our children needed?" Count barked.

"Aye chill out, my nigga, don't be raising ya voice at my mama," Waayil interjected, staring at Count hard.

"They raised you to be soft I see, Waayil," Count snickered.

"Ain't nobody soft, nigga, it's about respect. And ain't nobody about to disrespect my moms, I don't give a fuck who it is," Waayil hissed. His voice wasn't raised but I knew he was heated.

"Okay, settle down," my father said, as Yikayla massaged Waayil's shoulders. My dad then looked Count's way and added, "Technically, at that time, Count, Waayil and Nusef were ours and we had the right to decide what was best for them. We let them see you in prison as a courtesy, it was not something we had to do, nor was it something that you had the right to get."

"I just think you did it on purpose to create a distance. Look at them calling you two mom and dad, but calling us by our first names," Dana scoffed.

"Well, I am their mother, and Theo is their father, Dana. You raised them for eight years and I'm sure they appreciate that. I raised them for a decade plus, so I do expect to be acknowledged as a mother figure," my mom said, eating her food.

"You said them seeing us in prison was a bad influence, yet my son still ended up in jail. How is that?"

"Okay, can we change the subject? This is supposed to be a nice dinner, not whatever the fuck is happening right now," I interrupted. It was too late though; my mom was already heated. You could see her pretty brown skin turning red in the undertones as she glared at Dana.

"It happened because sometimes bad things happen in life, that is all, Dana," my mom responded through clenched teeth.

"And how did he get caught? You called the police on my son? You wanted him to go to jail!" Count yelled.

"No, I called the ambulance for my brother and Waayil told the truth when they came and asked what happened! Don't you ever insinuate that I want something bad to happen to him! He is *my* child and I would never!"

"Oh my gosh!" Wednesday yelled when all hell broke loose.

My mother calling Waayil her child set Dana off, so before I could even process everything, Dana's hands were around my mother's neck. It was complete chaos as the women fell back in their chairs and onto the floor, tussling and rolling the fuck around. Waayil and I hopped up to pull them apart, because when my dad tried, Count got in his face and now them niggas were at each other's throats.

"Aight, y'all chill! Fuck!" Waayil yelled as he pulled Dana from my mother. I could not believe this shit right now.

"Get off me! Count, let's go!" Dana snatched from Waayil and grabbed her fur from the floor before storming out.

"Oh my goodness," Yikayla mumbled as she and Jonaya continued to stuff their faces while watching like this was some reality TV show.

I went to follow Dana and Count to the door, but before I could catch up, they'd rushed out. Emil walked in, and kind of looked at them, before closing the door behind himself. When he looked to me, I saw it appeared like he'd been crying and I couldn't help but to ask what was wrong.

"You aight, man?" I quizzed as he started towards me.

As he was passing me, he replied, "Mooney got shot and his family won't even let me in the room to see him."

"Shot? When?"

"Today, this morning," he sniffled. "I'm sorry about the dinner, I know it was important and ..."

"Nah, it's cool, E."

"What happened, bro?" Waayil came into the foyer where we were.

"Mooney got shot and his people won't let Emil see him or anything. Shit just happened today." As I explained, Emil started to cry and Waayil's thugged out ass pulled him in for a hug. This nigga was the definition of a Gemini because he was for real two people.

We stood there, and once Emil got himself together, Waayil let him go so he could head upstairs to his room. We took a moment before going back to the dining room, and everybody was eating and talking like nothing had happened.

"Mama, I'm sorry for all that, I swear I didn't think things would pop off," I said as Waayil and I sat back down at the table.

"No, honey, it's fine. Now that I look back, it was actually kind of funny," she replied smiling.

"I would have jumped in, Freya, but you had her," Yikayla joked, making everyone laugh.

Finally, the dinner had turned to something nice, and sadly to say, I was happy them muthafuckas had left.

~

The Next Evening...

I was closing down everything in the shop along with Waayil, when someone started knocking on the door. I looked to see it was Alba's ass, and pointed to the lit-up sign that read *Closed*. She had some shit in her nose, similar to a cast, and I remembered Waayil told me that Yikayla had cracked her shit.

I laughed when Alba yelled, "Nigga, open up this door!" and slammed her hand on it.

Putting the money up, I walked around the counter and unlocked it to let her crazy ass in.

"Fuck you want, ma?"

"It's cold as fuck out there, asshole!"

"Ain't my fault you hoes still wanna dress for the job, when it's cold ass polar bear pussy outside."

"Nigga, who the fuck are you calling a hoe? Ain't that the pot calling the kettle black? At least, I don't like ugly people."

What the fuck was up with everyone claiming I only fucked with ugly bitches? Shit was starting to fuck with a nigga's ego a little bit.

"Fuck you. Waayil is in the back. And if I hear you screaming for help, I won't come."

"I'm not here for him. I came to tell you something, but you have to promise to leave me out of it."

"What?" I frowned, interest piqued like a muthafucka. I couldn't think of shit that Alba and I had or dealt with in common, so what could she possibly have to tell a nigga?

"I know who shot you. It was Sax."

Bucking my eyes a little, I repeated, "Sax. How... how the fuck do you know this, Alba?"

"I know because he told me right out of his own mouth. I wasn't gonna say anything because I didn't want to be a part of it, but it was weighing heavily on my conscience. Not to mention, he came by my house this evening and said he was leaving town tomorrow morning and you need to catch him beforehand."

"I didn't know you had a conscience, shorty." I grinned. I was trying to stay calm, even though I was heated as fuck.

"You know what, fuck you, Sef."

"I'm joking, but thank you for telling me." I pulled her into a hug. She kept her arms folded during the hug to create distance, which made me chuckle.

"Fuck is going on here?" Waayil came into the lobby.

"Nothing. Get off me before you start making me see ugly people as fine too!" Alba shoved me off. "Bye, niggas." She stormed towards the door.

"Wait, where is Sax? At home now?" I called after her.

"Yeah, he should be packing still." She continued out.

I nodded and then turned to Waayil to say, "Sax is the one who shot me." An evil smirk spread across his face but I immediately cut that shit off and added, "You can't come. You're on probation, Yil."

"What? Nah, I have to! Now that I think about it, I'm sure Sax was the reason Alba knew shit about Yikayla's and my relationship, with his snake ass. Caught him at Alba's crib on suspicious shit. Plus, you don't even know that much about guns like I do, Sef! Fuck kind of brother would I be if I let you go in that muthafucka alone? You probably don't even have a gun." He frowned.

"Man." I waved him off.

"Do you?" He raised a brow.

It was silent so he bucked his eyes, awaiting my answer.

"I mean, no, but I was hoping to borrow yours," I said and he burst into laughter. "Aye, man, fuck you, aight?"

"Just like I thought, so I'm coming along." He laughed. "Stupid ass nigga. About to roll up on Sax with an empty clip probably."

I glared at the back of his head as he made his way to the back of the shop, ragging on me and laughing.

About twenty minutes later the shop was closed and Waayil took me to about four different spots, to meet with about seven different niggas. We had to drop our whips off at home, and hitch a ride with some sketchy ass nigga Waayil knew. Nigga had the nerve to offer me some weed. I wasn't smoking shit he smoked with the way his ass looked. Nigga looked like the human form of syphilis with a sprinkle of herpes. Then that nigga dropped us off in an area that looked like they lynched, skinned, and cooked Black folks all day, just for us to get some beat up ass whip with Florida plates.

"All that just to get a damn car?" I frowned as Waayil pulled onto the road. The criminal life was not for me. How in the fuck did niggas do this shit *all* day long?

"Yeah, nigga. See, I'm glad I came. You would have driven to him in yo' shit." Waayil shook his head as he handed me a pair of gloves and a black hoodie.

We parked a little ways down from Sax's house, and then walked up the street calmly. He had music blasting inside, and his wooden door was open while his screen stayed closed like always. I'd told that nigga how dangerous it was to be leaving only his screen door closed but unlocked. However, right now, I was happy.

I admit, I froze up as we started up his porch steps. I was used to just breaking my foot off in niggas asses, not killing them. But this nigga tried to shoot my girl, and ended up hitting me, so he had to go.

"Nigga, come on!" Waayil whispered harshly, when he realized I hadn't walked up the steps yet. "You wanna get this nigga yaself or let me do it?"

"I want to!" I yelled in a hushed tone.

"Aight, then bring yo' ass!"

I sucked my teeth but then hit the four small steps. Waayil nodded to the music as if he wasn't about to witness me kill a nigga, as he tightened the silencer on his gun. He entered the house with me right behind him, and there were two open suitcases sitting on the floor of the living room.

Sax came in singing along to the music, but when he saw us he turned to run. Where to, I don't know because the backyard door was to the right of us in the kitchen.

PHEW!

Waayil let one off into Sax's leg and he collapsed down. He then dragged a groaning Sax to the middle of the floor, and turned him over. He nodded down to him while looking at me, then stepped to the side.

I was prepared to shoot him, but before I did, I had to ask him a question.

"Please, Sef, come on," Sax cried, holding his leg which was bleeding profusely.

"Hurry the fuck up, Sef," Waayil hissed.

"Why did you have the gun aimed at my girl?" I inquired.

"I was just doing it for Rebecca. I thought I loved her and she hated Jonaya, so I wanted to get rid of her for her.... Bu—but it was all Rebecca's idea!"

I knew the last part was a lie, because he took too long to say it. Not to mention, he gave it away when he bucked his eyes as if he'd gotten an idea to lie, just before blurting that bullshit out. This nigga was dumb as fuck.

PHEW!

I let out one shot that hit Sax's chin, causing him to howl and me to jump back. Waayil started to crack up laughing, so I sent another one out. That bullet scraped the top of his head, causing him to scream even louder.

"Good Lord, muthafucka," Waayil chuckled before letting off two shots into Sax's head that killed him.

We hurriedly left out, since Sax had been screaming loudly as hell prior to his head shots, and once in the car, Waayil sped off while calling for cleanup.

"And you wanted to come alone." He glanced at me once he hung up, and started cheesing as he stared back at the road.

"Aye, at least my shots hit him." I watched him disassemble the burner phone and toss it out the window at a red light.

"Yeah. But this street shit ain't for you, bruh."

"And I like it that way." I nodded as we both chuckled. I now understood why hit men charged so damn much.

34

DREE

The station I reported the rape to called me back down so they could talk with me for a little bit. I was slightly on edge wondering what they had to say, and this time, I didn't have Canyon with me.

Back at school, a few people had found out that I'd reported that Sean had raped me, but no one said anything. I could tell by the few looks I got from people that they knew though. It made me feel uncomfortable not because they knew necessarily, but because it made me appear weak, which was the one thing I'd strived all my life not to be.

"Sorry about that wait, Miss Goode, I'm Detective Asher," a female detective came in. I think Canyon scared that Ted guy off because since then, I hadn't seen him. However, I was hoping with this one being a woman, she'd be nicer.

"No problem. Did you guys need something from me? I'm not quite sure what's going on with my report."

"Well ye,s we got the report, and we talked to the accused, but I have a few questions for you." She scooted her chair up closer to the table and opened her notepad. "Now according to my colleague's notes, you said you woke up in Mr. Ike's bed naked, but then, you got dressed and went home?" She read off her notepad, and then looked up from it to hear my answer.

"Yes, that's right."

"What about the next day?"

"Well, I... I think it was a weekend, so I just did some studying and that was it. I don't really remember what I did the next day. Uh, why?"

"Miss Goode, did you ever go to a doctor or a hospital to have them look at you? Or did you just go on with your life?"

"I guess, I just went on with my life, but that was because I was confused."

"Confused?"

"Yes, I didn't know if what he did was in fact rape, so I kept it to myself. And I was embarrassed about it as well."

Frowning, she placed her pen down and clasped her hands together, before saying, "So how is it that now you feel like it's a rape for sure? Or are you still confused?"

"Okay," I exhaled. "Let me rephrase that. I was never confused. I knew something was wrong because when I woke up, I felt groggy like I'd been drugged or like I'd drank too much when I hadn't. And I could feel that I'd engaged in sexual activity, but I kept telling myself I didn't know if it was rape to make myself feel better. I did not want to be seen as some rape victim, can't you understand that?"

"I can, Miss Goode. But what you have to understand is there is a time limit on rapes, honey. I mean, we need evidence to even help you, which you have none of, since you were *confused*. You didn't get a rape kit, you continued to interact with the man you're accusing of rape—"

"No, no I did not. I stopped the relationship I had with him."

"Well, according to him, you showed up at his home telling him about a baby you were pregnant with. And that baby is no longer, so we don't even have proof that the two of you even slept together.

According to him, all he did was perform oral sex on you, which you ran out in the middle of."

"First of all, I didn't show up at his home, I saw him at school and told him about the baby. But I only said something so he'd know. It wasn't like I was trying to be with him! I had someone I was interested in already, which is why I didn't want to sleep with him in the first place! I ran out during the oral sex, which was ages ago by the way, because I wasn't *there* with Sean yet! That's why he drugged me because time and time again, I'd been resistant to his advances for sex!"

"Really?" she raised her brows. "Miss Goode, to the court this will sound like a drunk, college girl who accidentally slept with a man she didn't want to sleep with, because she had a boyfriend already. And in order to keep your boyfriend or someone you're interested in from leaving you, you want to cry rape."

"That is not—"

"I'm not saying that's what happened, honey, but that is exactly what it sounds like and that is what they will play on. Your case is weak, and all you're going to do is put yourself out there to look like a reckless liar. Is that what you want, Miss Goode?"

I was quiet for a moment.

"No," I whispered. "But I don't want him to get away with it. And he's harassing me at school."

"Well, you should have thought about that when you were too *embarrassed* to say anything. Now, we have nothing to support your case, so unfortunately, you would come out on the losing end. I say to put this behind you. You're a smart girl, in law school, and like you said, you have someone who you have interest in. Just forget about this, and if he harasses you again, record it or something. But other than that, we have nothing to help you."

Wiping the lone tear that had traveled down my cheek, I got up from my chair and left without another word. That bitch actually tried to hug me but I dissed her ass as I left out of the room.

Class was done for the day, and since I didn't have Canyon anymore, I went straight home.

When I got in my bedroom, I lied down on my stomach and just buried my face into the pillow. No one was home but my parents, so I cried as hard as I wanted to.

I was so deep into my sobbing, that I didn't notice my stepfather had come in, until I felt the other side of my bed sink a little.

"Oh, I'm sorry did I bother you, I—" I shot my head up from the pillow.

"What's wrong, baby?" he frowned. He looked different out of a suit. Instead, he was wearing joggers, a wife beater, and a plaid robe with some socks on.

"Oh, I umm, I got a bad grade on a quiz and—"

"Dree, I have never heard you cry that hard, and I've been in your life since you were seven years old. Even the time I didn't get you a happy meal because you only played with the toy and didn't eat the food, you didn't cry this hard and you cried pretty hard that day," he smiled which made me chuckle. "So tell me."

Feeling helpless, I decided to just tell him what happened. I explained everything about Sean, from the day I met him and how much time we'd spent together. As cringy as it was, I even told him how I didn't want to sleep with him and after denying and denying, I woke up in his bed naked.

"And now everyone I talk to is acting like I'm just some woman scorned, trying to bring harm to this wonderful do-gooder. He has too many people on his side, at least his parents do."

"Firstly, Dree, I want you to know that you're not weak or a victim just because some knucklehead took advantage of you, baby. A man that needs to rape a woman is weak, and you remember that. That boy is lucky I'm shot up and have a reputation to protect, because I'd snap his neck if I didn't. Secondly, Sean's parents are not the only well-connected people around here."

I nodded with a smile, and whispered, "True."

"Now, who gave you a hard time?" His brows were furrowed.

"The Dean at school, and then two other detectives down at the police station. They all made me feel bad for what I was doing, or like it was too late to say anything."

Standing up, my stepfather said, "Write down their names for me."

"No, don't go down there to say anything, Daddy. Canyon did enough of that, and I don't want any more trouble."

"Just write down the names, baby. I don't do anything; I have people that will do it for me. And where is Canyon? I haven't seen him in a while."

"Canyon and I are broken up. It was never meant, I'm starting to see."

"Usually, I would agree because I don't like the thought of any of you dating, or being in relationships, or doing anything that says you're growing up, but I like him. He's a good guy, and for some reason, he loves everything about you." He snickered and so did I.

Smiling, I replied, "I will write down the names for you."

I didn't want to talk about Canyon. I couldn't get his loosened belt out of my mind for anything.

I jotted down the names on a Post-It for my father and then handed it over to him. Once he left, I grabbed my iPhone and unblocked Canyon's number. About five minutes later, a text came through from him.

Canyon: *Dree.*

It wasn't much, but it made me smile. I knew he'd been blowing me up because, whenever I didn't answer, he'd always just text my name or call.

Me: *What?*

Canyon: *I didn't sleep with anybody. I was about to, but I couldn't.*

Me: *So where are you?*

Canyon: *Outside.*

My eyebrows dipped as I got up and slipped my feet into my Nike slides, before running out of my room, down the stairs, and out the door. I saw him getting out of his car, looking so fresh and handsome in a simple sweater, jeans, and tennis shoes. He came up the driveway, then the steps, and up to the door, to tower over me with his hands in his pockets.

"Can we stop breaking up?" he cheesed as he leaned in the doorway.

"I don't know. Where is my make up gift?"

"Gift?"

"Yes. A ring or bracelet that says you're sorry. I know you got me one, right?" I folded my arms.

"Well, I didn't do shit. But your gift is at the same store my gift is at, that you were supposed to get me for lying about Neil."

"I didn't lie, I just didn't tell you. I don't even know why I did what I did with him."

"Because Luna was having my baby."

I shrugged. "Yeah."

"So you gon' let me in or are you trying to pull some Titanic shit and let a nigga freeze while you stay warm?"

"Sorry," I laughed as I stepped back.

As soon as the door closed, we started to kiss heavily, so I stopped and led him to the downstairs bathroom. As soon as we got in, he bent me over the sink, lifted my skirt, and pushed my panties to the side. I was slippery wet as I felt the head of his dick knocking at my opening. I gripped the sink as he pushed his way inside of me, while sucking on my neck.

"Damn, baby," he mumbled as he started to pound into me feverishly.

It was cold, but our bodies began to warm up as he slipped in and out of me, while my pussy hugged his dick. Pushing my leg forward some, he dug deeper inside of me before pumping me harder and faster. My hands were starting to hurt from grasping the sink edges so tightly as he beat my pussy up from behind.

"Ahhh," I sniveled as I released on him.

He slowed up to get a view of my juices on his thick rod, before picking his pace back up and pounding me so hard that I had my forehead against the medicine cabinet. Soon enough, he'd exploded and so did I. It was then that I realized we didn't use a condom.

"We forgot," I panted, feeling too weak and tired to move.

"Forgot what?" he inquired.

"A condom!"

"Nah *you* forgot, I wanted to hit raw." He laughed and I slapped his arm before cleaning myself up. He did the same, and after we washed our hands, we kissed a little bit before exiting the bathroom.

The next night...

Canyon and I were attached at the hip again, and for a moment, I'd forgotten about how sad I was yesterday, dealing with the Sean thing.

Currently, we were in the den watching a movie, and eating some snacks. It was crazy how I used to only enjoy VIP in the clubs, or going to nice expensive dinners. But with Canyon, I was seeing there was a lot more to relationships than having money or getting nice things. I was thanking God that He didn't let me miss out on a man like Canyon, because I would have been sick.

"Why the hell do white people always say their piece, then run out the room when they get mad? No way my mama would have went for that shit when she was alive. She would have snatched my ass up before I even hit the corner." Canyon frowned at the movie as he shoved popcorn into his mouth. He looked my way and asked, "Did you hear me?"

"Yes, I heard you, crazy, and I don't know. I guess it's just for dramatic effect," I chuckled. "They want the person to know how mad they are."

"Hey, Dree, can I talk to you?" my dad walked in. "Hey, Canyon."

"How you doing, Mr. Vaughn?"

"No, it's fine. You can say what you have to say in front of Canyon," I replied.

"Well, I made some calls yesterday and a lot this morning. I was able to get the authorities to search Sean's parents' home, and collect the security footage."

"Security footage?" I sat up since I was lying on Canyon's shoulder.

"Yes, apparently they have cameras in the house because they have a lot of hired help and they want to, of course, keep track of them." Jasper paused and sighed. "They were able to get the video footage of you being there that night, which was a close call because it was two days away from being automatically deleted from the vault, since the recorder only holds so much."

"What did they see?" Canyon inquired.

"They saw him slip something in your drink, Dree, they saw you pass out on the couch, and then him carrying you out and up to his bedroom. The also saw what happened in the bedroom, and we all pretty much know what that is."

Hearing this made me feel good in a sense because now I knew for sure that I was right. A tiny part of me still felt like maybe I'd told Sean in a drunken state that he could sleep with me, but now it was proven that I was knocked the fuck out. On the flip side though, I felt furious towards him that he would actually do that to me.

"So what now?" I asked.

"Now you have a stronger case, and now the ball is rolling."

"Oh my gosh thank you, Daddy!" I jumped up and hugged Jasper, who chuckled before kissing my forehead.

"Of course. That's what I'm here for." He kissed my head again, and then turned around to leave the room.

"So you call him daddy too?" Canyon furrowed his brows when I sat down next to him.

"Shut up! You know you're my real daddy." I winked.

"You better stop before I have to take you in that bathroom like I did yesterday." He squeezed my thigh while biting on his lip.

"Maybe I want you to."

I had never seen that nigga move so fast, but it was like within seconds, he was carrying me down the narrow hallway and into the bathroom.

35

———————

WAAYIL

Tonight Nusef, Eko, and I were out at this club to see one of my homies who was performing. There was a whole lineup tonight, but I was only here to see the homie, Donte, sing. Nigga was trying to get me a slot, but I shut that shit down with the quickness. I had no interest in attracting attention for my singing. I loved to draw and that was it. I only sang for my girl these days, and maybe at a couple family functions… nothing else.

"I feel like I can't even vote for that nigga no more," Nusef scoffed.

Currently, Eko was telling us how this nigga named Troy Garrick tried to push up on Rori. I'd never heard of his ass, but Nusef and Eko had since he'd ran for mayor four years ago and lost. I was locked up at the time with other shit on my mind.

"That's what the fuck I said. And Rori wouldn't let me beat the nigga's ass," Eko chuckled angrily.

"Just get at that nigga once she finishes the internship and shit you know?" I replied, bobbing my head to the music. "But don't tell him who you are or what you're doing it for. Gotta protect Rori's rep."

Eko nodded in agreement.

As I scanned the area, I noticed a girl and her friends watching me. We made eye contact, and she waved. I simply gave her a nod, before looking the other way. I'd just gotten rid of all my woman problems, and I didn't need anymore.

Shit, I thought I was gon' have to murk Zia, but when her ass found out her father got murdered, she left town. I think she'd been living down in Atlanta until I was released, so she was happy as hell to go back now that her pops no longer held the reins on her life.

"Hey, are y'all here alone?" The girl approached the table with her three friends.

"Why? You gon' buy me a drink?" Eko quizzed with his ignorant ass.

Laughing she inquired, "Why can't you buy me a drink? Or you?" She looked down to me.

"I don't have any money," I replied with a serious face. It was quiet, before Nusef and Eko started cracking up.

"Huh?" she frowned.

"I'm broke. I don't have any money for you to get a drink. If I slide my card, it's going to decline, ma. It's only lint in my pockets and nothing else," I elaborated further for her slow ass.

"Oh damn." Her homegirl sucked her teeth and walked over to Nusef.

"Damn, so why are you in the club when you ain't got no money?" She turned her lip up as Eko waved her other homegirl off.

I sipped my drink and then set it down. "Because I'm looking for a bitch to take care of me. Is that you?" I inquired as Nusef and Eko chortled loudly as fuck.

"You know what," she mumbled as she turned around and walked off.

"Nigga, you had a straight face the whole damn time," Eko chuckled.

"Shit, I was serious. I mean a nigga is far from broke, but if I'm gon' cheat on my girl, it better be for a bitch that's ready to pay some bills and put down payments on whips. Otherwise, fuck I need her for? I got good pussy, head, and conversation for me back at home."

I wasn't like the rest of these niggas; fucking up a happy home just for a piece of pussy. And 90% of the time, the pussy you cheated with was never as good as what you already had.

"This nigga is crazy. How the fuck are we twins?" Nusef laughed along with Eko.

I noticed when we were done conversing, that Roscoe was up on stage. He'd finished his weak ass set, and was walking off. Shit had to be weak if I didn't even notice his ass was up there. I watched him walk down, slapping hands with a few niggas, and decided I was gon' beat his ass. Nigga had been asking for it, and he'd hurt my girl too many times not to finally get the business.

"Be right back," I said, standing up and polishing off my drink.

I walked over to where Roscoe was, and when he spotted me, he shook his head and sighed heavily.

"You follow me here?" he asked, scowling hard for his homies standing by him. I heard footsteps behind me, and when I glanced over my shoulder, I saw Nusef and Eko walking up.

WHAM!

"Ah!" Roscoe screamed like a bitch after I slapped the shit out of him.

"Don't you ever ask me some shit like that again. Fuck I look like following yo' bitch ass anywhere, bruh?" I hissed, offended that he even thought I would follow him anywhere. I wouldn't follow that muthafucka to the promise land, let alone to a damn club.

Realizing he was looking like a bitch by clutching his cheek, he dropped his hand and charged me. I waited, giving him time because I knew this fight would be like taking candy from a baby. When he got ready to swing, I decked his ass right between the eyes, and the way he stumbled back had him looking like Ricky Ricardo doing the salsa. Again, I waited until he gained some composure, and when he came at me again, he actually landed a punch.

"Aww shit," I heard Nusef say as I slowly turned my face back towards Roscoe, tapping my lip for blood.

Chuckling, I nodded and said, "Finally, muthafucka."

WHAM! WHAM!

I gave his ass two more punches, then slammed his ass to the ground and put my shoe on his neck as he groaned.

"Whatever other bitch you got hiding out with a kid of yours, you'd better make sure that bitch stays hidden, muthafucka. Because if Yikayla comes to me about another female that you had on the side, I'm gon' whoop yo' ass again, bruh, you got it?"

"You figh—fighting me for hurting yo' girl? The fuck?" Roscoe stammered, blood covering his lips and dripping from his nose.

"Nah for hurting my best friend. Now heed to this warning, unless you wanna feel like this again. And the next time I see yo' bitch ass at the park, you better have my nigga, Lonan, witchu." I stared down and then pressed my foot into his neck some more. "Aight?"

"Yeah, aight, man!" his voice was a bit muffled because I had my foot on his neck.

"Hey, stop all of this!" Some old ass white man came up about two seconds too late, trying to break up some shit that was done.

"Nah, everything is good, right Roscoe?" I removed my foot and he struggled to get up.

"Yeah, yea, it's good."

Nusef, Eko, and I walked off, and when I looked back briefly, I saw his homeboy run over to help him up. Niggas were scary as hell, because they didn't make a move when I was over there. Never would I be hanging with a bunch of bitch ass niggas if I couldn't fight like Roscoe's ass. Them the type of niggas that wouldn't even bring sand to the beach because they're so damn scary.

The club resumed and after two more acts, the homie went on. When he was done, we had a few drinks, and old girl from earlier tried to slither her way back over. Shit was crazy to me how she was still interested after the shit I'd told her.

Around midnight, we all went our separate ways, so I could lay up with my shorty. I even had Lonan get in with us.

~

About a Day and a Half Later...

Nusef and I were in the shop closing everything down along with Rebecca. This nigga was trying to clown on Rebecca's new boyfriend, and I knew why. I chuckled at his ass, and once Rebecca left, I locked the doors.

"Damn, you a hater, bruh," I said.

"I ain't no hater. Not my fault that nigga be rocking whack ass hats." He shrugged, making me laugh harder.

"It's cool for you to be jealous, mane. You was fucking with her for a long while and you loved her."

"So you'd get jealous if Alba moved on?"

"Nah, see that's different. I barely wanted Alba when I had her ass," I replied, making him chortle and shake his head. "But Rebecca was a good girl, just not the one for you, so it makes sense that you're bugging a little bit."

"Yeah, I guess so." He smirked and zipped the moneybag before going to lock it up in the back.

Once everything was locked up and put away, I decided to drop by my parents' crib since it was only 8pm. I knew they were going out on a date, but since my sister Midori was home for a visit, I wanted to see her.

When I walked in, no one was downstairs, so I went up and heard the TV on in Emil's room. Stepping inside, I saw him watching and looking lifeless as fuck so I sat down on the bed next to him.

"You seen Mooney yet?" I inquired and he shook his head to say 'no.' "I mean, well, at least he's alive, and when he gets out, you can—"

"I talked to him, Waayil."

"Oh, well, shit, that's good then, right?" I smiled, but I dropped it when he didn't return the gesture. His eyes were still on the TV but I could tell he wasn't *watching* it.

"He told me to leave him alone. Called to say his family was suspicious of our friendship and we couldn't kick it no more."

I honestly didn't know what the fuck to say. I didn't know how niggas dealt with other niggas. Now, if he needed advice on some of these hoes, I had him, but another nigga? Shit, how the fuck could I help with that? Only thing I knew how to do with another nigga was play cards or whoop his ass. And I'm sure neither of those would bring about the desired results.

"Damn, well, aye if he's too scared to man up to his family, then he ain't the one for you, bruh." I gripped his shoulder.

"Thanks," he replied somberly.

Standing up, I said, "I'm gon' go holla at Midori. Let me know if you need anything, aight?"

"Yeah, aight." I walked out but he called my name, so I stopped and came back to his doorway. "I love you, Waayil."

"I love you more, bro." I half smiled, happy to see that he seemed to be warming up to me again.

He nodded and then I left to go further down the hall. I heard Midori on the phone, so I peeked my head in. Her eyes widened as she smiled, which made me chuckle.

"Yil!" she shouted and hung the fuck up on whomever she was talking to. She jumped in my arms and I hugged her tightly. "I missed you!"

"Why are y'all so loud?" Wednesday peeked in before coming further into the bedroom.

"Hater," Midori sucked her teeth as I let her down.

"I missed you too. You looking aight?" I pinched Midori's cheek.

"So what has been going on while I was away?" Her eyes darted back and forth between Wednesday and me.

"Uh... nothing," Wednesday and I replied simultaneously. I didn't know if I felt like telling every damn body about what Wednesday did. Enough people knew, which meant it was a chance the police could find out, and we didn't need that.

"I'm thinking about coming to school down here because I still ge—"

POP!

We heard a loud ass gunshot within the house, so I darted out of the bedroom. Rushing down the hall, I burst into Emil's room to see him cocked over with a big ass hole in his head and blood pouring from it.

"Emil, man, fuck," I said lowly as I moved closer to him just as my sisters ran into the room screaming at the top of their lungs. "Fuck..."

36

———————

JONAYA

Ever since Emil killed himself, everyone had kind of been low-key. We tried to act normal sometimes, but it was hard. Emil and I were never extremely close, but I did hang with him a lot when I was younger. Wednesday, Midori, and the twins were distraught as hell, and of course, their parents blamed themselves.

The funeral was yesterday afternoon, and for the first time, I'd seen Waayil and Nusef cry. I couldn't help but to do the same as I stared at Emil's lifeless body in the casket. It was unreal.

Then, of course Mooney showed up with his injured self, and almost got his ass whooped by Waayil, so he hightailed it out of there and didn't look back.

The whole thing was a mess, and I think Emil's siblings felt responsible for not paying more attention to him; especially Nusef, who'd given up on his relationship with him. But Emil was doing his own thing. Everyone was living their own lives, so none of this was their fault. That boy had been depressed for almost a year and was so secretive. Shit, I didn't even know he was gay until a little bit ago, when Nusef told me how he almost beat Mooney up at the house.

"Do you want something from the store?" I asked Nusef who was relaxing on the couch watching TV.

"Nah, I'm good."

"You sure? I know you ran out of chips. I can get you some." I smiled and kissed the corner of his mouth. I hated seeing him like this, but I understood it.

"I'm good, Jo."

I nodded and got up to go the store because he didn't have shit here, and I wasn't about to stay here and starve.

I made it to the grocery store, and since I had a list, I was able to pretty much get in and out of there with no problem. As I loaded everything up into the trunk and closed it, someone sacked me and started dragging me backwards.

"Help!" I yelled, flailing my arms as the person continued to take me somewhere.

I felt them put me in a car, but before I could react, we were pulling off at a high ass speed. I kept screaming 'help,' as if someone could get me from the moving car, while trying to remove the sack from my head. They tied the shit or something, just that quickly because I couldn't figure it out and I was starting to panic.

The car came to a stop, and I heard the driver get out before coming to my side and yanking me from the vehicle like a rag doll. They picked me up bridal style, as I wailed on them, trying to whoop their asses. I was wondering why they were so gentle with me, despite me going nuts.

"Put me down!" I screamed but I knew it was muffled.

Finally, I was placed to my feet, and the sack was snatched off my head.

"Surprise." Marquise smiled.

"What the fuck!" I barked and started swinging on him. "What the fuck is wrong with you, nigga!" I shouted as I continuously hit him.

"I just wanted to talk to you, Jo!" He attempted to block my blows.

"Talk? Talk! You sacked me and kidnapped me from the parking lot of a grocery store because you wanted to talk? What the fuck is wrong with you?!"

"You've been ignoring me, so I had to do what I had to do!"

"Oh my gosh, something is wrong with you, Marquise! Seriously!"

"Can you just relax so I can say my piece, please? I shouldn't even have to do all this," he had the nerve to say.

"Exactly! Little note, nigga, if you gotta kidnap her for a conversation, she don't want you, bruh!"

He inhaled and exhaled sharply, before gripping my shoulders and making me sit down on the couch. I wanted to leave, but shit I had to hear what the fuck he had to say now. He went through all these damn changes, so it'd better be good.

He reached into his pocket and then dropped down on one knee. For a moment, I was flabbergasted, but then I burst into laughter.

"Marquise, get your ass up."

"Be quiet and let me talk, damn." He opened the ring box. "I wanted to offer you this ring, to promise you that if you come back to me, Jonaya, I will always be good to you. I love you, shorty, and I can't see—"

"Wait, hold up. You kidnapped me from the grocery store just to give me a *promise* ring? Shit, the least you could have done was propose." I clamped the box back and stood up. "Take me back to the store, Marquise."

"So that's a no? If you turn me down again, Jonaya, I ain't coming back for you, ma." He rose to his feet.

"Good, nigga! I don't want you to! Now, take me back to the store!"

"Look me in my eyes and tell me you don't love me anymore and that you don't wanna be with me."

I gripped his chin wearing an uninspired expression, and said, "I don't love you, I never did, actually, and I don't want to be with you."

Snatching his face from me, he yelled, "Hurry up and get in the fucking car!"

Chuckling, I followed him out the house and let him drop be back off at the store. Bitch ass nigga barely let me get out of the car before he pulled off and made me scratch my damn leg.

I walked back to my vehicle, shaking my head at the fact that no one called the police after seeing my ass get sacked and thrown into a vehicle while yelling 'help.' These niggas in Memphis took 'no snitching' to another level.

I drove back to Nusef's place, and texted him to come help me with the stuff.

"What the fuck took so long?" he asked as he brought in the last of the bags and locked the door.

"I... this bitch tried to play me with my damn coupons," I lied. I thought about mentioning Marquise, but decided against it. I think if Nusef heard what he'd just done, he may beat him to death. And Marquise didn't need that, he was just lost.

"That's because the fucking coupons you try to use don't even be for the right product. I told yo' ass about that."

"And I told you it shouldn't matter! If I have a coupon for Colgate, I should be able to use it for any type of fucking Colgate!"

"Not if the coupon says whitening Colgate, Jonaya. You can't go get the two-pack peroxide version!"

"I do what I want! Colgate is Colgate, aight?"

He was about to respond, but instead he started to laugh. I hadn't seen him laugh in almost two weeks, so it made me happy.

"Damn, we're fighting about coupons already, shorty? We need to save that shit for when we're old and don't have shit to talk about," he smiled.

He pulled me into him and we shared a couple kisses before hugging again but more tightly.

"I love you, Sef."

"I love you too, baby." He kissed the top of my head. "Aye, before you and Rebecca, did I only fuck with ugly bitches?"

"Umm... why, babe?"

"Waayil and Alba act like I only fucked with ugly hoes. Then I asked Eko, and he dodged the question. Canyon just said we had different tastes sometimes, which ain't really an answer. So?"

I was trying my best not to laugh.

"You know I never really looked at them, Sef. They always had such nice bodies that I never made it up to the face," I lied. My baby definitely *did* have an ugly bitch streak until Rebecca.

"Hmm..." He squinted his eyes like he was thinking.

"But back to what we were doing," I said before slowly pressing my lips against his.

37

EKO

A Month and Some Change Later...

Now that Neo was gone, the last thing I had to do was murk Gavin. The nigga had been out of jail for a minute, but I just had no idea. The streets say he'd been out since before I killed Neo, which was obvious, since he was Gavin's only connection to the outside world.

I could easily let that nigga live since I wasn't fucking with that dope game shit anymore, but Gavin was like that bug that always kept coming back. He would lay low for a minute, then try to pop his ass back up out of nowhere. Life was too good for me right now, as far as personal and business, so I wasn't about to let that nigga fuck it up for me.

I'd been distant as fuck from the traps and all that shit because, like I said, I wasn't gon' be a part of that life anymore. However, I did still talk to the homies over there, and they let me know that Gavin was there right now.

I'd put the word out prior that I was looking for his ass since he'd been MIA. I'm pretty sure that once he found out Neo was dead, he started to panic and went into hiding. He was counting on that nigga for everything with his bitch ass. Gavin didn't know how to survive on his own, which was why I didn't understand his wanting me out of the game. He could never get to the level Neo was on and run shit. They'd overthrow his ass in a hot second.

I pulled up to where the trap was and swooped into a park. Getting out, I made my way down the street and saw the homie, John, who had called me. He nodded his head to say what's up, and then towards the house, to let me know Gavin was inside.

"Good looking out," I said lowly as I slapped hands with him.

I entered the house to see Gavin and couple of other niggas on the couch laughing and talking. All that shit ceased when they saw me, and of course, Gavin had to hop up and puff out his fucking chest to put on for these young niggas.

"Fuck you doing here, bruh? You don't do this shit no more, remember?" Gavin said, then looked around at everybody while snickering. Them niggas were scared though, so they didn't make a peep.

"You know what the fuck I'm here for; to get rid of yo' ass. You was talking all that hot shit to me and to my girl, so I came to see what's up."

"Well, then—"

"Aye, y'all get the fuck up outta here!" I barked at the two niggas sitting in the living room. Before I even finished my sentence, they were hopping up and darting out.

"Now, who's tough?" Gavin had pulled his gun out during the split second that I'd looked away to tell them niggas to scram.

"Negro, please," I scoffed. Gavin was a bitch and he knew it.

POP!

I sent one through his forehead before he could say another word. I didn't come here to talk with my heat out, or to exchange clever lines, like in an old western film. I came to get rid of this nigga so I could fully move on with my damn life.

I dialed up my nigga, Pat, using my burner app, so he could bring the crew to come clean Gavin's ass out. Once they came and did what the fuck they had to do, I headed home because Rori was there, and I knew she would be complaining if I made her ass wait too damn long.

I wasn't even parked all the way in my driveway before she came outside, with her purse on her arm, rushing to the passenger side to get in.

"Fuck you doing, ma?"

"Take me to the store real quick please, babe."

"Why the fuck you ain't go? You got your new car, courtesy of Jasper's rich ass, here."

"I was gonna take my car but then I saw you. Yours is already on and running, so just take me. I need to go. I feel my period coming and I need some medicine and toiletries to stash here."

"You *feel* it coming," I repeated and shook my head as I reversed back out of my driveway. "How the fuck is that possible?"

"I feel the cramps a little, so it'll be here tomorrow. So if you want some pussy you better get it tonight."

"Stop making yo' shit sound like a damn food order. Me smashing you is supposed to be sporadic. I ain't making no damn appointments." I looked her way as we came to a red light, and she smiled and shrugged. "Cute weird ass."

When we got to the store, Rori of course, wanted to hold hands as she led me to the aisle with all kinds of different tampons and pads. She was fucking with me, being extra by showing me some cup shit that you were supposed to shove up the pussy.

"Rori, get what the fuck you need before I leave you."

"Alright, alright." She dropped down to grab the box she wanted.

Just as I looked at the other end of the aisle, I saw Jenni appear. I hadn't talked to her ass since I let her know that if she fucked with Rori again, I was gon' knock her ass out. She left her alone, and I hadn't seen her ass since.

"Come here, bitch!" Rori snapped me from my thoughts as she took off running after Jenni. Jenni dropped the package of bacon in her hand and sprinted off.

I booked it after Rori, hoping to catch her but she was fast as fuck. She slipped down the chip aisle, and Jenni's stupid ass slipped and fell on her ass. She grabbed a bag of family sized chips, before tossing it at Rori to slow her down, but Rori barged through that shit like a linebacker.

"Baby!" I shouted trying to catch up to her.

By the time Jenni got up, Rori was pounding her damn face in, and slamming her into the foods.

"Ahhh!" Jenni screamed and cried as she attempted to block Rori's blows.

"Girl, you better windmill!" some old Black lady said to Jenni, before rushing off the aisle like she was afraid to get hit. Rori was moving so damn fast that her movements almost appeared to be blurry.

"Rori!" I barked, yanking her off Jenni who was fucked up. I even had to take a moment to process all the injuries on her face.

"I told you I was gon' catch you, bitch! I told you!" Rori hollered as I carried her out the store, running at full speed.

I put her ass in the car, and then jogged around to get in on the driver's seat, so we could get out of there in case the police were called.

"Baby, I swear yo' ass is crazy." I chuckled, zooming away from the store.

"I told you! I told you, I was gon' catch her ass!" Rori laughed excitedly like she'd just won the Super Bowl.

"Damn, baby, it's been months though. I thought the shit was over with," I laughed.

"Nope. I dreamt about beating that bitch up *every* night, and now, finally I can be at peace."

Taking her hand, I kissed the palm of it while keeping my eyes on the road. For some reason, that stunt Rori pulled, made her seem even more perfect to me.

I took her to another store, and this time, we peacefully made it in and out. As soon as I pulled into my driveway, the homie texted my burner app letting me know he'd found Troy Garrick's address.

I thought for a moment on how to get there, since I didn't wanna plug that shit into my GPS, and then zoomed back out of my driveway.

Now that Rori had graduated and finished the internship, it was time for that nigga to pay for kissing on her. Granted, she told me he kept it professional ever since, but I didn't care. Rori was mine and I was the only nigga approved to kiss her on the lips and anywhere else.

"Eko, where are we going?" Rori shouted, closing my passenger door since she was getting out when I pulled off.

"You'll see."

I finally got to Troy's, and before getting out, I said, "Stay here." I made sure to park down some so he wouldn't see Rori, just in case his eyesight was just that good or some shit.

Rori tried to fuss, but I closed my car door and jogged down the street and up his long driveway. He had a cool little family home that I nodded in approval to. Ringing his doorbell, I waited patiently, until I heard someone unlocking it. Just my luck, it was him, wearing a confused expression.

"May I help you—"

WHAM!

I punched the shit out of him, and then turned my ass right back around to walk to my car as he groaned in agony and called out for who I guess was his wife. Bitch.

38

———

YIKAYLA

The Next Afternoon...

Ever since Shanna hit me up about those dresses for her bridesmaids, I'd been getting a lot of messages from other people that wanted me to make clothes for them. I wasn't quite done with all of Shanna's dresses yet, but one was finished and after she posted it to her Instagram profile, it was like my DMs blew up. It was to the point where I had to create an email account for inquiries. That, in combination with me being pregnant, was just too much while working for Jerica. So today, I was going to give her my notice to let her know I would be leaving in two weeks. I wished I could be gone today, but I had to handle things the professional way.

"Hey, Yikayla," this girl named Trish waved to me. She'd replaced Brynn, who quit after I beat her ass. She claimed she couldn't be around me and all this crap. I thought Jerica would have let me go but she didn't.

"Hey, Trish, is Jerica back there?"

"Yep, she is."

I walked towards the back and ran into Jerica's husband

Desmond. As usual, he was smiling all hard while looking me up and down, lustfully. That was another reason I was happy to get out of here; that nigga was making me sick to my stomach.

"Hi, Jerica, can I talk to you for a moment?" I knocked on her already open door.

"Yeah, sure, Yikayla, what is it?"

"Well, I wanted to talk to you about my job here. I've really loved working here, but right now I have a lot of—"

"Jerica!" some woman barged into the room, interrupting me.

"Hi, Dolores," Jerica stood up to hug her. "Guess who made the best dressed list?" Dolores smiled and held up a magazine.

"Wow, but we can talk about that later. Let me just finish up with Yikayla okay?" Jerica explained to her.

Yeah, bitch, rude ass.

"Jerica." The lady shook her head with a smile. "You are always being so modest. Look at me on the list here in this beautiful gown that Jerica designed and made for me." The lady flipped to the page and showed me.

My brows dipped upon seeing the exact dress that Jerica told me no one would wear.

"Dolores, let's talk in a second, honey." Jerica snatched the magazine from me and tried to hand it back to Dolores but I yanked it back.

"Did you seriously steal my design?" I frowned. I was in utter disbelief. I'd been looking up to this bitch for the longest, and she was nothing but a fucking fraud.

"I didn't steal it. Was I inspired, maybe a little." Jerica shrugged one of her shoulders.

"Wait what is going on here?" Dolores inquired.

"Inspired? Inspired? This is my exact dress!" I flipped back to the page and showed her. "This is not an inspiration but my *exact* design, Jerica! Same fabric choices and everything! What the fuck!" I stared at the picture, utterly mortified.

"Maybe, I subconsciously—"

"You didn't *subconsciously* do shit! You purposely told me my dress wasn't good so I wouldn't make it and send it off. I cannot believe this shit. And to think, I saw you as an idol."

Dolores was looking at Jerica like she didn't know her during this whole exchange.

"Jerica, is that her design?" Dolores asked.

"Maybe if you weren't so disrespectful to other people's relationships, things like this wouldn't happen you," Jerica replied, confusing me.

"What? If this is about Brynn, Roscoe was mine well before he was hers, okay? Get your facts straight!"

"No, it's about Desmond, my husband, and how you blatantly flirt with him. He told me about the club and how you were all over him."

Dolores was watching the exchange with her jaw on the floor.

"What!" I exclaimed. "Firstly, that club incident, where he was trying to get with me, happened way before I knew he was your husband! Secondly, I do not flirt with him! He is the one who is always licking his lips at me and even asked for my number!"

"Chile." Dolores clutched her chest in astonishment.

Embarrassed, Jerica said, "You need to leave my establishment, Yikayla."

"I will but best believe you're gonna owe me some fucking money for selling my damn dress to someone, you thief." I turned to leave but then turned back and said, "Oh, and I quit, bitch," before throwing the letter I brought into her face. I smiled to myself when it slapped her ass.

I kept old girl's magazine as I stormed out of the fashion house and got into my car. I was so fucking mad, I didn't know what to do. The only reason I didn't beat that bitch up was because my career and reputation in the industry was way more important right now. I knew if I blacked her eyes she'd tell everyone, and Dolores would cosign, since she was a witness. I did not wanna be known as the feisty, ghetto bitch who fought people, before I even got my feet wet.

I stopped by my parents place since they'd been watching Lonan for me, so I could get some sewing done earlier. When I walked in, I heard music coming from my dad's bar, so I went down there to see my parents dancing, while Lonan sat there playing on his baby iPad.

I was happy to see them coming back together. My father saw the faults in his ways from leaving my mama here alone instead of making her ass go. My mother of course saw her flaws too, and somehow, they were able to move past the drama. I guess that was what marriage was all about. When the good outweighed the bad, sticking it out was the best option. Not to mention, my mom's ass kissing helped a lot. Also, she sang like a bird on Buddy's ass, proving where her loyalty lied. She said things weren't completely normal yet, but she would keep working my dad over.

Picking Lonan up, I kissed his fat cheek before asking, "What is going on here?"

"What does it look like? We're dancing," my mother smiled. She was loving Jasper's time off just as much as we did.

"Come on, honey, dance with me." Jasper waved me over, letting my mom's hand go.

"No, Daddy, I'm not in the mood. I just found something out and I'm not feeling good about it."

"What happened?" My mother made her way over and took Lonan from me, just as my father grabbed my hands to slow dance.

"I can't talk and do this." I chuckled.

"Yes, you can. Try it." Jasper smiled down at me.

"My boss, Jerica, stole my dress design. The same dress that she claimed no one would ever wear."

"Well, sweetheart, if someone who already has a career in fashion is stealing from you, imagine how good you'll be once you're on her level," my mom replied, slow dancing with Lonan.

"You think so?" I let my dad spin me.

"She's right, Kay. If someone of her caliber felt the need to steal, that meant it was really good."

"Yeah, well, I'm still gonna sue her."

"As you should." He leaned me back.

I did feel a little better about it because what my parents said was true. However, if Jerica thought she was gonna get away with making money off of *my* design, that bitch was in for a wild ride.

But for today, I would enjoy my life because right now, pretty much everything had fallen into place. Even Roscoe had some act right these days.

39

WAAYIL

"Hey, guys, Dana is here." Chiara peeked her head into my office. Nusef and I were going over some events and shit, and other plans we had for the shop.

"Fuck does she want?" I hissed.

"Send her back here," Nusef replied.

Chiara nodded and then went to get Dana. A few moments later, Dana appeared, smiling like she didn't attack our mother and then disappear for months.

"May I sit?" she asked.

"Go ahead." Nusef stood up to close the door as my mother sat down in the extra chair in my office.

"Waayil, Nusef, I wanted to apologize for the way I acted at that dinner. It was just frustrating to see that you guys had done so well without me. I know I wasn't there to raise you for the majority of your life, but hearing you call Freya 'mom' and me Dana was just too much in combination with everything else."

"You gotta get over that, honestly. What did you expect, for us to stop calling her mom and start directing that name towards you?" I frowned.

"Funny enough, yeah. I thought when I got out, everything would be the same. And not just with you two, but with your father as well. But everything is different so I have to get used to it."

"You do," Nusef said. "And that includes Jonaya and Yikayla. You can't be disrespectful to them, Dana, or this ain't gon' work."

"I actually like them. I was just frustrated that so many decisions were made with your lives, and I had no say so in them. So I was trying to grasp at anything to have authority over. All of this was because I was jealous," she smiled and chuckled breathily. "I wanted to believe that Freya and Theo didn't do a good job raising you two, but they did."

"You good," I nodded. "What's up with you and pops? That nigga was acting like he ain't want shit to do with us."

"Well, it seems he met someone while in jail. Not..." she laughed when I bucked my eyes. "Not literally in jail, but through a pen pal system. Some woman, she's about thirty years old. He wants a divorce and I'm gonna give it to him."

"I can whoop his ass for you," I said, making Dana and Nusef laugh. I was serious though.

"No, honey, but thank you. I'm actually okay. He's not the same man that he was, and I'm not the same woman, of course. It's sad that prison kind of ripped us all a part and changed us, but that was the risk we took by engaging in criminal activity, huh?"

"Well I'm glad you're taking it like this. I wish he would get at us though, but it's cool, I guess." Nusef shrugged.

I agreed. I had a dad in Theo, so if that nigga Count wanted to be free, I was fine. I was a grown ass man anyway and wasn't in need of an additional father.

"Thanks," she exhaled. "I heard about your brother and I'm sorry about it all. I know all of you guys were close."

"We were," I nodded, thinking about Emil. I still couldn't believe he was gone. That shit still fucked with me, because I felt like there was more I could have done for him.

The other day, I ran into Mooney and fucked his ass up, but I didn't tell anybody. I just couldn't let his ass walk around without doing shit, so I did him in. I knew Emil killing himself wasn't Mooney's fault, but he had a hand in my little brother's depression for sure, so he deserved it. Plus, I just didn't like that nigga.

"You hungry? The three of us can go to lunch or something," Nusef offered.

Smiling widely and making her dimples appear, Dana said, "Yeah, I'd like that."

~

That Night...

CRASH!

I tried. I tried like a muthafucka to let this shit go and move on. I told myself on countless occasions that this shit had ended well for me. But me being the type of nigga that I am, I just couldn't live with the fact that I'd let Alba's hoe ass get away with fucking with my mental for months. All the stress her ass put on me from having me think I'd gotten her ass pregnant was about to come back and bite her in the ass. I was thankful to Yikayla for breaking her nose, but that was Yikayla's revenge... I needed mine.

The brick I threw through Alba's window with my gloved hand, prompted her to come open her front door. I saw her looking through the screen as I stayed off to the side with a ski mask pulled down over my head. She stepped out, and turned to her left to inspect the damage done to her window as she shook her head and cursed under her breath.

"Stupid assholes!" she hollered down the street, and then looked the other way, hoping her stupid lying ass could find the perpetrator. But little did her snake ass know, I was right on the side of her porch, twisting that young silencer onto the front of my gun. Muthafuckas hopefully learned not to come for a nigga.

PHEW! PHEW!

"Ahh!" Alba hollered, collapsing to the ground unwillingly after I sent two into her kneecaps. Blood was gushing from her knees like a crazy, and I wasn't sure her ass would be able to walk again.

Her loud ass screams seemed to boom over the whole damn city of Memphis as I hopped the gate discreetly and booked it to my car. I didn't want the bitch to know it was me simply because I knew her ass would snitch. She had no reason not to, and plus, I was fine with being the only nigga knowing I got her ass back. I didn't care what these other muthafuckas thought.

Cranking my car up, a smile spread across my face because I could still hear Alba's cries in the distance, along with some frantic neighbors.

I lit a blunt, turned up my music, and inhaled deeply before pulling off. I could finally live peacefully.

I SLIPPED on some boxers since I'd just gotten out of the shower, and then climbed in the bed next to Yikayla. I ran my hand up her short nightgown so I could touch on the small bulge in her stomach. I couldn't believe I had gotten the love of my life pregnant. A baby that came from Yikayla and me... that shit was wild to think about, yet exciting.

"Can I ask you something?" she smirked.

"Aww shit," I groaned. "Fuck you wanna know, ma?" I smiled.

"Did you ever do anything with Chiara? I mean, women don't act that thirsty for a man unless they got something."

Really, Kay? Months after you slapped the girl?

"I let her suck me off but it was while I was still with Alba and fresh out the pen. That was all, I promise."

"Ugh! Don't touch me!" she pushed my hand from her stomach.

"So what now, you gon' leave me because I let her suck my dick ages ago? Nah. I don't think so." I shook my head.

"Yeah, I am leaving. I don't like you anymore." She pouted.

"But you got my baby inside you, so how the fuck is that gon' work?" I chuckled, grabbing at the waistband of her panties and pulling on them.

"I don't know, but I'm getting me a new man."

Taking her panties off and tossing them to the floor, I replied, "Can I eat yo' pussy one more time before you leave?"

She nodded her head 'yes' with her freaky ass, and smiled when I started to laugh.

"So you don't like me, but I can eat ya pussy? You ain't shit, shorty."

She shrugged with a chuckle as I started to kiss on her inner thighs, while placing them on my shoulders. I trailed my lips all the way to her box, and just enjoyed the heat radiating from it along with the scent. Pecking her lower lips, I slowly swiped my tongue between them, before attaching my mouth to her clit.

I licked and sucked on her pussy with so much passion as I moaned at the taste and the texture. She released, wetting my facial hair up, and I just kept going, loving how gushy her pussy got. She exploded again, legs shaking hard on my shoulders as I kissed her thighs.

"You still gon' leave me?" I asked as I released my dick and forced my way into her tight wet hole.

She shook her head 'no' while nibbling on her lip and digging her nails into my arms.

"That's what I thought." I plunged the rest of my dick into her, making her whimper, as I started to suck on her lips.

Yikayla Goode would forever be mine.

YIKAYLA GOODE

One Year Later…

Tonight was the grand opening of Waayil and Nusef's second tattoo shop, and I think for everyone this moment was extremely surreal. For as long as I'd known the twins, they'd always talked about running a tattoo shop, now here they were, opening a second. And the best thing about this one is that Chiara didn't work here. Yeah she kissed my ass now, even had a man of her own, but I would never like that bitch.

Anyway, I was so happy for the boys; especially my baby because there was a time where he'd thought he'd lost it all.

The shop was filled with all kinds of people; friends, family, colleagues of others, and even some kids were here. This was more of an afternoon slash evening thing so that everyone could attend.

"Mommy, the phone?" Lonan smiled at me with his adorable self. I still wasn't used to him being able to talk so well. He was only two years old, but he talked better than some of these niggas I knew.

As far as his daddy, he was now engaged to Shamaria, who was pregnant. Yep, RJ's mother, Christelle's, sister. I guess their kids would be cousins slash brothers. Roscoe was just a mess and would forever be. Christelle was heartbroken, but I tried to warn her dumb ass long ago. She didn't even know about Brynn either, but maybe that was best.

As for Brynn, that bitch packed up her and Haven's shit, and moved to Knoxville. I didn't care she if stayed or left, and sadly, neither did Roscoe, even though she had his daughter. He claimed he didn't believe Haven was his anymore, but I think it was just an excuse not to fight for his child. Plus, he didn't have enough money for all the children he'd created, so Haven being gone was less work on his pockets.

I passed Lonan my phone as I adjusted my baby girl, Yorri, in my lap. She was the cutest little chocolate baby in the world, and possessed her father's same honey colored eyes. She was well behaved too, and I noticed that this time around was easier for me because I actually had the father around to help.

My phone buzzed, and I saw it was yet another email from a potential client. Ever since Shanna, it seemed like I'd turned into a designer overnight. I now had a place like Jerica's, thanks to my stepdad convincing me to get a bank business loan, and I even had an assistant.

The name of my line and fashion house was Goode Girl, which I thought was the cutest thing when Waayil suggested it. I was really coming up. Plus, that whole lawsuit I filed against Jerica and won, did boost me a little bit too.

Jerica had gotten a bad rep after people found out she'd stolen from me because then, all kinds of allegations started to pour in, like the fact that she didn't make her own dresses, and that some of her one of a kinds, *weren't* actually one of a kind. I, for one, always had my suspicions about how she was able to hand sew so many damn dresses, but that was none of my business now.

I couldn't believe I was an actual designer some days, and that my father actually supported the dream now too. I think him getting shot made him look at life differently. He still worked a lot, but because he was so well established, he didn't need to do as much to still make a nice amount of money. My mother was happier too, and I guess all of her philandering ways was just because she was crying out for attention. She actually did love my father.

"Why are these nachos so good?" Rori came and sat next to me, kissing Lonan on the top of his head.

The music in here was pretty loud, but I made sure to sit away from the speakers. That also meant away from the food, which I was eyeing.

"Are they? They look good as hell but I wasn't sure since Dana was in charge of all the food with her crazy ass," I replied.

Dana, the boys' mother, had come around. I was hesitant at first because I didn't like what I'd caught that bitch saying about me, but overtime, I'd come to see that she actually was a nice person. She was still a little crazy, but I think that was just her personality. Her and my mom got along quite well, and it was nice to see my mother with a friend for a change, instead of a fuck buddy.

"Yes very." Rori rubbed her belly.

She was pregnant by Eko but still in grad school. I was so proud of her for sticking it out, even though she was with child, just like I did when I got pregnant with Lonan. I knew it was hard as hell, but she was doing very well. She was also working as a policy analyst for the time being. After working with Troy Garrick, who was the mayor for a short time, Rori just built up her resume from there. Troy didn't last because some girl named Scarlett came out and told that she'd been having an affair with him. Things got so bad he was forced to resign. I didn't pay enough attention to the scandal, but I knew the details because Eko's ass had an odd interest in it. He was so interested, that I almost felt like he was behind Troy's downfall.

Her man Eko's barbershop was the place to be. Not only to get your haircut, but even if you wanted to catch a little something. He too, would be opening another shop in a couple weeks, so he was making way more cash than he used to when he was just a manager and a dope boy.

I made eye contact with Dree who was by the food, and she rolled her eyes when she realized why I was staring her down so hard. I smiled softly when she grabbed an extra plate to make me one.

Canyon had really changed her, because a year or two ago, she would have never stepped foot into a tattoo shop opening party. Canyon was literally the only one for Dree, because he could handle her. Any other man, Dree would be wiping the mud off her shoes on his ass. Canyon wasn't having that though. I guess that was why they'd run off and eloped; they were meant to be.

It was also good to see Dree and Jupiter back close again, which I thought would never happen unless pigs started to fly. Even crazier was that Dree and Canyon's baby mama got along. Canyon had lucked up for real because most men could not say that; not even Roscoe. I tried to be cool with RJ's mom, Christelle, but she was too whiny and wimpy for my liking.

And speaking of extra women, Alba didn't come around much anymore after Waayil shot her in the knees. He didn't tell me it was him when it first started spreading around, but after Wednesday's foot woes, I knew my baby was behind it. It was hard not to chuckle seeing Alba walking around with a damn walker for six months, but that's what you get when you fuck with Waayil Christian.

Dree was still in law school, but she didn't have to deal with Sean. He got sentenced to only five years in jail because of his parents' connections and wealth, but he didn't even last that long on the inside. Because Waayil knew some niggas on the inside, Canyon was able to get some money to the right people to pay Sean back in the same way he'd violated Dree. However, they'd gang raped him so severely, that Sean became paralyzed from the waist down. He eventually passed from some type of complications. I wanted to feel bad, but I couldn't. But it was a shame to think about he went from a promising law school student, just to end up the way he did all because he wanted some ass. Niggas.

"There, brat." Dree handed me my plate and was about to sit next to me, but Canyon grabbed her arm and sat there instead. He then pulled her into his lap, and I smiled as they whispered something to one another before kissing.

"Thank you," I said, but Dree wasn't paying me any mind.

"My little baby!" Jonaya shrieked as she came from the crowd and grabbed up Yorri. She kissed her cheeks multiple times, and then started to sway with her to "Privacy" by Chris Brown, while singing along.

"Please don't sing that nasty shit to my baby," I said, chuckling. She just rolled her eyes and continued.

Jonaya was in her senior year of college, and she and Nusef were still going very strong. They were like the same person in one relationship, which was weird but adorable. I smiled as Nusef came behind Jonaya to dance and sing to Yorri along with her. My baby was enjoying it, smiling and giggling at them two.

"What I tell you about this greasy shit, Rori? You need a salad, baby." Eko walked up frowning, before sitting next to Rori.

"Leave her alone, Eko." Waayil and Nusef's mother, Freya, chuckled and shook her head.

"Thank you, Mrs. Samuels." Rori nodded and then made a face at Eko.

"Yikayla, Waayil wants you to come over by the front desk." Wednesday approached, smiling way too hard.

It took me a minute to get over what she'd done to Waayil, but when I saw he'd completely forgiven her, I had to as well. I initially thought she just did the shit on purpose, but then I had to remember that I knew Wednesday. She wasn't a bad person; she was just a girl who made a really bad choice that turned out to be horrific. If I were her, I would hate for people to dislike me forever over one bad decision that was a mistake. And with Emil gone, now was the time to cherish your family while you still had them.

"Come on, Kay!" Midori rushed over to help Wednesday get me to go over to where Waayil was.

Midori was now going to college in Memphis because she was too home sick up in Rhode Island. And after Emil killed himself, she didn't want to be away. She felt horrible for not having been able to spend time with him when she could.

I let the girls lead me to where Waayil was, and when he saw me, he grinned and picked the microphone up that was nearby.

"Everybody, can I get your attention," he spoke when the song faded out and the deejay cut it off. "Y'all know how I feel about this woman right here; my best friend, my girl, and now my beautiful daughter's mother."

"Pussy whipped," Eko coughed.

"You damn right," Waayil nodded while smiling.

"Waayil." I bucked my eyes at him because my parents were here. Yeah, we had a baby but you still wanted your parents to see you as innocent. At least I did; mainly, my dad.

"Yikayla, baby, I love you, Lonan, and of course, Yorri more than anything. We've been through every stage of a relationship that two people can be, and I've never had a bond this strong with anybody that wasn't Nusef. Everything is coming together perfectly right now, and has been ever since I got released and got you back into my life. So by saying that..." he set the mic down and then reached into his jean pocket to pull out a ring box.

"Waayil." I inhaled sharply and covered my mouth when he opened it.

"Wait, let me see." My father stepped up to inspect, making everyone roar with laughter. "Okay, go ahead."

"If you're wondering, yes, I did ask him," Waayil smirked at me, dimples showing the fuck out and hazel eyes glistening up at me. He looked so good in his crisp polo and dark jeans, with a few sparkly pieces on his neck and wrist. "Will you marry me, Yikayla?"

"Of course," I chuckled, hating the tears that were running down my cheeks because I actually wore makeup today.

Waayil slid the ring onto my finger, as Lonan rushed over to get a closer look at the chaos. Waayil got up to kiss my lips a couple times, before he scooped Lonan up and kissed his cheek. Jonaya handed me

Yorri, as everyone surrounded us to get a look at this big ass ring Waayil had gotten me, while the deejay cut the music back on.

"Way bigger than mine," Rebecca joked, and playfully frowned at her husband, Zaire. We just snickered at her, before feasting our eyes back on this big ass rock sitting on my hand.

Waayil was right about us having been in every stage of a relationship. We'd been friends, best friends, crushes, lovers, boyfriend and girlfriend, parents, and now we were engaged. Actually, all of my sisters and their significant others had been through a couple stages themselves. But... I guess that was why our love was the realest.

FIN

BECOME A VIP READER!

*To join my mailing list text **SHVONNE** to **66866** and stay up to date! Also, join **Shvonne Latrice Reading Group** on Facebook!*

9 781966 375302